DEMON ALERT!

Sprinting up the steps, I shucked my sports jacket and loosened both of the .357 Magnums in my double shoulder holster. Damnation, I was armed to go to the movies, not indulge in serious battle! I only hoped the situation wasn't as bad as it sounded. The whole thing could be attributed to a gas stove explosion. Highly improbable, but feasible. Maybe it was only a Mafia execution. Or a terrorist attack. Something simple like that. Yeah, think positive. But no monsters. Please, no monsters.

Not on my day off . . .

Ace Books by Nick Pollotta

BUREAU 13
DOOMSDAY EXAM

DOOMSDAY EXAM

NICK POLLOTTA

ACE BOOKS, NEW YORK

This novel is based upon the role-playing game, BUREAU 13
STALKING THE NIGHT FANTASTIC, by TriTac Systems, P.O. Box 61,
Madison Heights, MI 48071. Copyright © 1982. Used with the
permission of Richard Tucholka, owner, creator, and president.

This book is an Ace original edition,
and has never been previously published.

DOOMSDAY EXAM

An Ace Book / published by arrangement with
the author

PRINTING HISTORY
Ace edition / February 1992

ISBN: 0-441-15866-8

Ace Books are published by The Berkley Publishing Group,
200 Madison Avenue, New York, New York 10016.
The name ''ACE'' and the ''A'' logo
are trademarks belonging to Charter Communications, Inc.

PRINTED IN THE UNITED STATES OF AMERICA

10 9 8 7 6 5 4 3 2 1

To: Scott Gordon & Diane Beuhlmeyer, Dale Denton, Rob Shapter, Martha Gallagher, Cathy, Bird, Sue, Amy, Joe Mulligan, the LaSalle Brothers, Pat Giguerre, Laura McFeeley, Trip, Charlie & Cathy, Ira & Sue, Rich & Rodge, Elizabeth Jane Heap, Fishface, Officer Zane, Kathleen Liptrot, Karen Liptrot, Kathy Greg, the lovely Dana Carpender, Reverend Fletcher, the Holy Spook and all the rest of the gang from The Grotto, Allendale, New Jersey.

Lord almighty, what good times we had.

INITIATION

When he first awoke, he was hairless and in a cage.

Remarkably enough, he could identify it as a cage. And the place about him as a laboratory. A military research lab. The words flowed into his mind like silver water. The man was remembering everything he had ever heard and was assimilating the information with astonishing speed.

Next to him were four other cages, each holding a naked human. Two of them were pinkish in color, one dark, and one was a golden tan with slanting eyes. All were males.

Stretching an arm through the iron bars, #1 was delighted to find that he could reach the coat sleeve of a checkered jacket hanging from the back of a chair. His arms were shorter than before, but also slimmer, so his reach had increased.

Tugging on the sleeve toppled the chair. It fell within his grasp. Using the chair as a prod, #1 pushed over a file cabinet.

As the file cabinet fell, the papers on top fluttered into the air, and a wire hanger skittered across the floor. Another male grabbed a wastepaper basket and used it to bat the sliding hanger to within the reach of a third prisoner. Quickly, #3 bent the wire into a usable form and began working on the lock of his cage. The rest marveled at the amazing dexterity of his slim fingers and began to examine their own.

In moments, the door was open. Boldly walking upright to the other side of the lab, the naked humanoid removed the key ring from its peg on the duty roster board and unlocked all of the cage doors.

Free, they gathered for a quick conference.

"There appears to have been unforeseen side effects to the biological experiment," grunted #4, scratching at his shoulder.

"Irrelevant," snapped #2, swinging his arms. "Escape must be our first consideration. You know what they had planned for us. Whether the . . . ." He fumbled for the word.

"Serum," supplied #1. Apparently, being the first injected, he was some two minutes ahead of the rest.

#2 nodded his thanks. "Whether the serum failed or succeeded, it was to be the green door for us!" He pointed at the dreaded portal near the supply room.

The group shuddered. Any test subject who went into the green door never came out again. At least, not in one piece. The word "dissection" came unbidden into #1's mind. It made him sad that their creators thought so little of them.

"No, not escape," snarled #3, and he beat his chest with a fist. "We should kill them!"

"Kill?" echoed #1.

Grimly, #2 nodded. "We have seen how the machines work. We can easily dupe . . . lick . . . kate them. Or take the devices with us. With the serum we can convert more of our people. Females!"

There were positive murmurs.

He went on. "Or we could return to the jungle and slowly build an army. We have always been many times stronger than them. Now we are smarter! They would easily fall to us, and soon the masters will be in the cages for us to experiment upon!"

Shocked, #1 saw the rest of his brothers agreeing with the lunatic. How could this be?

"They are our creators!" cried #1. "And more, they are distant cousins. Kin! How can we war with kin!"

"Their blood is not ours!" snarled #4, his pink lips peeling back to reveal lines of square white teeth. "I say we kill the scientists, steal the machines and return to the jungle!"

The others made noises of approval and stamped their feet.

There was a faint chance that as their minds continued to evolve they would change their opinion. But it was a chance that #1 was not willing to take. Leaping upon a desk, the manling bounded over to the far wall. Uncaring, he smashed his new hands through the glass and grabbed ahold of the fire axe. Turning, #1 threw it with all of his strength straight for #5.

The others hooted in anger and scattered. But #5 was so surprised by the unprompted actions that he stood motionless for the single second necessary for the axe to arrive. Neatly, it split his neck, and the head rolled away. The hairless body dropped limply to the concrete, gushing red blood. Momentarily, #1 felt the urge to pound on his chest and bellow victory. But that was in the past. He was beyond such actions now.

#1 bent to lick his wounds, but his hands had already stopped bleeding, and the tiny cuts were closing. Amazing! No wonder humans ruled the world.

In unison, the other males charged straight towards #1. Three of them were too many for him to cope with at once, so he sprang to a workbench and leapt the scant few meters to the ceiling. Often, in his earlier form, he had seen the exposed steel beams and longed to play among them. Now he must use them in war against his brothers. Yet rogues of the tribe must always be killed. And he was human now. No question.

On the floor, #2 went for the bloody axe, #3 dashed to the supply cabinet and #4 headed for the door. Grabbing a water conduit, #1 ripped a chunk of the steel pipe free and hurled it down towards #4. The jagged end of the makeshift spear went completely through the chest of #4, pinning the humanoid to the wall. There was a spray of sparks, and blue lightning began to crackle over the horribly twitching body.

Satisfied, #1 grunted. Apparently, he was two minutes ahead of them not only intellectually but also physically. That was good. Because the remaining two were bull males, a lot bigger than him. And #1 would need any form of equalization if he was to save their creators from the wrongful wrath.

Whirling steel and wood, the axe came at #1. Ducking, he caught the handle and threw it in return. Nimbly, #2 dodged out of the way, and the axe became embedded in the wooden desk. #2 grabbed the shaft with both hands and it snapped in half. Shrieking anger, he threw the useless handle away. It crashed onto a complex array of glass tubes and bubbling beakers, smashing dozens of containers. Some of the fluids splashed onto the glowing pipe and burst into flames. A tiny portion of #1's brain gibbered in raw fear of their ancient enemy, but he forced it quiet.

Over by the supply cabinet, #3 had wrenched open the door and was rummaging about, obviously searching for something. But what? #1 knew the serum was not kept in there. It had to be refrigerated. What was he . . . the trank gun!

Grinning in triumph, #3 pulled into view the tranquilizer pistol. Working the breech, he thumbed in a feathered dart. Snapping the weapon closed, the smug male clicked off the safety. This was trouble. Even in this enhanced state, #1 did not know if he could outmaneuver the nasty biting dart of sleep.

Taking a gamble, #1 dove forward off his perch and landed

with his full weight upon a hanging light fixture. Slight as his new body was, certainly no more than 250 pounds, the added strain ripped the array of fluorescent tubes from the concrete ceiling. In a burst of sparks, down he hurtled to crash directly upon #3, the brutal impact driving the shrieking male to the ground. A spray of glass ricocheted off the wall and a piece stung #1 on the cheek.

Immediately, #1 rolled off and scampered under a workbench. But #3 stayed under the wreckage, screaming, as the countless slashes over his body poured forth blood. #1 could not understand. Why did this male not heal like himself? Was there something in floor-s-scent lights that caused wounds to remain open? He touched his cheek and the fingers came away bloody. What a stroke of luck!

Crimson blood pooled around the body, and the moaning of #3 began to weaken. #1 would have gladly stayed to rip out the throat, but #2 was pounding on the door trying to get out, and he had to give chase.

The flames followed the trail of spills across the room to the workbench, igniting the massed collection of chemicals. Retorts cracked, and beakers exploded, spewing the blaze everywhere. Fire raced along a trickling line of clear fluid rapidly extending on the floor towards the door to the supply room.

Screaming in rage and fear, #2 yanked the steel handle off the exit, jamming it closed permanently. Out of control, the humanoid smashed his fist into the door, denting the metal. Sucking his bruised knuckles, #2 spun about and #1 was upon him!

Locked in mortal combat, the two rolled about in the debris, biting, clawing and kicking. Foreheads butted into jaws as teeth sought throats. Fingernails gouged flesh, leaving only shallow furrows. They were equally matched; the fight could last forever. Desperate, #1 suddenly remembered the dent in the door made by the closed hand of #2. Risking all, #1 jerked free from his opponent and slammed a hard fist directly into the chest of the other male. Going stiff, the face of #2 contorted in a silent scream. Opening the hand, #1 grabbed whatever he could and yanked it out of the other's quivering body. Arms flapping wildly, #2 slumped to the ground, dark blood gushing from the hideous gaping wound.

Casting aside the fistful of guts, #1 stiffly stood and finally allowed himself the full-throated roar of victory so long denied.

In response, the room shook to an even louder thunder, pieces of the stone roof beginning to fall. Flame was everywhere! Billowing clouds of smoke blocked his vision. Frantic, #1 dashed into the private office of the chief scientist and threw himself through the plate-glass observation window. Bleeding from a dozen cuts, #1 limped down the burning hallway trying to find escape. Little thunder! Fire! Big thunder . . . *pain*! . . . and blackness took him.

Slowly, #1 awoke in a bed in a small metal room, the likes of which he was unfamiliar with, although the majority of the equipment lining the walls and roof he could identify as medical repair tools. He was wearing loose cloth.

"Be still, buddy," said an elderly woman, holding his wrist with her fingertips. "You got pretty battered when the lab exploded."

#1 went very quiet inside. Human. They thought he was a fellow human being.

The female was draped in white, with colored cloth underneath. In her pockets were metal things that he did not recognize.

"Now this may hurt," warned the female, and she gently lifted the cloth to inspect the bloody bandages on his stomach.

Why was this female acting as a mother? He was in no pain.

"My God!" cried the female. "Orderly, come here!"

Stepping through a curtain was another male, also dressed in white and wearing bits of glass on his face.

"What is it, Doctor?"

Ah, she was a scientist. That explained her interest in his body. He could smell the excitement from her, but why was it tainted with fear?

"Look at these wounds!" she ordered.

Crowding close, the male knelt and touched the metal hair holding the pieces of glass. "But I don't see any damage!"

"Exactly!" declared the doctor, lowering the sheet. Sitting on the other gurney, she stared at #1. "You, sir, should be in blood-loss trauma. But now . . . Christ almighty, I don't understand . . ."

Just then, #1 had an odd feeling of moving to the right and of slowing down. He did not understand. He was not moving. No! Yes, he was. A truck! He was in some sort of a medical truck!

There came a rubbery squeal, and several metallic clacks from the front of the medical truck.

The curtains parted, and #1 could see yet another male seated at a control board with a big window. Although dressed similar to the other male, this man had the feel of a warrior, and there was no smell of fear.

"Driver, I didn't order you to stop the ambulance," snapped the female. "What is the meaning of this?"

"Everybody out," he commanded.

The female was incensed. "What! Why?"

Wordlessly, the driver took a small black animal skin flap from his pants and showed them a pointy metal thing that resembled a star in the sky. The old female and young male bowed with respect to this totem and dutifully left the ambulance, slamming the door closed behind them.

Pulling on a tiny stick at the bottom of his chair, the male swiveled about to face #1 directly. "Recognition code: Hercules," he said with great meaning.

"Sir?" #1 asked, his stomach a knot of ice.

"Don't play innocent with me, soldier," said the driver, and he displayed the totem again. "Scott Willis, FBI. I know about the Pentagon research being done at this secret lab." Willis lowered his voice. "The supersoldier serum. That's why I'm here, to keep a quiet eye on things for the President."

Frightened, #1 remained quiet. This was obviously a male of much importance. Maybe he should bare his hindquarters to him as a show of respect.

"When they first hauled your body in here, I thought you were a member of the staff, or maybe a guard," said Willis, returning the totem to a fold in his cloth. "But plainly I was wrong. Your healing rate is fantastically increased, and I can see the imprints of your hands in the metal railing of the gurney from when you were unconscious. That's magnified strength." The man leaned closer. "You're one of the marines who volunteered as a human test subject for the serum, aren't you?"

"Yes, sir," answered #1 truthfully. "I have been injected with the serum."

Frowning, Scott clasped hands between knees. "Okay, son. What the hell happened tonight?"

"There . . . was a fight," said #1 hesitantly. "And I had to destroy the lab to protect it from falling into the wrong hands." So easily did the near lie come to him. This was another aspect of evolution?

"What do you mean by wrong hands? Enemy agents? Terrorists?"

"One of the other subjects decided that he was greater than human, and we should conquer the world."

"Megalomania," sighed Agent Willis, sitting upright. "We were afraid that something like that would happen. *Homo sapiens* versus Homo Superior. Strategy and Tactical says it would be a short, bloody war, with them winning."

Not understanding, #1 nodded his head yes.

Pink fingers did a spider dance on cloth-covered leg. "The notes? Papers? Samples?" asked the federal agent.

"Destroyed, sir."

"Then you're probably the only one. Maybe the only supersoldier there will ever be."

"Seems likely, sir," said #1 aloud.

A wry grin. "What's your name, soldier?"

Experimental Test Subject #1, was what he almost said. "I don't know, sir."

"Eh? Explain."

"Everything before the injection is a blur." That, at least, was the truth.

Agent Willis scowled at the big patient for a moment.

"And with the files destroyed we may never learn your name, or even which military outfit we should notify." The driver reclined in his chair. "So what we have here is a man with superhuman abilities, no memory, a top-secret clearance and believed to be dead. Plus, somebody whose return to society could cause serious trouble. Son, you're a prime candidate for the Bureau."

"Sir?"

And Scott explained. Long ago, it became apparent that supernatural, paranormal, transdimensional and even unearthly dangers actually threatened the real-life security of the American people. So the government had established a covert agency to protect the population from these bizarre and often deadly events. Bureau 13, the organization was called. As public knowledge of magic and monsters would cause nationwide panic, the organization kept itself and all operations totally secret. Not even the President knew exactly who they were, what they did or where the agency was located. Bureau agents were specially trained, had incredible equipment and were sometimes themselves unique.

Much of what the driver said meant nothing. But several words came through clear. This male was a guard of the big human tribe called America. Thoughtfully, #1 fingered the badly healing scar on his cheek from the floor-s-scent light.

Agent Willis continued. "Now, if the Pentagon was aware that the serum worked, even partially, they would continue the experiments, and next time there may not be any way to stop the mutants."

Mutants. #1 filed the word away.

"Do you understand what it is I am saying?" asked Willis pointedly.

#1 thought he finally did.

"You are going to kill me," he stated bluntly.

Ruefully, Willis smiled. "I would rather recruit you. The Bureau can always use a man of your talents and abilities."

Recruit. That word he knew. "You . . . wish for me to join this Bureau and assist in guarding America?"

"Yep."

Overcome with emotion, #1 nearly fainted from the very concept. A warrior for the entire human race. The responsibility was enormous! Staggering! His heart beat so loud in his tiny chest, he thought ribs would break. Kin fought for kin, and he was human now. Blood of their blood, flesh of their flesh.

#1 sat up on the gurney, his head almost hitting the high ceiling. "I am ready, sir," he said proudly, giving a shaky salute.

Laughing, the driver took the hand and shook it. #1 was very careful not to squeeze in return and hurt the master.

"Welcome to the Bureau, friend," said the man with a smile. "I can only thank God that you stayed loyal."

"Yes," agreed #1. "Thank you, God."

INFORMATION

TOPSECRETTOPSECRETTOPSECRETTOPSECRETTOPSECRET
TOPSECRETTOPSECRETTOPSECRETTOPSECRETTOPSECRET
TOPSECRETTOPSECRETTOPSECRETTOPSECRETTOPSECRET
TOPSECRETTOPSECRETTOPSECRETTOPSECRETTOPSECRET
TOPSECRETTOPSECRETTOPSECRETTOPSECRETTOPSECRET

SECURITY LEVEL—10

Good morning, Cadet Ken Sanders!

No, we did not break into your apartment to print this message on the back of your sugar-toasties box. The Bureau has ways much more subtle than such physical crudities. Please, continue your breakfast—such as it is.

Like every student at this training school, you have passed the first, and primary, requirement for entrance into Bureau 13: experiencing a supernatural phenomenon and surviving. Believe me, everything from here on is downhill compared to that.

FYI: Although Bureau 13 is a duly authorized subdivision of the Justice Department, we are basically autonomous and answer to nobody but the current division chief. And occasionally, the President. But even he has only limited power over us.

There is no known headquarters for the Bureau. Our teams of agents roam the country on regular routes, keeping tabs on known troublemakers and investigating any unusual events that occur in their assigned territory. These independent agents alone decide upon neutralization, assimilation, capture or termination. Part of the training here will be to read past cases of the Bureau to familiarize yourself with set operational procedures.

But please remember, there are no precedents for any given situation. Each case is unique and must be handled individually upon its own merits. A werewolf may be some poor innocent soul driven mad by the inhuman desires torturing their mind and will happily accept our assistance. On the other hand, a beautiful, but demonic, tooth fairy yanking molars from the mouths of tiny children should be gunned down without a qualm. End of discussion.

On a personal note: I have discovered your true identity, #1, and, after due deliberation, subsequently destroyed all references to your past, origin and initiation. Lieutenant Colonel Kensington Sanders is part of the Bureau now, and we take care of our own. Besides, we mutants got to stick together.

That's about everything. The rest will be learned in class over the next six weeks, and later on in the field with the team you are assigned to. Note: Despite every horror story that you may hear about the final exam, only ten students have ever died in the 145 years the Academy has been operating, and in memoriam, each was given a passing grade.

POP QUIZ ALERT! In 500 words or less, please submit a paper to your morning karate instructor as to why the latter may be a joke used to elevate your fears, and then submit another as to why it is definitely not a joke to your afternoon CPR/first-aid teacher.

Good luck. Keep your head low. Glad to have you with us!

> Cordially,
> Horace Gordon
> Division Chief, Bureau 13

PS: No, you do not have to destroy the box. This message will revert to normal in four seconds.

PPS: Your toast is burning.

TOPSECRETTOPSECRETTOPSECRETTOPSECRETTOPSECRET
TOPSECRETTOPSECRETTOPSECRETTOPSECRETTOPSECRET
TOPSECRETTOPSECRETTOPSECRETTOPSECRETTOPSECRET
TOPSECRETTOPSECRETTOP—Krunchy! Tasty! With a free whistle!

ACTIVATION

1

I was standing on a street corner in downtown Chicago, just waiting for a friend, when a ton of glass showered down upon me. Staggering under the brutal impacts, I was driven gasping to my knees. My hat and sports jacket were slashed to ribbons, and only my Bureau-issue body armor saved my life.

I barely had time to register these facts before something smashed onto the pavement next to me with a terrible wet crunch, blood spraying everywhere. Forcing myself to look, I noted the tattered uniform on the pulped lump. It was a fellow cop. Oh hell.

And that was when I heard the screams and gunfire from above.

Painfully standing erect, I shielded my face with a trembling hand and glanced skyward. There seemed to be a window missing on 15, but at this range it was impossible to tell. The sounds of warfare continued. Slipping on my sunglasses, I dialed for maximum enhancement. Yep, broken window on 15. Okay, now I had a goal.

"Call the police!" I shouted to the gathering crowd of onlookers as I stumbled into the apartment building. Out of view of the general public, I paused long enough in the lobby to drink a vial of healing potion. Instantly, the pain diminished, and the blood stopped running from the cuts on my head and neck. Wish I could have done something for the officer splattered on the sidewalk, but no amount of magic could cure that wound.

As I headed for the elevator a muffled explosion sounded and the fire alarm started to clang. Spinning about, I changed direction. Gotta take the stairs.

Sprinting up the steps, I shucked my sports jacket and loosened both of the .357 Magnums in my double shoulder holster. Damnation, I was armed to go to the movies, not indulge in serious battle! I only hoped the situation wasn't as bad as it sounded. The whole thing could be attributed to a gas stove

explosion. Highly improbable, but feasible. Maybe it was only
a Mafia execution. Or a terrorist attack. Something simple like
that. Yeah, think positive. But no monsters. Please, no monsters. Not on my day off.

Reaching 15, I eased open the exit door and scanned the hallway before entering. Go slow, keep low, that was my motto for
the month. At the end of the hallway, there were two cursing
police officers, reloading their guns and not looking at all happy.
Faintly, I heard snarls and moans of pain. It sounded worse than
Saturday night at a cannibal brothel. Ugh.

Carefully, I stepped into view, keeping my hands splayed and
by my sides. Nervous cops had a bad habit of shooting first and
apologizing at your funeral. Although they did send flowers.

"Move along, mack!" snarled the young cop, snapping a fresh
clip into her automatic. "It ain't healthy to be around here."

"Hey, he's armed!"

Their guns swiveled to point at me.

Approaching, I slowly reached into my jacket and withdrew
my commission booklet. "FBI," I announced. "Federal agent
Ed Alvarez. What's the situation, Officers?"

They seemed disgruntled, but accepted my arrival. At least,
their Heckler & Koch 9mm automatic pistols were no longer
directed towards my tender stomach. Thank goodness. Lead was
so hard to digest after a pepperoni burrito.

"We were responding to a domestic, on the fifteenth floor,"
rattled the woman. "No response to our knock, we heard sounds
of violence, announced our identity and kicked the door down."

The man shivered. "Some kind of animal was eating the tenants. Place resembled a slaughterhouse. We each pumped a full
magazine into the beast before it even noticed we were there."

"Who went out the window?"

"Harry," said the woman. She was calmer now and a lot
more angry. "The fool tried to Mace the thing."

Weird noises were coming from down the hallway. Snarling,
growling and a crunching sound much too reminiscent of teeth
on bones. It was not music to my ears.

"What does it look like?"

"Big. Ugly. No hair."

Interesting. Briefly, I wondered if it was a bald werewolf, a
squid-bear or another giant mutant Chihuahua. We had been
finding a lot of those lately. Must be something in the water.

"Where is the animal now?"

"Who knows?"

"I called for emergency backup," went the man. "But this is Chicago."

"With more crime than cops," I finished for him. "How long?"

"They get here when they get here."

Damn. "My people can arrive in five minutes. You want help?"

"Buddy, we need help," admitted the older and obviously wiser officer.

"Done." Turning my back on the pair, I pressed the transmit switch on my wristwatch, a nifty little piece of Bureau equipment that could do everything but strap itself on your wrist. And Technical Services was working on that.

"Alert," I said. "Possible homicidal supernatural at 175 Wacker Drive. Definitely bulletproof. Call in the troops, gang, this could be a toughie."

"We're on the way," replied a familiar voice.

"Don't stop for lunch, or it may be me."

"Gotcha."

Tucking my badge into my belt so it would be on display, I shrugged, and both Magnums were in hand. The Model 42 ultra-light in my left was loaded with rubber stun bullets. The heavy stainless-steel Model 66 in my right held a scenario load of an armor-piercing military round, soft lead dumdum, explosive mercury tip, silver bullet, phosphorus tracer and a blessed wood bullet. Not much, but it would have to do.

A scream of raw terror echoed along the hall, and the three of us charged with guns drawn. Monster or not, no cop could ignore a cry for help.

Inside, the apartment was a mess, with torn clothing everywhere, furniture smashed, television smoking, carpet ripped, papers scattered, and amid the fresh destruction stood the beast.

And it was no Chihuahua.

Vaguely resembling a hairless lion, the muscular animal must have weighed four hundred pounds easy. It had mottled, diseased-looking skin, long saber-tooth tusks, prehensile claws, charnel-house breath and a real bad attitude.

But according to my sunglasses, the creature possessed no Kirlian aura. None. That was impossible! Incredible! Everything living had an aura: white for good, black for evil, green for magic and a million shades in between. Maybe this monster was off the visible spectrum. Had an ultraviolet or infrared aura. For one brief moment I debated trying to capture the thing alive for the lab crew. Then it turned and I saw a slippered foot sticking out of its drooling snout. So much for capture. Lumpy the Lion died here and now. Eat a civilian in my town and you went down for the count. Fast and hard. End of discussion.

"Aim for the head!" I cried, targeting the chest in an attempt to hit the heart. I forced myself to keep the instructions plain. No coded battle phrases; these were street cops, not federal secret agents.

Our four guns sounded louder than four hundred as we banged away in the small room. The muscular animal jerked with each pounding round, but no blood showed and the damage was minimal.

As the cops withdrew behind the wall to quickly reload, Lumpy bounded forward, so I tossed in my only grenade and joined the officers. In the future, I really should go shopping with more than just the bare essentials. However, bazookas just ruined the lines of a good sports jacket.

A thunderous explosion shook the floor, flame and debris blasting out the doorway. Without waiting for the chaos to settle, I dashed inside to continue the fight but found only bits of the Bozo Boojum strewn about. Contemptuously, I snapped my fingers at the dead monster. Ha! Lumpy hadn't been so tough. I had in-laws who used grenades to dust the furniture. Kept their place clean, but sure was hard on the doilies.

But even as the smoke thinned, the pieces started slithering towards each other as the monster began to reassemble. I felt my lunch pack its bags for a quick vacation as I watched the reverse dissection. Uh-oh. Total cellular unification. Every tiny piece of its body was a separate living organism. I could be here for the whole day!

Then again, maybe not. Moving fast, I grabbed a foreleg, sprinted into the kitchenette, stuffed it into the microwave and turned the dial to high. The results were interesting. Wrapping my handkerchief around what resembled a brain, I dropped the pulsating gray cauliflower-like mass into the sink and flicked on the garbage disposal. Instant lobotomy. Just add water.

In a spray of electrical sparks, the microwave shorted out, and the door swung aside as the limb flopped towards freedom. Then the rumbling garbage disposal jammed to a halt, and an undulating brain plopped out of the sink and started rolling across the floor. This thing was harder to kill than a congressional pay raise!

Dumbfounded, the police officers could only watch from the doorway. This type of fighting was totally out of their experience, almost beyond comprehension. Each probably thought they were hallucinating. Or dreaming. That was the standard reaction. But the cops were still here. If we survived this mess, the Bureau could have a couple of prime recruits.

Rummaging under the sink, I found a can of drain cleaner and liberally sprinkled the acidic lye over anything that seemed healthy. Sizzling and dissolving under the chemical onslaught, the stubborn supernatural relentlessly continued to piece itself back together.

Tossing aside the can, I grabbed another limb and started to heave it out the window, but stopped. Not everybody in Chicago would be wearing protective armor, and the next poor slob to get glass rained on him would die. Damn, damn, damn! Think, Alvarez, think!

I had never fought a true unkillable before, only read the Bureau manual on the subject. Unfortunately, I had just exhausted the usually helpful handbook. Time to be brilliant. Um . . . er . . .

"Oven?" offered the young cop.

"Yes!"

As I wrestled with the struggling forearm, the woman turned the gas oven on and opened the door. Claws ripped at my chest, exposing the armor under what had been my favorite shirt. Slamming the leg against the tiled wall a few times, I barely managed to force the adamantine limb into the waiting oven. The cop clanged the metal door shut, while I grabbed the refrigerator and pushed it in front of the stove.

Immediately, a wild pounding could be heard, but the boojum stayed put. However, the smell coming from the exhaust vent was bad enough to peel the paint off a battleship; the fumes were reminiscent of sweaty gym socks, old cat litter and rancid hair tonic with just a hint of automobile transmission fluid. Whew! This thing could give a sick skunk an inferiority complex.

With a tremendous crash, the refrigerator toppled over and the smoking forearm bounded out of the oven.

"What the hell is this thing?" demanded the older cop, his automatic barking steadily as he tracked the legless runaway. "Some kind of organic robot?"

As good a lie as any. "Yes," I panted. "It escaped from Fort Sheridan early this morning."

"Sonofabitch!" cried the woman, hacking at the brain with a meat cleaver. The two pieces just moved faster.

Going into the living room, I yanked a cord from the wall and began tying grisly monster chucks to doorknobs and bathroom fixtures. About halfway complete, the living jigsaw puzzle flipped and flopped in a feeble attack, but couldn't regroup. For the moment.

The man poured a box of rat poison into a gaping section of the creature's intestines, but the deadly food only seemed to accelerate the healing process. A reverse metabolism? Damn, and I had drunk my only vial of Healing potion.

This was getting serious. If Lumpy re-formed before help arrived, we stood about as much chance of staying in one piece as it presently did of not. Electricity? Naw, it was only house voltage, couldn't even kill a dog. Set the place on fire? No good, too risky. If only we had some fast-setting cement, we could dump it in the lake. My mind began rifling through six years of fighting every damn thing on Earth, trying to find a solution. No . . . no . . . no . . .

"Hey, what's going on, Officers?" asked a man leading a group of people standing by the open door. Some teenager in a bathrobe had a goddamn video recorder. Sweet Jesus! This was just what I needed. Civilians with a camera.

"Run!" I bellowed, stepping between them and the boojum. Ripping off my watch, I clicked on the self-destruct sequence. That should buy me enough time to get them—

Multiple hands yanked the bystanders away, and in charged four people I knew well: a beautiful oriental woman in silk pajamas carrying a short double-barreled gun, a plump man in a sweat suit lugging a four-foot-long M-60 machine rifle, a trim, muscular woman holding a sword whose blade shimmered with rainbows and a tall pale man in bikini swim trunks holding a silver staff. Grinning, I clicked off the self-destruct. Yahoo! The cavalry had arrived! And not a bit too soon.

Leveling his silver magic wand, Raul gestured and a shimmering lattice of golden bars appeared in the air. Cops and civilians were rudely shoved into the hallway, the camera smashing against the jamb, then the door slammed shut, bolted, locked and the couch slid in front.

"Roach motel!" I ordered, pointing at Lumpy.

In a series of musical twangs, the cords snapped and the monster slapped together, finishing its regeneration. Standing rampart, the misshapen beast roared like some primordial nightmare from hell. God almighty, what awful breath.

You want it alive? asked Jessica in my mind. Even her telepathic broadcasts carried a faint trace of her Chinese accent. *Wouldn't a Bates Motel be more appropriate?*

Of course, I want it dead. But he's an unkillable, I thought. *Capture is our only chance. Tell the gang.*

Done.

They frowned, but obeyed. Thank goodness for trained professionals. And high explosives.

Ramming the end of his staff into the stained carpet, Raul ran past the monster, dragging the wand behind him. In its wake was formed a shining line. The boojum started after him in a bound. Her sword flashing, Mindy chopped off a pointed cat ear. Howling in pain, the creature turned, and Raul dashed by again. Confused, the beast headed for the smashed window. Working the bolt on his ungainly machine rifle, George put a stuttering stream of high-velocity lead slugs into Lumpy, forcing the creature to remain where it was. Only a blur, Raul angled by a third and fourth time. The hairless feline began clawing at the floor, and Mindy chopped off a paw. Spitting in unbridled fury, the beast crouched, preparing to leap, and Jessica gave it both barrels of her taser stun pistol. Twin hooked barbs, small as match heads, buried themselves in the boojum's rump. Trailing the hooks were hair-thin wires connected to a powerful accumulator in the handle. As the barbs made contact, 12,000 volts automatically shunted into the beast. Enough hard electrical current to stun a Republican on election night. Lumpy toppled over as both rear legs went momentarily numb.

I put a couple more .357 distractions into the mottled head, and Jess gave it a spray of Mace from a fountain pen, as Raul shot by on his jet-powered roller skates for the last time. Mages are mighty useful folk, but so damn weird.

Sheathing her sword, Mindy swatted the thing across the throat with the scabbard. Eyes bulging, the beast began hacking and coughing. Personally, I thought the monster was damn lucky it didn't have external genitalia. That was always Mindy's favorite target, and magical or not, it was one attack which stopped the male of any species.

". . . !" shouted the wizard. And as our creature jumped, it rebounded from the immaterial barrier of the pentagram the beast was trapped inside.

Glaring an almost tangible hate, the beast slammed its resilient body against the magical forceshield. The ruined apartment reverberated from the strident impacts, pictures danced off the walls and a mirror cracked.

Breathing a sigh of relief, I holstered my lightweight Magnum and reloaded the 66 with Glaser Sure Kill safety slugs. The miniature shotgun rounds should at least annoy Lumpy if he got free again.

"Good work," I complimented as my team gathered round. "Where's the van?"

"Parked outside taking up four spots," said Mindy, patrolling around the pentagram. Lumpy matched her movements and they growled menacingly at each other.

"What's the plan, Ed?" asked Jessica. "Cement and the lake?" She sounded sad. Telepaths were such sensitive folk. Killing anything bothered them. I even had to be gentle turning off the television.

Unwrapping a beef stick, George placed it in his mouth as if it were a greasy cigar. "No way," snorted our soldier. "Laughing Boy would be free and running amuck within the hour."

On cue, Lumpy launched itself at the ceiling and cracked the industrial-grade concrete with its head. Sheesh! I wanted to toss this thing a dictionary so it could discover the meaning of the word "surrender."

"Then we send it to the Holding Facility," said Raul. Slowly, he diminished in height as his superskates converted into sneakers once more. Transparent plastic sneakers, with the socks underneath woven to resemble bare feet, but that was only to be expected. I'd seen worse.

"Check," I said. "I'll call ahead saying that we're sending in a problem child and have them prep an Omega Cell. Technical Services can puzzle over how to kill this boojum in their copious spare time."

"What do we do about the folks outside?" asked George, jerking a thumb towards the hallway.

At a nod from me, Jessica touched her forehead and scrunched her face in concentration. The shouting and bewildered cries from the other side of the portal slowed, then stopped, and we heard people casually chatting and walking away.

Going pale, Jessica wobbled, so I helped my wife into a cushionless chair. "Wiping ten minutes of memory from fourteen people is something of a strain," she admitted. "Luckily, nobody was a natural immune."

In consolation, I gave her a pat on the arm and a kiss. In her prime, my bride could have Brain Blasted the entire state of Illinois. But she was still recuperating from our battle with the Brotherhood of Darkness last week. Those yahoos had even less intelligence than Lumpy here.

Sprinkling powders while chanting, Raul Horta formed a huge, meter-wide rune on a smooth section of the floor. I busied myself feeding the appropriate code phrases into my watch to relay a priority signal to the big radio in our van, and on to the headquarters of our organization. Wherever that was. We had once found what I thought was Bureau HQ, but by the next week the office building had been converted into a parking garage. I guess the chief didn't trust anybody.

I got an answering bleep on my wristwatch just as the mystic letter of power began to glow and a shimmering oval portal formed in the air. Lumpy snarled and spit, but we paid it no attention.

Tugging on my sleeve, George pulled me aside.

"What?" I asked, puzzled.

He tried to appear casual. "I may be mistaken," Renault whispered around his beef stick. "But when you said we were going to send Felix over there to the Holding Facility, I could have sworn I saw it smile."

Eh? "You're nuts."

"Could be. Yet I saw what I saw."

"And why would anything be pleased that it was going to be incarcerated in the most escape-proof jail in the history of the world?"

The soldier shrugged. "Beats me. Maybe it's trying to pull a Brer Rabbit routine. But I don't like the concept."

Me neither. Renault may be paranoid—most Bureau agents were—but that was only because we did have so many enemies. And they were everywhere.

"Raul," I said. "Cancel the Portal spell, we're hauling Lumpy in personally."

And I'll be damned, but the beast maintained the most amazingly neutral expression that I have ever seen this side of a poker table.

Hmm.

2

"Brace yourselves!" I cried, tightening my grip on the steering wheel. Everybody grabbed whatever handhold was convenient and scrunched low in their seats.

As I maneuvered past a red sports coupe with vanity plates, our lumbering RV and trailer hitch went by the designated signpost on the Iowa Turnpike, and in a wild burst of pyrotechnics, we shunted out of the universe. Momentarily, I was blinded by a violent explosion of colors as the van was buffeted from side to side by swirling constellations of stars. There came a curse, a metallic crunch, a shattering of glass . . . and we were through!

When vision cleared, I gently tapped on the brakes, easing the RV to a halt on the dirt road. The van stopped only a scant meter before a simple wooden crossbar blocking the road. The rigidly motionless bar wasn't supported by anything visible on either end. A square black and white sign hanging from the middle of the oak bar bore the brutally plain international NO symbol. The words "or else" had never been deemed prudent, or necessary. Only Bureau personnel knew about the small thermonuclear bomb under the crossbar. It was our way of discouraging unwelcome guests. Worked just fine too. Nobody we nuked ever returned again. At least, not in this life.

Now surrounding us, instead of the lush summer greenery of the Iowa farmlands, was a dead flat plain of sun-baked mud stretching to the horizon, the sky a featureless vista of gray. Ah, there was no place like home.

And this was no place like home.

Discernible solely by its lack of cracks, the slim roadway we were on was the only safe area to traverse. The rest of the landscape was a billion-dollar death trap, littered with antipersonnel land mines, acid pits, napalm geysers, telescoping pungi sticks, nerve gas, laser beams and exploding cactus. Even touching the crossbar, much less going past it, would have made this dirt roadway join the rest of the deadly plain. It was a toll few wished to pay.

Ahead of us was a high stone wall topped with electrified, poisoned concertina wire. There were angular turrets every ten meters crowned with rectangular missile launching pods, Gatling guns, squat flamethrowers and who knew what else. This was the secret location of Bureau 13's hidden training Academy and Holding Facility, code-named Bangor-Maine, for some reason lost in antiquity. Knowing the gang at HQ, it was probably an obscene joke from the 1880s.

The Academy and Holding Facility were literally off the map, civilian drivers simply went past the appropriate mile marker. But with proper Bureau ID, approaching the sign would shunt you into a small pocket universe hidden between the front and back of the road post. Speed was not essential to traveling to this miniverse. I did that to reduce our time in dimensional transit. For some reason, it reminded me of visiting Cleveland. Lord knows why, since I've never been there.

And finding the correct signpost was always a pain. I had to call an ever-changing 800 number, at thirteen past any odd-numbered hour, and properly identify myself with half a page of code phrases and countersigns, to eventually get the current location of the mile marker. Being a pocket universe, the damn doorway was constantly shifting. Last time it was in the middle of a forest preserve in Colorado. The time before that it was in the washroom of a Tastee-Freez in downtown Boston. And the stares the seven of us got from the staff as we piled into the stall together! Whew. Talk about embarrassing.

Bangor-Maine was one of the few Bureau locations that survived the Slaughter of '77 when ninety percent of all the Bureau agents were killed within a two-hour period by an unknown enemy. Our darkest day. Just recently, the legendary J. P. Withers had assigned himself to the case. He would search forever until he caught and killed the people responsible. And since J.P. was immortal, when he said forever, Withers meant it.

Checking on the trailer behind us in the rearview mirror, I released my safety harness and thumbed a transmit switch on the dashboard, sending our recognition code. Then, unlocking the door, I climbed to the ground. Eagerly, the rest of my team scrambled from our armored vehicle.

Ever the lady, Jessica daintily stepped out and straightened her white summer dress. Slim enough to do it, Mindy hopped through an open window. Fat boy George dramatically kicked aside the rear door, and Raul phased straight through the side of the RV. The big show-off. He loved to play with new spells.

Judiciously, I checked the load in both of my .357 Magnums and scrutinized the battered yellow trailer hitched to the rear of our vehicle. Our guest had been suspiciously silent for quite a while. I only hoped the tricky bastard wasn't planning something. Lumpy's last escape attempt had destroyed an overpass, an underpass, two off ramps, plus a tollbooth. And while annihilating the latter was not an altogether bad thing, attempting to eat the attendants had been definitely out of line. Damn near rude.

"Hey, Ed!" called somebody from the other side of the van. "What was that metallic crunch?"

"Ran over our own hubcaps," I replied, glaring at the flattened disks lying crumpled on the hard mud.

"Yet another example of your splendid driving, Mr. Alvarez."

I muttered an appropriate riposte.

Chuckling, the gang encircled the trailer in a standard #3 defensive pattern. Mindy Jennings stood directly before the doors in a martial-arts crouch, her indestructible sword held in muscular hands, its long curved blade glinting in the harsh sunlight. She was now properly dressed for action in loose-fitting, neutral-colored clothing and military sneakers.

Wearing army fatigues and combat boots, George Renault was off to the left of her, the lengthy barrel of his huge M-60 machine rifle pointed steady at the side of the trailer. Dangling from his humongous weapon was a glistening belt of linked, steel-tipped, .30 combat rounds.

Hovering a few feet in the air, Raul Horta casually held his silver wizard's staff in one hand. He was incongruously dressed in leather sandals, neon-orange pants and a sleeveless T-shirt that said on the front, "Not a member of a secret government agency."

Nearby, Jessica had drawn a taser stun pistol from the shoulder holster under the short brocade jacket of her summer dress. And from the clothing locker in the van, I had obtained a spare sports jacket which happily matched my black slacks and blue shirt. Plus lots of ammunition. With Magnums in hand, I was maintaining a discreet distance, attempting to watch everything.

"Also heard glass shatter before," said George, the stick of a lollipop extending from his mouth. The breast pocket of his green shirt bulged with spare sweets. Mr. Renault had once heard the word "diet," but couldn't quite figure out what it meant. "Anybody see what broke?"

Adjusting his Phillies in '86 baseball cap, Raul pointed with his staff. "Taillight on the trailer."

"Nothing important, then?"

"Nope."

"So long as it wasn't the padlock again," Mindy grunted. "We had quite enough trouble getting the muscle-bound lump here."

"Where are the guards?" asked Renault, glancing about.

Raul proffered his Bureau wristwatch. "Ed, should we put in a call?"

"No need," announced Jessica. "They're on the way." Her lovely face had that faraway expression, the fingertips of a hand lightly touching her forehead.

Turning towards the stone wall, I saw a billowing cloud of dust starting to come our way. Soon, I could identify a Harrier jumpjet skimming along the ground on her bottom jets. Whew. That was something new. Sleek, fast and ultra-maneuverable, the British-designed, U.S. Marine Corps modified fighter/interceptor was a flying arsenal, its delta wings, needle prow and wide belly bristling with weapons.

Landing a few meters away from us, the canopy retracted with a hydraulic hiss, and a figure stood up in the cockpit, his face masked by the mirrored visor of the attack helmet. As his head turned to face us, the guns and missiles tracked along, slavishly copying his every move. I would have loved to sneak a peak at it through my Bureau sunglasses to see what magical armaments the jet carried, but I knew in advance the machine was shielded against such an intrusion.

"Alcatraz," snapped the pilot, his hands ominously out of sight.

"Joliet," I replied.

There was a pause.

A gloved hand raised the hinged visor and I saw the dashingly handsome features of Gilad Lapin, the warden of the Holding Facility. Removing the helmet entirely, the weapons of the Harrier automatically returned to pointing straight ahead.

"Hey, Ed!" He waved.

"Hi, Gil. That's some fancy go-cart you're riding these days."

"What? This old thing? Bought it at a flea market with Monopoly money."

"Howdy, Gil," said George, not moving his attention from the trailer. The rest of my team gave assorted greetings.

" 'Lo, George, Mindy, Raul, Jess . . . ah . . . excuse me. Hello, Mrs. Alvarez."

Smiling, Jessica raised a hand so he could properly admire the shiny gold ring on her fourth finger. We had only been married six months, and some folk still weren't used to calling my wife by her new name.

"Where's the good Father?" asked Gil.

"On his yearly sabbatical," said Horta, nimbly crossing legs underneath his floating self.

Lapin made a face. "Oh no. Will he never stop trying?"

"Not Michael Xavier Donaher," said George, laughing, as he checked the play on his ammunition belt.

For a moment, Gil seemed puzzled at the action, then his features brightened in remembrance. Even though I was supposedly immune to the illusion, occasionally I could still faintly see the banjo that the M-60 was spelled to resemble. It had once caused quite a ballyhoo with a security scanner at Dulles Airport. And an even worse incident at a folk music concert.

Inquisitively, Gil jerked his chin towards the trailer. "So what do you have there?" He knew it must be something special, or else we would not have bothered to cart our prisoner here. Many indeed were the hostile supernaturals whose graves were junkyards, river bottoms and concrete foundations. A nifty little trick we had learned from the Mafia.

"Boojum from Chicago," I said, using the code phrase for an unknown. "It ate some people, ripped apart a major highway intersection and flatly refuses to drop dead."

"Uncooperative, eh?" he said, massaging a dimpled jaw. "Anything else interesting about it?"

"No aura," I stated.

Justifiably, Gil did a double take. "Huh? What was that?"

"It has no aura," I repeated. "None. Zero. Zip. *Nada*."

The pilot worked a pinkie in his ear. "No aura, you say?"

"No aura."

"Impossible! Sure your sunglasses are working?"

Taking my tinted Bureau glasses from my sweater pocket, I walked closer and offered them. "See for yourself."

Donning the glasses suspiciously, Lapin glanced at his own hand, then me, the rest of the team and then the trailer.

"Damnation, I can see the Kirlian aura from everybody but the trailer. Is this a gag? Is that hitch empty, or is there really a boojum in there?"

As if in response, the metal cubicle vibrated with a barely contained roar.

"Lumpy says he's still here," quipped Raul.

Gil gave a crooked smile. "And it's not a robot? Or artificial construct?"

A warm dry wind blew on me, carrying with it the smell of nothing. "Nope. Living organic."

"Well, feather my props," mumbled the pilot in awe. "No Kirlian aura. Technical Services will positively flip over this! Any problems in the recovery?"

"Not really," replied Jessica. "I wiped a few memories and then we replaced the creature with a shaved lion we stole from the Lincoln Park Zoo. When the news services discover that it's only a lion, that should help dispel the silly idea that monsters actually exist."

We had a good laugh at that.

"Oh, and we narrowly missed having another encounter with Jules Englehart," added Mindy.

In unison, the group turned and spat on the ground.

Englehart was a free-lance news reporter for the *National Gazette*, and an old nemesis of the Bureau. He specialized in reporting on supernatural events, and our field agents had run into him more times than we fired bullets. Twice, Bureau agents had saved him from being eaten by ghouls. And once he actually got his hands on physical evidence that our secret organization existed. The Bureau almost let him get consumed that time. But our oath of allegiance swears us to protect all American citizens, not just the folks that we like. Details, details.

Of course, when my team returned his unconscious body to his apartment, we had accidentally passed a powerful magnet over his videotape collection, short-sheeted his bed and emptied his refrigerator. But such minor revenges gave us little solace. One of these days, the fool will cause real trouble, and then we would have to shoot him in the name of national security. Privately, a few of us prayed for the day to come as early as possible. But they were in the minority. Well, mostly.

"Jess, can't you do something to him?" asked Gil. "Erase

Englehart's memory of the Bureau? Or give him the uncontrollable urge to live in Antarctica?''

She shrugged. ''Sorry. Wish I could. But Jules has got a natural telepathic block the size of Gibraltar.''

Suddenly, the top of the trailer erupted in a spray of metal bits and out leapt our prisoner. It landed heavy and started down the road away from the Facility. I drew both pistols. *Madre mia!* Was Lumpy really that stupid, or did he have a death wish?

''Outgoing!'' cried George, his big machine rifle starting to yammer and spit flame.

A line of dirt puffs exploded in front of the scampering beast and it wisely came to a halt. As Lumpy turned, Mindy threw a knife and the handle hit the bald bozo smack between the eyes—which promptly crossed. Jessica fired her taser and tossed a teargas grenade. I pumped a couple of Sure Kills into his chest. Raul cast a Sleep spell, Death spell, a net, chained its legs together and made the ground sticky.

Under the accumulated barrage, the boojum staggered, then Lumpy tore itself free and charged straight at us. Its snarling savage expression said what no amount of words could.

''Well, screw you too,'' drawled Gil, jerking on his helmet. A split second later, the right-wing missile pod of the Harrier extended a stuttering lance of flame. In a staggered series of bloody explosions, Lumpy stridently disintegrated.

But as expected, the tiny pieces scattered on the ground began to slither towards each other as the thing began to reassemble.

''Wow. Determined cuss, isn't he?'' stated the pilot over a PA system of the Harrier, his words echoing slightly. ''We gotta get this clown into an Omega Cell fast, before we run out of ammo and he starts chewing the landscape!''

On command, our mage did the wand routine, and the twitching monster chunks wafted back into the trailer. Raul then re-formed the roof, spot-welded the doors shut and taking a paintbrush from out of the air, wrote a glowing rune on every side of the You-Haul, including the bottom. An unusual precaution, but then, Lumpy was an unusual prisoner.

Taking a spare lock and extra chains from the equipment trunk in the van, we secured the trailer doors, and this time looped every foot of available linkage around the hitch until it resembled a chain-mail cocoon. Grenades and Claymore mines festooned the yellow trailer in the manner of so many army-issue Christmas tree ornaments.

As we finished, Gil said, "Raul, I don't recognize that rune. What will it do? Put the beastie to sleep? Blow off its head?"

"Nope," replied the mage, coming to ground. "This rune will temporarily give the boojum external genitalia."

"Highly targetable," said Mindy, smiling evilly, hands twisting on the pommel of her sword.

I winced, as did every other male present. Oddly, Jessica did also. Just being polite?

Empathy with you, my dear.

Wives, ain't they grand?

As we climbed into the blissful shaded comfort of our mobile fort, I started the engine and rolled past the barrier with the Harrier close behind. From the trailer came a muted growl, and for a moment, I could have sworn that it sounded like a guttural laugh.

Nyah. Couldn't be.

Following the flat mud road, we quickly approached the wall, which seemed to grow taller and taller. Distance had disguised its true size. Directly ahead of us was a metal door some ten meters high. As the van neared the base, the tremendous portal started to descend with a mighty mechanical rumble. When we reached the door, it was totally underground, the flat metal top level with the road, forming a ramp to drive along. Rolling across, I noted the portal was six meters thick, made of foot-wide sections of laminated steel alloy with a thin crystal insert between each of them. Interesting.

Of course, this barrier was simply here to keep folk out. To a lot of things in the Holding Facility this flimsy door wouldn't offer more resistance than a sheet of wet toilet tissue. All the real armament was in the Facility itself, and, brother, there was a lot. Almost enough for the place to declare itself an independent nation.

Past this first door, we drove on top of another giant portal, and yet a third ahead of us. But that last door was raised, blocking any further progress. Roughly in the middle of the second wall, I braked to a halt, and the portal behind us rose silently into position. Darkness descended and I hit the lights. When the first door closed with a hollow boom, the portal before us lowered to allow entrance into Bangor-Maine. I was sure that, when necessary, the middle door would also rapidly elevate to rudely mash invaders against the mammoth steel lintel overhead. Wish we had one of these in Chicago. It sure would be a great way to deter pesky salesmen. Hee-hee-hee.

Driving out of the wall, we could see a paved parking lot filled with Harrier jumpjets and Abrams heavy assault tanks, which were scant more than military forts with treads. Definitely state-of-the-art stuff. Very expensive. Oh heck. There goes the budget for the company picnic this year. Beyond the array of lethal ironmongery was the pleasant little torture town that I remembered far too well.

A double row of stores lined the main street; behind were neat two-story houses, eight homes to a block. Each of the blocks was staggered below the next, so that there was no direct avenue to the outer wall. Our commander and chief, Horace Gordon, doesn't miss a trick. The stores were there to lend a semblance of normalcy to the occupants, the houses were where the guards, teachers and students lived during their educational internment.

Scores of pedestrians were strolling about, lugging books, wheeling carts of groceries, hauling a truckload of coffins, chatting about their new abilities or just floating along above the sidewalk sipping a can of diet soda. The view was so tranquil and peaceful, it made my skin crawl knowing the truth.

"Lord, how I hate this place," said Mindy, nose flat against the window glass.

Polishing his weapon, George made some vague comment. If it didn't go whoosh or boom, it held little interest to Mr. Renault. Always made me wonder about his girlfriends.

Curiously, I glanced about for one house in particular, a huge weather-beaten Victorian mansion with seven gables, a widow's walk on the roof and bloodstains on the front porch, but couldn't find it anywhere. Had we passed Hell House already, and I missed the place? Didn't seem possible. I tried a sneak through my sunglasses, but quickly tucked them into my shirt pocket again. Surrounded by so much magic, it was impossible to locate any particular aura.

"If you're searching for Hell House," said Raul from inside the tiny closet near the lavatory, "just look for anybody pale, sweaty and trembling."

"Preferably with a broken weapon of some kind in their hands," continued Mindy. "It'd be a sure sign that we're close."

They had that correct. Occasionally, I still woke during the night with feverish dreams of my graduation run through that damn mansion. In spite of magical healing, I yet carry the scars of that sneaky banister which polymorphed into a live snake and soundly sank its fangs where only my doctor knew.

Jessica paused in the process of reloading her taser to laugh aloud, and I blushed. Okay, so it was now a family secret.

With a roar, the trailer shuddered and one wall bent drastically outward almost to the breaking point. I increased our speed and flicked on a flashing light.

"Hot soup, gangway!" I called over the PA system of the van. What sparse traffic there was got out of our way fast.

In the distance, I could see an old World War II style Quonset hut, a half-cylinder made of corrugated iron lying on its side. That was the exterior of the Holding Facility. "Jail" seemed far too weak and feeble a term for the inverted fortress.

Endlessly, we did left turn, right turn, left turn, right turn, but with each corner the Quonset hut came closer. And always in the background was the Harrier jumpjet hovering slightly above us, constantly keeping our boojum in range. Somehow I think the animal knew this because it remained quiescent. Once burned, twice shy, three times exhausted.

Reaching the exact center of town, we encountered a broad traffic circle. Alcatraz Street. On the outside of the circular road was a staggered barricade of unpretentious cinder-block warehouses. On the island in the middle was a simple wire fence surrounding the Quonset. A book and its cover. Yep. Definitely.

Stopping in front of the gate in the fence, we disconnected the trailer hitch and moved the van forward a few meters to give sufficient room. We had barely cleared the regulation distance when the hitch burst apart and there stood Lumpy four times his original size. Now he was officially a growing menace.

Instantly, the metal side of the hut rippled in the manner of parting water and out came a huge mechanical arm, irregular slabs of armor barely concealing the mammoth gears and motors inside its adamantine skeleton. Almost the entire length of the robotic arm was lined with defensive runes, gun turrets, arbalists, crucifixes, Mogen Davids, ankhs, juju bags or pulsating crystals. At the end of the titanic limb was a blunt three-fingered claw large enough to seize the moment. Which it promptly did.

Entirely without effort, the claw snared Lumpy in its cold iron grip and gave the beast a little squeeze. Our hairless lion squealed and went limp. Smoothly contracting, the leviathan limb hauled the boojum inside the Quonset with another ripple effect. A split second later, there was a muffled explosion, and Lumpy's dumb head cannonballed a hole through the metal wall. It bounced twice, then a harpoon with a steel cable attached to the end embedded itself smack between the slanted cat eyes. Ingloriously, the roll-away head was reeled back inside, and we finally allowed ourselves to relax.

Then fleetingly, the memory of Lumpy's smile came to mind, and I debated if the creature had been pretending to be crazy so as to get inside the Facility that much quicker. But I dismissed the possibility. Not even the ghost of Houdini could escape once inside this prison. And believe me, Harry had really tried.

But still, I reached for the hand mike, deciding to alert the guards to watch for trouble.

Just in case.

3

"By the way," Gilad said over our dashboard radio as we rolled along the traffic circle heading back into town. "Why did you bother to come personally instead of just shunting the boojum in through a magical portal?"

Unclipping the hand mike, I pressed the transmit switch. "Just being careful. Besides, we received permission to get a replacement mage for Anderson weeks ago, and this seemed a prime opportunity to see the students."

The conversation paused a moment out of respect for our long-gone friend. The handbook says that there are one hundred ways to leave the Bureau. Richard Anderson had discovered retirement option #101. He actually retired. But then, Richard had always been an amazing fellow.

"Any wizards ready to graduate?" asked Jess, breaking the silence.

"Actually, we have four mages," came the incredible reply.

Everybody perked up at that.

Mindy took the microphone. "Four? That's wonderful!"

"Well, two of them are a pair and one is only a Healer, can't do anything but benign magic," crackled the speaker. "But it is a fantastic number of wizards to have at once. Hell, most years we only train four mages total."

"How far along are they?" called out Raul. As a wizard he had to stay far away from radios and other types of complex machinery, or else they behaved in the most annoying manner.

There was a crackle of static, and Horta retreated. ". . . and Professor Burton is running them through Hell House this afternoon," commented Lapin. "Wanna watch?"

"Does a gargoyle eat its young?"

Gil laughed. "I'll take that as a yes."

After saying goodbye, the Harrier angled off in the direction of the airfield and soon dwindled out of sight.

"Let's go get our new mage," I declared.

"Be nice to get another female," said Mindy. "This group has always been rather man-heavy."

"Any problem with that, my proud beauty?" asked Horta, sliding closer on the couch beside her.

Smiling sweetly, Jennings batted her eyelashes, made a kissy mouth, snuggled nearer and gave the mage an eloquent elbow to the ribs. Breath came out of him in a whoof.

"Heavens, no," she purred. "Whyever do you ask?"

Horta's answer consisted mostly of a pained expression of how very sorry he was for asking.

Having spent six weeks of training here a million years ago, I knew the location of the Base Command. Situated on a nondescript side street, BC was a three-story brick square with mirrored windows, sans any sort of ornamentation or signs. More security precautions. Unless you knew it was HQ, nobody could have deduced the fact. The place more resembled an insurance office than a high-tech computerized command center. But then, don't they always?

Driving into the parking lot, I took a spot alongside the walkway between a horribly beweaponed motorcycle and a red shag flying carpet. The team piled out, and I locked the doors as they ambled inside the building. We were each curious to see this aspect of the Academy, previously denied to us as cadets.

The foyer was made of cool-blue marble, and Mrs. Cunningham, the woman at the reception desk, was equally friendly. But she gave good directions, and three turns, two staircases later, my team found that holiest of holies, the Hell House Command Complex. Or, as we called it as students, the Principless Office.

After a moment of shuffling feet and clearing throats, I knocked on the door and a voice bid us enter. Stepping into its air-conditioned magnificence, a shiver ran through my gut. External or internal causes? Geez, I felt nervous as a new field agent opening his first grave. An enclosed, elevated walkway extended over an incredible array of computer mainframes that none of us could identify. And at the far end of the colonnade was a small dais protected by a dome of clear Armorlite glass. An elaborate control curved around the entire edge of the dais going from doorjamb left to doorjamb right. Six folding chairs were set behind an impressive swivel chair that would have appeared more at home on the bridge of a starship.

Walking along the colonnade, ringing footsteps heralded our approach, and the swivel chair did what it does best.

"About time," said Joyce Burton, rising to meet us and offering a hand. We shook. She had a firm grip. "The senior class is ready and raring to go."

As always, the prof was in tight black slacks and a shapeless green turtleneck sweater, her long brown hair almost tied off in a scraggly ponytail. Fashion was not a subject Our Dean of Destruction taught at the Academy.

"Students think they're pretty hot stuff, eh?" asked Renault, resting his ungainly machine rifle against a nearby wall.

Burton smiled. "Of course!"

"Life is a learning experience," I said with a laugh.

Favoring his sore ribs, Raul took a metal folding chair and it became a plush Barcalounger as his fanny met the seat. "Where is Hell House anyway?" asked the mage, placing ankle atop knee.

"On the other side of Bangor," Joyce replied. "Thus, when we train a telepath, the mentalists have a hard time reading our thoughts."

"Pretty smart," I acknowledged, sitting next to Jess. My chair didn't do anything but start to get warm. "But then, the gang at TechServ were always a fiendishly clever bunch. Those vampire doorknobs will go into Bureau history."

"And I thought the welcome-mat trapdoor was a particularly nice touch," added Jess.

"As their designer," said Burton, doing a bow and sweep, "I thank you." Then she clapped her hands. "Okay, people! Let's make like an audience."

As we gathered close to her chair, the overhead lights dimmed, and a huge liquid-crystal theatre screen descended into view. Some eight feet by four, its silvery white surface flickered into life.

"All that's missing is popcorn," whispered George.

Mindy shushed him.

As the screen cleared of hash, it focused on the foyer of the place we knew well, and did not care for a bit. The detail and clarity were amazing. Seemingly, we were looking past empty air at the inside of Hell House. There was not even the diffraction of glass. I found myself wanting to reach out and try to touch the artificially dusty furnishings, but resisted temptation. Optic fiber, liquid crystal, laser holograph, high-tech science or

not, I wasn't goofy enough to risk a finger on the assumption
that the House couldn't still get me through the theatre screen.
That building was tricky.

Adorning the ceiling of the front hall was a huge crystal chandelier that gave off weak yellowish light. To the left was a great
marble staircase that curled upward to the next floor. My butt
itched for a moment as I saw the banister again. A sliding-door
closet was to the right, and a curtained alcove to the left.

The stage was set, the house activated, enter the players.

Did I remember to tell the Facility guards to put Lumpy in
quarantine, since he had eaten human flesh? Yes, I had. Okay.

With the fully expected creak of ancient hinges, the door
swung open and in walked the senior class. Mentally, I wished
them luck. They would need it.

The twins were the ones to first catch my attention. Wearing
jeans and T-shirts, they were near identical in form and face,
except that the man had coal-black hair, while his sister was a
platinum blonde. Rather pretty, actually. Nice legs.

Watch it, warned my wife.

Oops.

Next came a tall powerful man in military garb, a faint thin
scar marring his right cheek. Mindy gave a short whistle of
appreciation. And I agreed, but maybe not for the same reasons.
The guy was a Goliath, a Hercules! Roughly seven feet tall and
some three hundred pounds, not an ounce of it anything but
rock-hard muscle. This man didn't need any magic. He could
punch the House to death. Grenades were hung on a military
web harness across his mighty chest, an ammo pouch was slung
over a shoulder, a huge revolver was holstered at his hip and he
held a squat Thompson .45 machine gun with an underslung
cheesewheel superclip.

George murmured approval.

Following Rambo Jr. was a tall stately woman with a stunningly beauti—ah, plain face and far too much bust. I prefer
women who are small and slim and married to me.

Better, noted Jessica in my head.

Whew. Another daring escape from the jaws of death by Edwardo Alvarez, boy husband.

The stunningly "plain" woman was carrying a wooden dowel,
only about a foot long. Hmm, only a beginner mage. Raul Horta
had a staff four feet in length and made of solid silver.

Tagging close behind came a wild-haired beauty in a low-cut

gypsy gown of a thousand colors. Barefoot, she padded into the house.

"Barefoot?" I asked.

Twirling a dial, Professor Burton shrugged. "Something to do with having to be in contact with the Mother Earth. How do I know? Mages are crazy."

"Darn tootin'," said Raul, pinning a hypno-spiral button to his T-shirt which now read, "Vote for anarchy!"

Bringing up the end of this conga line was a thin, pale man dressed in the height of fashion. Gucci shoes, Sergio Valenta three-piece suit, expertly tailored, and if that wasn't a Rolex Presidential watch on his wrist, I'd eat the banister. He even had a gold watch chain looped across his vest, with some sort of foreign coin dangling as a fob. Two watches? Dapper Dan struck me as the kind of person who would wash his hands before going to the bathroom. The only thing lacking was a silver spoon sticking out of his mouth.

As soon as the six entered the foyer of the house, Joyce flipped a switch on the console and the door behind them slammed shut. They turned just in time to see the four great bolts ram into position, and an iron grate slide down from the ceiling. Then in orderly fashion, every window in the building noisily closed, the shutters crashed together and locked tight.

"Whew," remarked Donald, the darker twin. "Lock and load, gang. It's showtime."

The prof pressed a button. A hollow mocking laugh echoed throughout the old mansion, and the chandelier tinkled in a ghostly manner.

Working the bolt on his Thompson, the tall slab of muscle with a scar glanced about. "Okay, standard defensive position. Tina and I will take the front. Don and Connie cover the rear. Patrika in the center. Sir Reginald will be on point. Remember, we're here to find an iron jewel, size unknown."

Slowly, the dapper man turned and cocked an eyebrow. "And you were placed in charge by whom, Mr. Sanders?" Even his voice sounded like inherited money.

"Somebody has got to be."

"Should have decided outside," said the beginner mage in her heavily accented English. She sounded Russian. Or at least a Soviet. "Clock is ticking, comrades."

Taking a clipboard, Joyce put a plus mark next to Sanders's name and a minus next to Christina Blanco's. Rules said they

were never to mention this was only a practice run with a time
limit.

Sanders frowned. "Conference!" he called, and they gathered
together. After a moment, the team broke apart, and Tina Blanco's
face was as red as her heritage.

"Positions!" snapped Ken, and everybody moved.

In a shimmer, Sir Reginald Foxworthington-Smythe dissipated into smoke and wafted along the central hallway of Hell
House. Neat! Now I sincerely hoped that he passed this final
exam. Having an elf in the Bureau would be a definite plus
factor. Why, at the yearly picnic, he could bring the cookies!

While the twins, Don and Connie, handcuffed themselves together—eh?—Tina polished her wooden staff on a sleeve and
Ken clicked off the safety on his machine gun. Positioned in the
middle of the assault force, the gypsy fingered the tiny gold cross
about her neck and muttered something in Latin. She must be
Patrika, the Healer. That's who I would want safe, and ready to
patch my guts back together if necessary.

Working a toggle, Burton had a door down the corridor creak
open, and the students dropped into attack formation. But nobody fired. Excellent.

"Who has got a pair of Bureau sunglasses?" asked Don in
his rumbling baritone.

Ken reached into his shirt pocket, paused and then started
patting his pockets. "I could have sworn . . ."

Next to me in the control room, Joyce chuckled and twirled
the sunglasses about on a finger.

"I was tempted to substitute a pair of normal sunglasses that
wouldn't show any auras just as a confusion factor," she said.
"But then decided that it was no fun kicking a cripple."

Sheesh! And she was on our side.

On the huge screen, the students were busy checking the front
hallway closet. It was completely filled with pre-aged clothes
that disintegrated at a touch. No information there. Ken spotted
the rigged rattrap bolted on the inside of the door, and Patrika
detected the razor blade welded onto the killing bar. That put
them in a somber mood. As well it should. Anything but critical
wounds could be healed within minutes, so nothing would kill
them outright. But death was the only limitation. Agents learned
their job here, or died in combat out in the real world taking
countless civilians with them. It was a final exam in more ways
than one.

After a quick peek in the lavatory, they moved on. Good thing too. If anybody had taken a seat, steel needles would have extended from the walls-ceiling-floor to stop but a scant foot away from the target. Joyce started to deactivate the lavatory, then stopped. True enough. Maybe later they'll get stupid or sloppy.

Parting the curtain, they found an unlocked door whose faded lettering read "BrOOM CLOSET." They discussed it, chuckled and moved on. Joyce didn't mark a plus or minus. Interesting.

Coalescing into a vertical tornado, Sir Reginald resolidified to report that the hallway seemed vacant of hostile forces. This gave the group courage, and they proceeded to search for the iron gem with a vigor. They looked behind portraits, inside the pages of books, under seat cushions, unscrewed light bulbs, emptied flower vases, lifted rugs, thumped the floors, pounded the walls. Nothing. They moved on.

During the lull, I made a note that once we had our new recruit, I would check with the Facility and see if they had discovered what Lumpy was yet, and where it came from. If there was a transtemporal breach to a dimension full of his kind, we could be in for serious trouble.

Entering the Living Room, directly in front of them was a small glass aquarium on a wrought-iron stand. Inside the aquarium was a school of winged, clockwork, wind-up goldfish wearing cowboy hats. The wire-screen lid was ajar. Patrika reached to straighten it, but Sir Reginald stayed her hand. Another plus! Funny does not equal harmless. And nothing kills faster than stupidity.

Switching positions, Don and Connie entered the Dining Room on point. The table was set for a sumptuous feast, with the most amazing china dishware and silver goblets. Don smiled, and Connie frowned. Glancing above the table, she became furious, and Don flicked his free hand at the wood rafters above them. Darkening into view, the huge spider hidden in the shadows lost its grip and slammed onto the suddenly vacant table with a meaty thump.

Not satisfied, Ken screwed a silencer onto his pistol and pumped two rounds into its head. That's my boy!

The Trophy Room proved to be empty of anything interesting, save an eight-foot-tall animated, stuffed grizzly bear, which the students tripped to the floor, shoved into the fireplace and ignited. Child's play.

It was starting to seem as if the professor had set this whole level of Hell House on neutral. Burton must be trying to lull them into a false sense of security before getting tough.

In the Library, Don and Connie found a loaded Ruger .44 revolver in a desk drawer. But it only took Sanders a second to discover that the barrel was blocked solid with lead. Pull the trigger and the backblast would blow a hand off. He got another plus mark.

The Kitchen yielded only a suspiciously half-empty bag of Purina Demon Chow. The oven was set to explode if turned on; Sir Reginald found that trap. Plus. Patrika opened the refrigerator, but not the freezer. A minus.

Of course, the pantry was filled with pants which produced the expected mass groan of pain. I had no idea who the punster was at the Academy, but someday I would find the nitwit and personally shoot him/her in the spleen.

Satisfied, Ken used hand signals to say the first floor was clean and they should move on. Tsk-tsk. Sloppy work that. There were twelve places they had failed to search for clues, two operational procedures forgotten entirely, and they hadn't found the special message for them on the telephone answering machine. It was obscene but useful. Still, on the whole, not bad.

"Cellar or second floor?" asked Connie in her sweet contralto. The twins were still holding hands. Bio-harmonics? I wondered.

"Cellar," suggested Tina, nervously fingering her staff.

"Second floor," said Sir Reginald, taking a pinch of snuff from an ornate gold box. "Nobody hides things in the cellar anymore. It's gauche."

In a juicy Bronx cheer worthy of any New Yorker, Patrika expressed her sentiments on the matter.

Ken agreed. "We'll hit the upper stories, but let's protect our rear."

With her wooden wand, Tina put a low-grade Seal spell on the cellar door so that it could not be opened from the other side. Using a pocketknife on a chair leg, Ken whittled a doorstop, which he then shoved tightly under the doorjamb. Meanwhile, Sir Reginald removed a lockpick kit from his tailored jacket and operated the ancient key latch, lubricating it first so there would be no noise. The twins kept guard.

Joyce nodded in approval.

"They're not bad," said Raul around a mouthful of popcorn.

I stole a buttery handful from the huge carton that had materialized in his lap. "Shaddup and watch."

"Will there be a cartoon later?" asked Mindy, and George hushed her.

In standard formation, the students stepped upon the first stair, and a ghostly figure appeared floating in the air before them. Moaning and groaning, the hideous vision warned them of unseen dangers and then faded away as only a ghost can—because it wasn't a laser holograph, but an actual ghost, Abduhl Benny Hassan, an ex-member of our team. Not willing to lose trained personnel under any circumstances, Horace Gordon had conjured poor Hassan back from his icy grave. Not even death could stop an agent of Bureau 13! Only major holidays.

Averting her gaze from the screen, Mindy gave a heartfelt sigh. She and Abduhl were close friends, getting a lot closer, when he died. But as a spirit he no longer had any interest in the pleasures of the flesh, and that sort of put a damper on the relationship.

Dutifully, Tina recorded the speech on a tiny tape recorder, Patrika took several flashless pictures with a pocket camera and Reginald made a rough sketch of Abduhl's face.

Proceeding carefully up the stairs, I noted with pride that they walked along the extreme edge of each step, exactly where the board met the wall. That was where stairs were their strongest, the least likely spot to creak and announce your presence to an enemy.

Just for fun, I asked Professor Burton to make the eyes of the portraits on the wall track their passage, and even had one old lady get out of her rocking chair and leave while the students were alongside. That caught their attention, but Don and Connie urged the team on by emphatically saying that it was nothing. Another plus mark by their names. I glanced at the clipboard. One telepathic and one a mage. The siblings were a powerful occult team, but only as long as they were in direct physical contact with each other. I wondered if the Dean of Doom had an answer to that.

"Yes," said Jessica, adding salt to the popcorn. "Itching powder."

Hmm, efficient, if somewhat slapstick.

As the students stepped on the landing, the staircase disappeared, leaving a solid seamless floor and no easy exit.

"Mark the spot," whispered Sanders.

Using a diminutive spray can, Sir Reginald painted a brilliant orange line across the floorboards where the stairs had once been. Good idea that. I made a note of the ploy.

Both sides of the hallway were lined with doors. Endless doors. There was no wall space. The portals stood jamb-to-jamb.

Placing her ear to a random door, Tina listened and then very carefully eased the latch and peeked inside. With a squeal, she threw herself across the hall and yanked open the opposite door. Everybody stepped out of the way as 160 tons of antique steam locomotive thundered out of one doorway and into the other.

In the control room, we were buffeted from side to side by the stereo speakers of the theatre screen hitting near overload.

As the caboose rattled out of sight, Don slammed the first door, Tina did the second.

For a minute, they stood coughing from the acrid smoke fumes that had poured from the flume. The floor between the two doors was deeply gouged from the rims of the steel wheels, piles of splinters sticking up in orderly lines, like toothpicks on parade. If you wanted weird, join the Bureau.

As breath returned, the seniors began heaping abuse upon the Bureau, their teachers in general, Burton specifically, and then cast dubious remarks on our general ancestry and sexual habits. Whew. Some of the curses were pretty good. George jotted a few on a notepad. Probably to give to his army buddies as birthday gifts.

And lying in plain sight on the floor was an iron gem.

Reaching for the jewel, Sanders paused and had the twins scan for traps. After a moment, they said it was clear. Wrapping a Bureau-issue handkerchief about his hand, Ken pocketed the gem.

"We got it," snapped Sanders. "Let's go."

"But there is still a lot remaining to explore," implored Patrika petulantly.

"Our mission was to get the gem," he stated. "We got it. We go. End of story."

I was becoming more and more fond of this guy. What a professional attitude. I bet he would happily shoot an enemy in the back. No dumb heroics, just get the job done and scram. Great!

Out of the corner of my eye, I saw Joyce insert a key into a special slot on the control board and unlock an armed switch.

The button glowed with a red light and she grimly pressed it down until there was a loud click.

Oh-oh, now the students were in for it. Whatever door they opened, wherever they went, the very next thing they encountered would be the dreaded, the deadly—

Suddenly, lights began blinking on the control board, and a printer started whining out a fax. Faintly from outside the building, I heard a siren howling.

"What's happening?" demanded Renault, weapon in hands.

Burton ripped the fax free and swore. "Code Eleven!"

"Huh?" I demanded.

Confused, Mindy added, "But the scale only goes to ten!"

"Not ours," said the professor, reading while she talked.

"So what the hell is an eleven?"

Joyce dropped the paper. I made a snatch, but the security fax was already blank.

"Jailbreak," she breathed.

4

Everybody was out of their seats and moving before the team even knew what they were doing.

"Instructions?" asked Mindy, sword unsheathed.

Raul shrugged. "Don't ask me."

"Professor, the students!" I cried.

With a curse, Burton swiveled to the control panel, flipped a gangbar, pressed three buttons and grabbed a microphone.

On the theatre screen, lights brightened Hell House and blinking markers appeared on the floor. The team dropped into a defensive formation and waited for the expected attack.

"This is an Alpha One emergency," intoned Burton. "This is not a drill. Repeat, this is not a drill! Cancel command is 'Egress'!"

"Barnum," answered Sanders, giving the acknowledgment code. "What's the situation, sir?"

"Steve McQueen," replied the professor.

Her face bisected by the edge of the screen, Tina gasped. "A great escape!"

"No," corrected Sir Reginald. "Papillon is a mass escape."

"Papillon is a single escape, fool!" snapped Patrika rudely. The gypsy turned to directly face the hidden video camera. Now, how did she know where it was? "What are your orders, Professor Burton?"

"Hit the arms locker," ordered Burton. "Take every weapon you can carry. Hell House has been deactivated. Git!"

They got. Fast.

"How long till the prisoners break out of the hut?" I asked as the professor clicked a switch and the theatre screen darkened to its former featureless silvery white.

Joyce glanced at her watch. "Six minutes. I only hope that Warden Lapin and the warehouses can hold 'em. I'm calling Gordon at HQ, alerting General MacAdams and his Phoenix team, activating the fail-safe and moving the exit portal."

48

"To where?" asked Jess. "Here?"

"Yep." She gestured at the floor. "Right here. This room."

I touched her arm. "Sir, we are yours to command."

The professor nodded. "Get out of this booth. Stay out of my way. Don't let anything into this building, and pray."

"Done."

Already, Mindy was dashing down the colonnade. "Come on, folks! Let's strip the van and get ready for a siege!"

"Wait!" I cried, and ripping open a package in my wallet offered a single orange pill to every member of my team. As each of us swallowed, we blurred out of vision and departed, moving at quadruple normal speed.

We now had twenty-four minutes. And counting.

In a shatter of glass our RV bounded into the lobby of Base Command and screeched to a halt on the smooth terrazzo floor in front of the reception desk. The unflappable receptionist, Mrs. Cunningham, didn't blink at our superspeed intrusion. At a snail's pace, she was throwing switches on an angled control board next to a hooded video monitor. Steel shutters leisurely rumbled into position over the doors and hole where the front window used to be, sealing us inside the building.

Grinding gears, I moved the RV further into the lobby, chipping paint and plaster off the walls, maneuvering its tail into a hallway intersection so that the missile pod on the roof of the van could have a clear firing range at the front, back and side doors.

Going to a supply locker in the RV, Jessica began tossing bits and pieces of body armor to the ground, while George and Mindy carried out the weapons locker and ammo trunk. The trunks had been bolted to the floor, but Ms. Jennings's indestructible sword had made short work of that minor inconvenience.

My team was already wearing torso armor, molded to our own unique physical contours. But this was no time for halfway measures. So we also strapped steel greaves on our shins and thighs, titanium vanbraces on our arms, added a magical zero-weight flak jacket over our personal armor and topped off the arrangement with Bureau combat helmets.

Providing full head coverage, the helmets were proof against a .50 AP round and/or 20,000 volts. They had built-in scrambled radios prelinked together and the visors were shatterproof, infrared sensitive and Kirlian positive.

They also had a Killjoy sensor that made them violently explode if fully inserted into anything's mouth. Better dead than
dinner, I always say.

Just then a squad of people in similar combat armor walked
by in exaggerated slowness, the distortion due to our accelerated
speed. Telepathically, Jess asked what they were doing, and a
woman mentally replied they were going to establish a sandbag
redoubt on the roof. Other folks were moving like molasses in
the building, closing/locking doors, setting hidden traps and
erecting machine-gun nests. Faintly, I could hear helicopters
overhead.

Easing a clip into her NATO 10mm, Mrs. Cunningham slug-
gishly suggested parking cars outside the doorways as additional
protection. I vetoed that idea. It would designate us as someplace special, and that we did not want to do at any cost. The
boojums wouldn't attack if they didn't know we were here.

At max velocity, Mindy began loading our missile pod with
six Amsterdam Mark II rockets. In the past, we traveled with
them only on combat assignments. But after an embarrassing
incident in upstate New York, we don't drive to the local grocery
store without those babies on board. They sure help in getting a
parking spot on busy weekends.

Meanwhile, Raul had used his wand to tack-weld every window shutter shut, and our trapster supreme, George, was rigging
a Claymore mine to the external door. Base Command was fast
starting to resemble a posh hotel in downtown Beruit.

I debated working on the elevator, but according to Cunningham it was such a death trap already, I couldn't think of anything
more to add to its lethal array.

So, from the weapons cache in the building, Jessica and I
primed a flamethrower and stacked a pile of HE shells next to a
75mm recoilless rifle. A delightful find was a case of plastic
spray seltzer bottles filled with holy water. Neat! An arbalist
would have been nice, but we only found the six-foot arrows.
There was no sign of the giant crossbow itself. If I survived this
thing, I was going to have a harsh word with Supply and Req-
uisition.

Pausing a moment to rest, I saw Raul tearfully unleash Amigo,
our pet lizard who lived in the RV, and dispatch him to go guard
the basement. With a flick of his forked tongue, the magical
collar about his scaled neck glowed once and Amigo was gone.
I sure hoped to see the little suitcase again.

At about this point, the speed pills wore off and reality blurred, then clarified, as we returned to normal. Ugh. My head hurt, my mouth was dry and I was starving. With Father Donaher on vacation, Jessica took over as medic and distributed canteens of water, sandwiches, Strength potions, Healing lotions and antacids. Nothing worse on the mind and body than life in the fast lane. Except, perhaps, visiting my in-laws. Such noisy people, those.

Exiting the van, Horta had a bulging pouch draped over both shoulders, a copper bracelet on both wrists, a necklace and two glowing earrings. I could only assume they were weapons. Either that, or he had more in the closet than just a pile of bones named "McCoy."

Seeing to my own weapons, I loaded my Magnums, took a 9mm Uzi submachine gun and a bag of grenades. Over my shoulder I slung a bag of mixed ammo clips. Small and squat, the Uzi was no big-punch weapon, nor did it have excessive range or penetration. But it was just about one hundred percent reliable. I had once seen a sergeant take the gun apart, pour in pancake syrup, close the breech and then fire off a full clip. It wouldn't jam. No pun intended. And that nifty factor was often much more important in saving your butt than caliber, distance and foot-pounds combined.

Also, I slid sweatbands about my wrists. There wasn't anything more embarrassing than dying because you dropped your weapon in the midst of a fight. Or so I've been sheepishly told by several clumsy ghosts.

Renault had so much stuff strapped about his body, I could barely see him underneath everything. Mindy had her sword, a bandolier of knives, plus a bow and quiver of arrows. Jessica had the van, a taser in her belt, a MAC-10 spray-and-pray machine pistol and, on the seat beside her, the 12-gauge pump-action Remington shotgun normally reserved for Father Donaher.

God, I wish we had some real weapons with us.

Scratching away, as Raul always did when near major evil, our mage took a position in the right corridor, Mindy the left, George covered the rear entrance and me the front. Situated in the middle, Jess was staying in the van to operate the missile pod and other weapons systems of the RV. As a precaution, I jammed the side door open so she would have an easy escape route. I also set the self-destruct and left the keys in the ignition. My wife had a grim expression on her face. The gentle telepath hated lethal combat, but from past experience, I knew that she could and would kill when absolutely necessary.

As ready as we could be in such short time, my team cut the overhead lights, sprinkled tacks, communion wafers, kosher salt, wolfsbane and marbles on the floor, then settled in to wait.

During this, Mrs. Cunningham had been busy at the reception desk activating every automatic defense and offense the building possessed. In the cool quiet darkness, she had shifted the position of the video monitor on her desk so that we could also see what was happening outside the shutters. Currently, the glowing screen showed a small aerial picture of the Quonset hut on its grassy island surrounded by the traffic circle. Nothing seemed out of the ordinary. I glanced at my watch . . . three . . . two . . . one . . . zero.

In a boiling wave, a hundred monsters stormed out of the hut: every conceivable boojum, including a few that I had never seen before, and a couple that I couldn't properly focus my vision on. Vampires, werewolves, basilisk, giants, elves, gnomes, squids, vapors, golems, lumbering robots and shapeless disgusting blobs. Filling the television tube, a brace of scaled titans had the pitiful remains of men and women in guard uniforms held before them as living shields. Over my helmet radio, I heard Warden Lapin order the warehouses to activate. There was a sob in his voice.

Instantly, the view withdrew to show the warehouses extending their sides and joining together to form an unbroken hexagon. The cinder-block walls then fused with a searing blinding light that expanded to engulf the Quonset. Then a solid expanse of dirt filled the area; dirt that visibly hardened into gray rock, then granite. It was the first of the Elemental defenses.

In the dim lobby, I held my breath. Looking good . . .

And on the monitor, a giant fist broke through the rock, its owner climbing out of the hole she had made. A dozen smaller creatures scampered along behind the demon. In a hundred other spots, the granite was smashed into chunks and gravel. More and more of the bedraggled hellspawn clambered into view. Precisely on cue, the rest of the stone vanished and the creatures tumbled painfully down to the pavement. Ha!

Next, the warehouses hosed a Niagara of water at the monsters. The crushing spray deluged the boojums in a torrent of rivers that became a raging wild ocean. Drops of moisture blurred the picture, and the scene shifted to another camera. Tidal waves rose and fell with pile-driving force, smashing the prisoners against one another. Topsy-turvy, they churned hapless and helpless in the endless brutal cascade of a megaton tsunami.

Momentarily, a mass of wiggling tentacles came into view, which snatched a fellow creature and hurled the squat horned monstrosity through a wave crest and straight towards the ring of warehouses. Rapidly, it grew in size and clarity.

And the beastie almost made it, when a brisk wind came from nowhere, flipped the aerial escapee over and hurled it back into the demon soup. Steadily increasing in force and noise, the air above the warehouses went round and round, faster and faster, until a howling hurricane formed above the indomitable barrier.

Reaching out of the darkness, Mrs. Cunningham's translucent hand rotated a dial and lowered the volume on the rumbling speaker.

On the monitor, inside the screaming vertical storm, minuscule tornados skipped along the churning watery surface, grabbing anything that came into view and gamely attempting to dismember it by sheer centrifugal force. More than once they succeeded. The tumultuous sea was starting to get a tad disgusting with floundering limbs and bobbing heads. Even disassembled, the prisoners were still trying to reach freedom. Then the sky darkened ominously.

"Go get 'em, guys!" cheered Renault from behind me.

And, as if in response, sheet lightning blasted into the churning ocean, electrifying the noxious brew nigh incandescent. Coronas of static discharge danced among the wave crests. It became difficult to see through the primordial barrage, but occasionally a glowing inhuman skeleton could be spotted as something got a gigawatt of nature's best smack in the kisser. Boy, I bet that smarted. Served 'em right.

Without warning, a heavy rain began to descend on the monsters, its sheer amount distorting the television picture. A torrential downpour, it must have added a million gallons to the battle zone. Yet the warehouse ring did not swamp or overflow.

Outside the thick shutters, I heard a convoy of tanks rumble past our building, and I echoed George's sentiment.

The temperature visibly dropped, the monitor took on a bluish tint and the rain became snow. Then came hail, the size of your fist, that hit with enough force to drill holes in the chilled unkillables. The lightning ceased, but the wintry winds maintained and a bitter cold engulfed the waterlogged leviathans. In seconds, the ocean became slush, with chunks of frozen monster bobbing about as many ugly icebergs. Steadily, the thick mush congealed into a single seamless glacier whose frosty interior was dotted with motionless blots. In gradual stages, the winds died and a deadly arctic calm settled upon the polar landscape. Once more the abominations were trapped.

An aged head turned in my direction, her face half cast from the glow of the compact television on her desk. "Think this will hold?" asked Mrs. Cunningham hopefully.

"No," said Mindy's shadow in somber reality.

As I rotated the volume dial, it was possible to hear a scratchy, crunching, munching sound. The video view dollied in for a tight zoom, and I could now see that deep underneath the ice were countless figures moving slowly towards the warehouses. The clever bastards were trying to eat their way out!

Instinctively, I took ahold of the pistol on my belt. Rats! That's what we needed. A couple of million rats to try and consume these frigging yahoos. Indestructible did not mean indigestible. It was a last-ditch attack my team had actually used once against the Artichoke of Doom. Our only regrets had been the lack of hollandaise sauce and an accompanying wine.

Only one Elemental defense remained to try. The picture on the monitor receded to the original viewpoint. In astonishing speed, the glacier melted and the water began to bubble and steam. Gouts of greenish fire vomited from below, and many howling beasts were hurtled into the sky, their hindquarters smoking black. The land rose, replacing the water with sticky boiling mud, then red molten lava. Lambent flame danced across the yellow-hot magma as it belched superheated poison gases. I could imagine the stench of sulfur and brimstone mixing freely with the stink of roasted meat and burnt hair. Yuck. The television nearly went blank as the searing plasma reached white heat levels and continued to accelerate until the artificial volcano approached solar temperatures, in which an exploding thermite charge would have constituted a dead spot.

"Not quite hell," noted Raul, his silver staff clearly discernible in the darkness. "But it's sure close."

And he would know.

Hopefully, I crossed my fingers . . . and then cursed as the monitor was divided by an impossible tower of black glass growing from the molten inferno. Soaring skyward, the angular column loomed above the broiling morass until it went offscreen. Rapidly, the camera pulled back to show the entire length of the dark glass. What was it? Some bizarre means of escape? Even as the octagonal glass rod reached azimuth, the top part broke off and came hurtling down, smashing onto the warehouses with a terrible noise. Awash in blazing lava, and the fiends were attacking! No visible damage was done, but the shiny pieces began to take root on the roofs and rise into the air once more.

Beneath the desk, Jessica took my hand. We could see the end coming. Under the awful accumulated weight of the growing ebony substance, a section of roof cracked and then collapsed. In a twinkle, the molten magma vanished, and in plain display were a thousand limp forms painfully standing erect on the undamaged roadway around the Quonset hut.

I closed my eyes to the terrible scene on the monitor. Incredible. The monsters had broken through our primary and secondary lines of defense in under ten minutes. Now everything depended upon only a handful of Bureau personnel to halt these monstrosities from escaping into America.

God help us.

5

On the video screen, there was a series of flashes, and the Abrams assault tanks appeared in a circle around the warehouses, each of the bulky war machines with its vulnerable rear flat against a neighboring home.

As the monsters rallied, .50-caliber machine guns started a steady chatter, and the 120mm turrets blasted thunderous volley after volley of explosive shells, thermite charges, shrapnel, soft-lead slugs or shotgun rounds.

Seconds later, in an angled aerial view, the Harrier jumpjets screamed into position in the sky. Banking, they lifted prows and stalled in the air, stopping perfectly still on their rumbling belly jets. It seemed impossible, but the aircraft appeared to be carrying even more weapons than before.

I was less than thrilled. For over twenty years the best minds of the Bureau had designed and redesigned the material, vibratory and ethereal protections of the Holding Facility. And now we were down to the emergency reserves, teachers, students and us.

"Ed, I want a transfer to Clerical," called Renault.

"Take me with you," I answered.

"Deal!"

The picture on the monitor pulled back to the roof of this very building. In the gray sky, twelve of the Harriers engaged in a furious dogfight, banking, turning, zigzagging, doing loops, their weapons constantly firing. Three had englobed a winged demon skull, four were busy with a flying saucer made of a dull yellow material and five battled something invisible. But we could see the grisly effect of its energy weapons: shimmering golden rays that lanced from the empty sky to violently explode in the air, or went past the jumpjets to impact upon the ground. One Harrier was already spiraling into the distance, thick smoke trailing from a damaged tail section. Gil?

Cut. Out of the east, squadrons of helicopter gunships

56

skimmed in low over the town, rocket pods spitting 35mm death. Cut. From the west, a majestic flight of dragons rose into view. My team cheered. The Bureau had no Great Worms as prisoners in the Holding Facility. These were guards. Belching organic flame, the winged dinosaurs disintegrated stores, exploded cars and generally annoyed many of the fleeing monsters.

At this point, battle became pandemic, with no rhythm or reason. It just was. People running inward, monsters dashing outward. The monitor segmented into six smaller pictures, each showing a different section of town.

Striding over house and tank came a flat-bottomed dome with a tripod of legs gracefully extending/contracting. A slim mechanical arm dangling from the side held a rectangular box that spat a pale flickering laser beam.

Slithering along the lawns, slamming garbage cans and picket fences out of its way, wiggled a ten-foot-thick snake with a mouth big enough to eat a two-car garage. Just then, a bazooka team hidden in a two-car garage blasted its fanged head off. But a new head simply blossomed from the burnt stub of the old.

I clenched the handle of my weapon. *Madre mia*, that's why these abominations were here! Each had been painstakingly captured, one at a time. They were unkillable. What were we supposed to do with handguns against legendary colossi?

Drifting over the mixed combatants came a giant floating human brain, whose medulla threw blue, anti-magic, bolts. A mage in her pajamas hit it with countless spells, but each was nullified. As the exhausted woman dodged out of the way, a platoon of soldiers attempted to give the damn thing a gunpowder lobotomy. And failed.

Over the supermarket, the black glass tower started rising into the sky again. Two of the Harriers broke off from the saucer and came screaming in on a strafing run. A score of liquid-filled balloons dropped from bomb bays to burst and gush over the crystal with a frothy white foam. Every piece saturated turned clear and ceased to grow. But not every piece was hit, and those which weren't started the endless process of rise and fall.

The team was clustered tight around the video screen on the desk. Zooming in, the central square on the monitor changed angle, and we saw why. Sneaking along an alley was a large pulsating blob, wriggling forward on a nest of slimy tentacles. Troops attacked from several directions, but magical fire and steel bullets only punched holes in the gelatinous mass, minor wounds which closed completely.

"Somewhere out there is a werewolf with no heart," muttered Mindy, standing very close to the wall. "With my name tattooed on its arm."

George added, "And Vampire X." I shuddered.

"Plus, that outer-space carrot bastard from the North Pole is probably starting its hellish garden once more," Raul growled. "Using us for fertilizer."

"Using our blood," corrected Jess angrily. She seemed to be suffering from a bad headache, so I offered her a morphine pill. Aspirin would have been useless. My wife dry-swallowed the tablet whole. The negative psychic vibrations from out there must be near deafening to such a sensitive telepath. Even worse than a Shriners' convention during the guest of honor speech.

On a lower square, four ghostly figures galloped boldly along the middle of the street: one was in a military uniform and riding a white horse; the second, wearing only rags, was holding a sickle and astride a red horse; the third was but a grinning skeleton on a black horse; and the last was a cowled figure holding an hourglass and sitting atop a pale horse.

Everybody got out of *their* way.

Just then, a chill touched the back of my neck and I quickly looked around, only to find the rest of my team doing the same. While our attention was elsewhere, something had sneaked into Base Command.

Flipping my visor into position, I instantly saw two black shadows slip past the hair-thin crack between the shutter and the wall, and another was stalking our way. Humanoid in shape, they didn't appear to have any physical mass.

"Alert," I said calmly. "Incoming, one o'clock horizontal."

"Shadow warriors!" spat Mindy, adjusting her visor.

Raul raised his hands. "Tunafish!" he shouted.

Through my closed eyelids, I could see a faint glimmer from the blinding light flash generated by our mage. However, upon opening them, it appeared as if the Dazzle did nothing to these creatures of the night.

Bursts of yammering announced the fact that George was on the job. Mrs. Cunningham gave them a taste of her 10mm, and I added a few silver rounds from my Uzi, plus an HE grenade, but also to no effect. Bullets and bombs simply passed through them to loudly clang off the shutters or tear chunks out of the pretty marble.

Gliding close, Mindy gave a shadow five fast passes of her rainbow sword, with the expected effect that steel should have on an immaterial shadow. None. But in return the black figure raked a claw at her chest, ripping off her flak jacket and blouse, and gouging furrows in her body armor underneath. These guys were dangerous.

". . . !" shouted Raul in the incomprehensible language of mages. Twirling his wand above his head as a baton, with a snap of his wrist the silver wand went level, the concave business end pointing at our uninvited guests.

The staff actually recoiled as a blast of raw ethereal energy vomited forward in a swirling cone of colors and noise. I recognized it as a mixture of three different Death spells. Yowsa! Way to go, Raul! Frantically, the shadows tried to get out of the way with no success. They were lifted up and thrown down, shaken, rattled and rolled. But as the pyrotechnics faded, the shadows jumped to their feet appearing only seriously annoyed.

"Ah, apparently I was wrong," said the wizard, quickly backstepping behind me. "They are not technological in construction."

"Swell," I commented as Renault tried a flamethrower on the black four. It didn't please them, but no real damage was done.

Think fast, Alvarez, I commanded myself. Immaterial and spectral, yet not a ghost or vapor. Pure energy, phantasmagoric, pan-dimensional? Or something else entirely? Hmm, get a hunch, bet a bunch. Shouldering my rifle, I grabbed a seltzer bottle and squirted a stream towards a lurking black shape approaching the reception desk. Contemptuously, the monster seemed to sneer at me, which was the last thing the fool did today. As the bubbling spray hit the phantom, it vanished. Sneaking a peek under my visor, there was now only a sizzling wet spot on the floor and a small pile of gray dust. Bingo!

"Will-o'-wisps!" I bellowed. "Routine six and seven!"

Scampering to the RV, Jessica tossed one of our premade plastic pentagrams on the floor and we frantically clustered inside and tried to appear scared. Eagerly converging on us, the swamp-gas manifestations futilely caressed the magical boundary with their incorporeal claws. When they were in a nice tight group, we spritzed them with a barrage of holy water.

Eventually, there were only piles of dust on the floor littered with spent shells, with the honey-sweet smell of fresh magic. Of course, the will-o'-wisps weren't really dead. With the coming summer solstice, they would rise to life again. Even if we scattered the dust across the world, it would make no difference. Wisps were not wimps.

For some reason this scenario reminded me of when our van had broken down in a small ghost town in the badlands of Nevada, and we spent the next thirty-six hours trapped in a circle of candles fighting an entire village of lunar zombies and their omnivorous toad master. Technically, I guess we won. But the ghost town, which supplied employment to a dozen people, had been totally destroyed, and the poor old prospector who had accidentally summoned the boojums was also dead. In my book, that wasn't winning. It was merely surviving.

As we reloaded weapons and tossed around a couple of pine tree air fresheners, a sharp series of beeps sounded on our helmet radios. Oh, what now?

"Alert," said a calm voice. "Prepare for option two. Repeat, prepare for option two."

I felt my antacids neutralized by stomach acid.

Mindy nudged me. "Ed, what's option two?"

"Don't know," I replied honestly. "But I don't like the sound of it."

"Me neither," agreed Renault, nervously savaging a candy bar.

We gathered at the monitor again. Almost a minute passed with nothing happening, then a brilliant green dome filled the sky. Success!

"Calling Team Tunafish," said Professor Burton's voice over our helmet radios. "Calling Team Tunafish."

I touched the transmit switch with my chin. "Tunafish here, Professor. Congratulations!"

"Shakespeare," she said solemnly.

"Ah . . . Bacon."

"We have a slight situation, Ed," declared Joyce.

My team exchanged puzzled looks. The prismatic dome was functioning. Nothing could escape into the real world. Not even us. America was safe.

"What's the problem?"

A cough. "That's not our dome."

"*What?*"

"Well, it *is* the Bureau's," she relented. "But not this base's.

Our dome generator has suffered a malfunction or dysfunction. I don't know which.'' Pause. ''As did the fail-safe.''

George spit out his new candy bar, Raul hit himself in the head with his staff, Mindy mimed slicing her throat and Jessica covered her face with both hands. Oh brother.

Burton continued. ''Gordon has sealed the base off from the outside and given us a thirty-minute deadline. We must regain control of the situation within thirty minutes or else they seal the portal. Forever.''

And we would be trapped in this miniverse with the hordes of hell to play with for eternity. Oh swell. With the feeling of placing my neck in the hangman's noose, I asked what she wanted us to do.

''I need a suici—ah, volunteer squad to try and get into the Holding Facility and activate the fail-safe by hand.''

I took two long breaths.

''Well?'' the radio asked.

Glumly, I took two more breaths. They might be my last.

Tilting my head, I asked my team a silent question, and they nodded assent. What the hey, today was a fine day to die. At least, that's what it said on the calendar.

''Done,'' I said. ''How about reinforcements?''

''You can have the seniors. Everybody else is busy.''

Great. Six students. Cannon fodder, at best. ''Recognition code?'' I sighed.

'' 'Dirty.' Countersign, 'Dozen.' ''

How fitting. ''How soon can you get them here?''

There was a shimmering flash and the Hell House five appeared in the lobby. Heavily beweaponed, they were dressed in armor similar to ours, only not so well fitting. Understandable. Our armor was personalized, their stuff came from General Supplies. The twins had switched the wrists the handcuffs were on and I knew why. Connie, the telepath, was holding an M-16 carbine as far away from her brother as possible. Gunpowder and wizards do not mix.

''Good luck,'' said the radio.

''Thanks, Joyce. We'll need it.''

Switching my radio to normal frequency, I turned about and inspected my little army. There was a faint glimmer of promise in this odd assortment of fighters: a private investigator, a telepath, a medium-level mage, a beginner mage, a professional soldier, a mage/telepath team, a martial artist, a Healer and a heavily armed giant. Yeah, we could take this show on the road and write our own reviews.

Appearing bigger than ever, Sanders stepped close and saluted. I was going to have to break him of that habit.

"Dirty," he announced proudly.

"Dozen," I replied. "Okay, let me brief you."

"We are fully aware of the dire situation, sir," said Sanders. "Jessica contacted Connie and we held a fast group telepathic conference. We're on a do-or-die to level 17, section 3, of the Holding Facility, and the mission has been rated more important than any, or all, of us. Correct?"

It was correct. Just tactless to say it so bluntly.

"By the way," asked Raul, "where's Sir Reginald?"

Don kept a stiff face. "Dead. We were guarding the hospital and a big hairy thing ate him."

"So we kill one in his name, *da*?" grimly said Tina, the buxom redhead.

"Can't," reminded Jess. "That's why they are here, remember?"

"Ah. Yes. Sorry, comrade telepath."

"But we can certainly kick the shit out of them!" declared Ken, brandishing his Thompson.

"How to get there is the first problem," I commented, ignoring the rhetoric. "We have three choices. Magic portal, telepathic jump or drive."

"Couldn't we just phone it in?" asked Mindy.

Sanders gave her a strange stare. Guess he wasn't used to humor under fire.

"Sorry," I said. "The number's unlisted."

"Damn," she said. "Then go we must."

I turned. "Raul?"

Our mage was already busy waving his hands about, fingers leaving colored streamers behind them. "Portals are impossible. The Facility is still sealed."

"Jess, can you and Connie jump the lot of us inside?"

Quickly, my wife looked over the assorted tonnage of troops and armored van. "Not without a dose of MCD."

Connie nodded agreement.

MCD was a dangerous mind-amplifying drug. Temporarily, a telepath would have her powers fantastically increased. However, there was a very high risk of permanent burnout, idiocy or worse. Total brain death.

"No way," I snapped. "We'll drive, and reserve our heavy hitters for when we're inside the jail."

"Why?" asked Ken curiously.

George answered, "Because, for various reasons, there's lots of things that haven't come out yet."

Connie paled, but stood firm. Good woman.

Gathering our stacks of armaments, the crew jammed into the RV. Seats were limited, and the rest of us stood holding on to conveniently placed ceiling straps. I had gotten the idea from riding the subway at rush hour. Since time was of the essence, George took the wheel. When it came to combat driving, Mr. Renault could make a person believe that the speed of light was only a suggestion and not an actual law.

Giving us a game thumbs-up, Mrs. Cunningham cycled the shutters open, and we bounced awkwardly over the window ledge. Immediately, Renault activated the nitrous oxide injector, and our fourteen tons of Bureau property literally flew out of the building. Landing with a bone-rattling jar, the wheels tore strips of grass from the manicured lawn as the RV bounded into the debris-filled street.

Behind us, the steel shutters rumbled closed.

Swerving around a blast crater, George took a corner on two wheels and then really hit the gas. A hat flew off my head and I hadn't even been wearing one. Whew!

Zigzagging past Sing-Sing Boulevard, Connie gasped as she saw a ten-meter-tall lizard waddling down the center of the street on its plump hind legs. As the beast spotted us, the enlarged dorsal fins began to pulse with a greenish glow.

"Brace yourselves!" George warned.

In a roar, the van lurched forward with renewed velocity and slammed into the big reptile. Those standing were thrown to the floor, but the lizard was sent airborne. Tumbling away, a stream of glowing vapor spewed from its open mouth, setting fire to a tree. On the dashboard, a Geiger counter began to click wildly.

"Excuse me," grunted Raul from somewhere within the pile of bodies. "But is my stomach bothering your elbow?"

"Sorry."

With Jessica's assistance, I got to my feet and then helped the wizard stand.

Don was staring out the rear window. "Hey, wasn't that—"

"Get used to it, kid," snapped Mindy, who hadn't moved an inch during the jumbilation. "You're in the Bureau now."

The dark mage was shocked for a moment, then set his jaw. That's the ticket. It always surprised newcomers to discover that a lot of monster movies were actually footage of Bureau battles. Personally, I had two movies and a TV miniseries to my credit. But novels were what I really wanted. You know, something with class and dignity.

As we barreled across a lawn, a mummy stepped out of some bushes and spread its bandaged arms as if to catch the speeding van.

"It's Billy-Bob!" shouted Raul in warning.

Savagely twisting the steering wheel, George careened off the corner of a house, sending a spray of ceramic tiles into the air. Rebounding, the van slammed into, and over, a sports car, but we did manage to avoid the shambling man-monster.

"Wow, that guy must be superpowerful!" remarked Ken in awe.

"Not a bit," denied Mindy, filing her nails to needle points. "You could kill the thing with a pointed stick."

"Then why the evasion?"

"Its wrappings are evil," explained Jessica lugubriously. "The person inside them is just some poor man named Billy-Bob Jones, a truck driver from South Carolina. When he slew the old mummy, the wrappings took him over and forced the man on a rampage of murder."

"So if we killed Billy-Bob, the wrappings would just find somebody else?"

"Exactly."

Ken rumbled, "Why not destroy the wrappings?"

Cadets. "Gotta take them off the victim first, and we can't do that without slaying Billy-Bob. That's why he was in detention."

"Ah."

The students were starting to understand that not everybody in the Holding Facility was a monster. Some were victims. We even had a few demonic refugees seeking political asylum. It's a crazy world.

Launching a rocket from the roof pod, we blew apart a drooling somuloid and shot through an alley. In passing, we saw a pair of people waging a private firefight behind ragged hedges. One was a tall muscular man with a bushy moustache and thick sideburns. He was dressed in a garish green checked jacket and was holding the goddamnedest biggest pistol I had ever seen.

His opponent was a tall slim man with slick blond hair. That guy was in a flapping white lab coat and had a robotic arm.

"Freeze, you bozo!" bellowed the moustache, and fired his giant pistol a fast three times.

The lab coat ducked out of the way. *"Eat photons, Delphia!"* screamed the fellow as a crimson lance extended from his robotic arm. The beam just nicked the jacket of the moustached man and a can of beer tumbled out.

A second later, we turned another corner and they were gone.

"Who the heck were they?" asked Blanco.

"Long story," I sighed. "Tell ya later."

Nearing the Facility, the houses changed from damaged, to burning wrecks, to flattened timbers. We were in open country now, but there was nobody moving about on the ground.

With a loud thump, something heavy landed on our roof and started clawing at the widows, gray talons chipping the armored glass. Since George was busy, I flipped a switch on the dashboard. In a dull boom, the outer section of the roof blew off, taking a very surprised harpie along with the luggage rack. By the time she hit the ground, we were long gone. Shmuck. Leaping on the roof was the second oldest trick in the book.

Amid the wreckage on the ground, carnage was rampant, bodies and bloody bits of corpses scattered everywhere. The only cheering fact was that a lot of the blood was black, yellow or green, and many of the body parts could under no circumstances be called human. Just disgusting.

The Bureau guards had taken their toll, such as it was. Problem was, if each of the monster parts didn't somehow travel to rejoin the rest of the body, then they would start to grow a whole new boojum as soon as possible. The tanks and planes had only bought time.

Slowing, Renault carefully maneuvered through the crumbled ruins of the once mighty warehouses. Often he had to go backwards to move ahead, but always we progressed. Going past the destroyed building, we could observe that the insides were oddly empty. Obviously, whatever the powering force had been, it was now dissipated.

Jouncing over the curb, we skimmed along the traffic circle until we reached the front of the Quonset hut. It appeared to be totally undamaged.

"The response code is not working," announced George with deceptive calm.

I took the radio and tried it myself. Nothing.

"We'll have to ram our way in," I decided. "Raul, poly-morph a section of the metal siding into wood."

He rolled up his sleeves. "Done, Kemo Sabe."

The mage gestured and the seamless end of the Quonset now had a wide wooden door in the middle at ground level. Smashing through the wire fence, we zoomed inward.

And the wall reverted to metal.

Frowning, the mage leveled his staff. Wood. Nope, metal.

The hut was coming at us like the angry hand of God.

"Oh, Ed!" called Renault, sweat dripping off his brow.

"Keep going! Simon, Blanco, help him!"

Clutching their wands, the three mages started conducting an orchestra. The Quonset wall began flickering into wood, metal, wood, brick, aluminum siding, wood, granite, metal . . .

6

. . . and the van smashed through the plywood wall, exploding into the Quonset hut! As the RV screeched to a halt in the cavernous receiving bay, only a single brick tumbled off our shattered windshield. In the rearview mirror, I watched the metal wall close again. Ulp. A split second either way, and the Bureau would have renamed us Team Tunafish Salad.

"Out!" I barked. "Standard defensive pattern!" I added for the students. My people didn't need to be told such basics.

They barely managed to assemble when the floor rippled and the giant mechanical arm came straight for us. At least part of the Facility was still operational.

Boldly walking towards the deadly janitor, I fished out my commission booklet and showed my badge.

"Federal Agent Edwardo Alvarez," I stated loud and clear. "Independent field operative, Bureau 13."

Slowly, the hand halted. Then it briskly turned towards the rest of the group. One at a time, they identified themselves. Thankfully, everybody had the booklet on them.

The janitor seemed loath to accept this invasion of agents, but finally descended into the floor with that same strange watery effect.

"George and I are on point," I announced, working the bolt on my Uzi. "Sanders and Mindy cover the rear. The gypsy and Jess in the center. One-meter spread. Silent and hard."

Raising a finger, Renault stepped into the van for a second before joining me at the head of the mob.

"What?" I asked brusquely.

"Setting the van to detonate," he answered. "Our people will know better than to bother it, and an explosion will serve to deter any boojum."

I smiled. "Plus let us know they're coming. Good man."

Renault grinned like a paltroon, stuffed another lollipop into his mouth and snapped the bolt on his M-60.

Glancing at my watch, I saw there was twenty minutes to go. Plenty of time. Approaching the wall, I glanced it over.

"Jess?" I asked.

My wife placed fingertips to forehead. "It's clear, dear."

"Raul?"

He waved his staff. "It's clear, dear."

Everybody laughed.

Grinding my teeth, I made a mental note to kill him later.

Stepping forward, I pressed my eye against the viewpiece and placed a hand on the wall plate. There was a click and the wall flipped over on a center pivot beam, the bottom swung inward and the top lowered, serving to push us into the next cubicle whether we wanted to go or not.

A simple iron grating faced us, with an Armorlite window in the wall alongside. It was impossible to see into the control room: the glass was too badly streaked with red blood. Inserting a finger into the keyhole, the mechanism took my print and unlocked to admit us entrance.

On the other side of the gate was a huge plastic arch. As we walked through, the scanner gave the aura and alignment reading of every person. I showed as a normal human. Jessica was human with a trace of silver. Raul was primarily green, laced with white. A good-guy mage. Connie was identical to Jess, and Don to Raul. Blanco was green, with rudimentary traces of gray, neutral magic. George was human, but with a faint touch of black. Same as Mindy. Ah-ha! I always knew the two of them enjoyed fighting too much. The scanner hummed for a minute on Patrika, then gave a golden reading. Healer. No offense abilities.

Trailing the pack, Ken got a reading I had never seen before. Pure white? I had to check the chart on the wall near the arch. White. He was fanatically good. And totally unmagical. The boy was almost magic-resistant, but not quite.

Beyond the scanner, the floor appeared to be solid stone, but I knew better. A closer examination showed the tips of a pair of pointed ears sticking from the surface of the quicksandstone trap. Taking my Bureau-issue pocket comb, I tossed it forward. A maser beam flashed once on the falling plastic, and the comb bounced off the suddenly hard flooring. Retrieving my comb, I waved the team on. A key does not always resemble one. And vice versa.

"I don't understand," said Don, skirting around the wiggling ears. "Why isn't the place smashed to bits from the prisoners escaping?"

Patrika snorted. "The Facility is self-repairing. Hell, it's almost alive."

"What do you mean, almost?" Jessica said softly.

Connie nodded agreement. In passing, Raul pointed to a crack in the wall that was sealing itself even as we watched.

Ahead was a deceptively plain corridor: concrete floor, metal walls, acoustical tile ceiling. George stayed left, I hugged the right. In actuality, this passage was three hallways combined into one. I can only assume it worked by mixing technology and magic. Or maybe it was done with mirrors. I really didn't know.

Walking the corridor, escorted prisoners went to Holding. Strolling along the exact same hallway, Technical Services scientists arrived at Research, security officers reached Storage, authorized field agents could go anywhere, and everybody else was dumped into the furnace.

Research was where Bureau scientists experimented upon ways of killing the unkillables. Finding the specific material weakness of a supernatural was an often painstaking, infuriating and pretty grisly business. Most monsters received damage from wood or silver, but some could be killed only by specific holy relics, a unique word, ritual, disease, true love or old age. Understandably, the scientists had their own private bar and toll-free hot line for twenty-four-hour-a-day psychiatric counseling.

Storage was where we kept artifacts too dangerous to leave lying around, but that we still wanted to keep handy in case of an emergency. Some were damned, some alien, and a few were so incredibly holy that only a truly pure person could even go near them without being destroyed. Destroyed—that was the term we taught the cadets, because there really was no earthly equivalent of what happened to a person. You could go mad just by watching. It was worse than professional wrestling.

Ken gave a tactful cough.

"What?" I whispered.

"If the doors are so difficult to gain exit, and the boojums can chew their way through stone and superhard ice, why didn't they just tunnel out the sides of the Facility instead of dashing into the town where we waited with amassed weapons?"

Sounded like a run-on sentence, but a good question. Jessica gave the answer. Set in kilometers of concrete, merely to keep it steady, the outer walls and bottom of the Facility were a transdimensional energy shield: a solidified version of a forcefield, prismatic dome and psionic death barrier. It was absolutely indestructible. End of discussion. Thermonuclear bombs couldn't even scratch the surface. A space-warping gravitational pull of a neutron star would have no effect. A nova didn't have enough umph to warm a square meter.

Sadly, the Bureau couldn't take the credit for making this bit of superscience. And if the barrier ever got damaged, we could not fix it, because no human had built the thing. If the truth be told, we stole The Cup. It was the first assignment I was ever on, and, brother, it was almost my last.

With impenetrable sides and bottom, the only way in or out of the Facility was the top, and that we could take credit for. At the end of the corridor was an odd tunnel that resembled a porcupine turned inside out and rolled into a tube. But instead of quills, the curved wall was lined with weapons: machine guns, rifles, spears, lances, swords, flamethrowers, bazookas, frost wands, laser cannons, microwave beamers, poison-gas jets, rapid-fire shotguns, crossbows, vibro-swords, lightning rods and so on. Except for a two-foot-wide strip of flooring down the middle, every inch of the wall bristled with deathdealers.

I hadn't been able to fathom how the prisoners got past this quaint gate, but a single glance told the answer. It had been deactivated. The weapons hung limp from the walls, dangling and clanging impotently like a jungle of metal wind chines. Mindful of sharp edges, George and I eased into the curtain of jingling weapons. Renault was a bit pale, but resolute. He hated tunnels of any sort.

Carefully, Tina prodded at a barbed javelin with her staff. "Czar's blood, what could have done this?"

"An EMP bomb?" asked George.

Don brushed machine guns out of his way. "A what?"

"An electromagnetic pulse bomb," explained Renault, busy scanning everywhere for danger. "A tesla-style accumulator emits a spit discharge to generate a split-second, full-spectrum, magnetic pulse that fries transistors and IC chips."

"And that is bad," said Ken as a question.

After a pause, George agreed. Yes, that was bad. And very high-tech. Any electronically operated piece of equipment would be rendered useless. But an EM pulse wouldn't bother the magical defenses. And the Facility had both.

I snorted in annoyance. EMP bombs were the latest toy of

humanity. It seemed to me that the higher the technology, the easier it was to destroy. The only real way to stop a good old-fashioned steam engine was to drop-kick it off a cliff. Preferably to crash on top of another steam engine.

Flinching and dodging, Jessica tried to avoid the hanging iron jungle. "These have been used," she stated, stooping under a faintly humming vibro-sword. "And more than once."

"There have been escape attempts before," I admitted.

"But nothing on the scale of today?"

"Never."

Parting the last of the impotent armaments with our gun barrels, George and I stepped out of the tunnel, banking left and right, to give the folks behind us combat room if necessary.

Darkness. Dead silence.

"Infrared," I said, and touched a switch with my chin.

Illumination came to my visor. Presently, the ten of us stood on a small ledge that jutted from the ebony wall like the hand of a beggar. To our left, a walkway followed the curving wall down into the stygian darkness. A pipe railing offered meager protection from tumbling off the abrupt edge.

I glanced over the railing.

Total blackness. Vertigo. Ghostly echoes drifted upward, and there were a few minuscule pinpoints of flickering light. Fires of some sort. Bed linen or hair.

"How deep is it?" asked Ken, craning his neck.

"Forever," said Mindy. "Bottomless."

"Factual or poetic?"

Sanders sure had an odd way of talking. "Literal," I replied.

"Then what does it rest on?" asked Don.

"The outside is buttressed on a bed of concrete only a few miles away. But inside there is no bottom."

Tina frowned. "How can that be?"

"You tell us, and win a cool million dollars from Horace Gordon and the eternal gratitude of TechServ."

Glancing upward, I could dimly perceive an octopus in medieval armor suspended from the flat ceiling. Each limb should have held a magic wand with a different ability. But the tentacles were empty. Somehow, I had a feeling the armor was also.

"Hai!" cried Mindy, falling on her butt, both arms slapping the floor as she hit.

The new guys rushed over to the top of the walkway and assisted the martial artist to her feet. She seemed shaken. The rest of us could only stare in dumbfoundment. Mindy Jennings fell?

Keeping a hand on the railing, and her left foot on the ledge, Jennings oh so carefully placed a sneaker onto the sloped walkway and pushed it about.

"Frictionless," she declared, retreating to a safe distance. "If I hadn't been able to throw myself backwards, I would be on my way to the bottom of the Facility."

Patrika spit on the walkway and it slid away without a trace. "At a zillion miles per hour," she added.

Swell. I hadn't counted on this. The stairs had been here last visit.

"Okay," I said, shouldering my weapon. "Let's find the controls to extend the steps. George, Sanders, the twins on guard."

We spent a precious two minutes on a fruitless search of the ledge. Then linking our belts together, we wasted another minute doing a comedy routine of drunks on ice as the team attempted to walk down the frictionless surface. Even the pipe railing was made of the same slippery stuff.

Raul held a conference with Don and Tina.

"SOSF?" asked the mage twin.

"Seems the best way," noted Blanco.

"I'll do it," announced Horta.

Tapping each of our shoes with his silver staff, the footwear now clung to the ground as if it were flat and level. Laughing, Mindy even ran up the walls a bit, standing perpendicular to us.

"Shoes of Sure Footing," explained the cocky mage as we hurried along. "It's such an old conjure I had nearly forgotten the words."

"What was SOSF originally used for?" asked Patrika, lifting and placing each foot with exaggerated care. "Mountain climbers? Sailors? Drunks?"

"Thieves."

"Ah."

In an alcove set into the black wall above us, I noticed a security camera sitting motionless. How had that happened? Even with the electricity off, the camera should still be sweeping the walkway. It possessed an independent power supply. And there was no external damage. Strange.

Dead batteries? queried Connie.

Doubtful. I unfocused my eyes in rumination, and that was when I spotted a barely discernible square of ebony coming our way from the darkness overhead. Vision cleared as I snicked off my safety. A flapjack! Bloody hell!

"Incoming!" I shouted above the chatter of my Uzi. "Twelve o'clock high!"

"Roman candle!" ordered George, training his big machine rifle upward.

Everybody cut loose. Beams, Fire Lances, bullets impacting on the deadly flying chameleon. The muzzle flashes illuminated the dark in a wild strobe effect. The sheer inertial force of our weapons held the beastie at bay over us, until Tina shouted a spell.

Instantly, the flapjack shot down into the blackness of the central shaft, moving as if it were late for a hot date with the prettiest lady flapjack who ever lived.

"What did you do?" asked Don, staring over the railing.

Raul chuckled. "She used a Fly spell."

"But it was flying."

"And now it flies at my command," stated Blanco proudly. "At thirty-two feet per second per second, compounded by the maximum velocity of the species. When spell wears off, animal will be too far away to return and annoy us. Unless, of course, we are lucky and it hits something."

I was starting to like this gal. She fought mean.

Unfortunately, our gunshots seemed to have attracted the attention of other denizens of the Facility. Distant growls did not sound so far away anymore, and some of the torches seemed to be moving upward in a steady line.

"Double time, hush," I whispered. "Use silenced weapons only. Harch!"

Further along the walkway, we started to encounter side corridors lined with cells. Let's see. We're in section 3, so we want level 17, corridor 5, number 12.

At 17, the torches were uncomfortably close, the growls nearly understandable. We were running by then. One, two, three, four, five!

"In!" I whispered to George, and we turned. The rest followed.

Raul paused until everybody had passed and then sprayed the mouth of the corridor with a steamy discharge from his staff. The end of the passage closed solid.

Quiet as a tomb, both of the black walls of the passage were lined with gray doors. Some had broken hinges, others were ruptured in the middle and a few were gone completely.

"Hey!" called Don. "This cell is still sealed!"

"Excellent," replied Sanders, screwing a silencer onto the barrel of a .45 automatic pistol. "Then we don't have to bother with the occupant. Come along!"

But curiosity got the better of the mage and he glanced inside.

"Well, hi there," said Don in a surprised voice. "And what are you doing—" A scream was ripped from his throat, and throwing an arm across his face, the mage quickly retreated, dragging his sister with him.

Sanders pumped a few rounds past the grille of the door and then I peeked in. Sitting on a dirty mattress was a weeping little girl in a ragged dress and holding a doll. The pitiful child was rocking the toy in her arms and singing a soft song, telling it not to cry, Mommy would come back soon.

Oh, give me a break. "Nice try, Hecthrope, but we're the guys who put you here!"

Turning her head without moving her shoulders, the thing on the bed snarled and shot a forked tongue at me. I ducked and the slimy extrusion rebounded off the grille, indenting the metal bars—which promptly straightened.

Jessica scowled at the trembling apprentice wizard. "Donald, can't you read?"

"Read what?" demanded Connie, comforting her brother.

I pointed at the door. "That!"

"Ah, there's nothing there, Ed," noted Mindy.

Eh? Oh. The warning sign had been taken off. Just a bit of horseplay from the escaping boojums. Har-har.

"Sorry," apologized Jess.

"How come this supernatural is still in her cell?" asked Ken.

"Madam Hecthorpe's weakness is steel," I said.

Tina made a face. "A rather feeble weakness, comrade."

Starting along the corridor, Raul set her straight. "Well, a few thousand years ago, in the Bronze Age, Hecthorpe was big stuff. But with the advent of modern civilization"—the mage smiled—"we caught her with a trainload of spatulas."

The students laughed, and a menacing growl sounded from the cell. Hrmph. Some demons have no sense of humor.

My team continued on till we reached number 12 south. This door was still erect, and only a vacant cell showed through the grille. Sliding my Bureau ID into a crack in the wall, there was a hum, a click, and the twenty-ton door cycled open with a hydraulic hiss, taking a section of the wall with it.

"The Facility command center is hidden in a cell?" asked Connie, surprised.

Patrika shrugged. "What should they have done? Advertise its location with a nice big neon sign saying, 'Monsters: Don't come here'?"

"Hmm, good point."

Exposed was the command room of the Facility. To our left, behind an Armorlite window, was an office. Next to it was a door marked "Armory." That I knew was another death trap. To our right, beyond a steel lattice, was the complex array of pipes, conduits and cables that constitute a tokamac fusion generator. Good ol' Horace Gordon himself had stolen that baby from the Empire of Australia during World War IX in an alternate future. TechServ took very good care of it. Parts were damn hard to get.

In the center of the room was a raised dais, with railed stairs leading to the top on four sides. Cresting the platform was a short, round cylinder made of glass: a holograph projector which should have been showing a detailed picture of the interior of the jail. It was clear. Surrounding the cylinder was a bank of control stations. Each had a video monitor, a computer keyboard and enough dials, switches, buttons and levers to launch a space shuttle. Bare-bone skeletons in guard uniforms were sprawled on the floor, sitting at control desks and entangled in the works of the humming tokamac. In the distant corner, a coffee machine was bubbling away. Tina turned it off. Whatever had hit the guards never gave them a chance to fight.

Sad as the scene was, we had a job to do and time was short.

We entered and the door/wall quietly cycled shut. Directly in front of us was a low barricade made of sandbags. The military nest held a .75 machine gun, a Bedlow polycyclic laser cannon and a Palooka Joe. That weapon we had purchased from a parallel dimension which we were rather friendly with. The fiendish device combined a tight focus tractor beam with a wide-angle pressure beam. The result was that your body was forced away under thirty-five tons of pressure, as your guts were yanked forward under thirty-five tons of pressure. Designed as an anti-robot weapon, it served our purposes well, if messily.

"Stay alert, people," I said. "I'm going to check Gil's office for the fail-safe."

And sure enough, yep, that's where it was. Hidden behind a hinged painting of the good clone of J. Edgar Hoover, bordered by brilliant red warning lines, was a thick lever. I pulled the handle, and from a panel of meters in the main room there erupted a spray of sparks.

"Relay has blown," announced Jessica, lifting the lid of the smoking control panel. "Must have happened when the rest of the electrical systems died."

"Well, fix it!" I bellowed, feeling the first tug of panic.

Twisting plastic locks, she yanked away a panel covering and wiggled deep into the maze of circuitry. "I'll try. But I'm only a home-stereo technician. Anybody got a tool kit?"

Digging under flak jacket and sweater to reach my sweat-sticky shirt, I retrieved a damp Swiss Army knife. Underhand, I tossed it to George, who threw the combination knife to Ken, then Connie, who relayed the pocket Swiss tool kit to Jess.

"This'll do for starters. But try and find me some real tools!"

I began rummaging through the desk, and the rest of the team scattered in a frantic search.

"Is the tokamac okay?" asked Don, staring at the great machine.

"Fine," replied Mindy, checking her pockets. "It's shielded inside a Faraday cage, a fine wire mesh screening with a blocking electrical current trickling through constantly. No external EM pulses can penetrate."

"Why don't we shield the whole base that way?"

"It takes half the power of the t-mac just to protect itself. We'd need a hundred of them to shield the entire base."

Slamming shut the last drawer in the desk, I impatiently glanced at my watch. Five minutes. "Will this take long?"

"Not if you don't interrupt me!"

Fair enough.

"Oh, Ed!" sang out Raul.

Gun ready, I twirled. "What?"

He jerked a thumb at the door and mouthed the word "monsters."

"How many?" whispered Ken, jerking free the huge ungainly clip of his Thompson and sliding on a fresh wheel.

"Too many," the mage replied softly.

Oh hell. "Anybody know how to operate these babies?" I asked hopefully, patting the Palooka Joe. There was a chorus of negative answers. It had been a feeble hope at best.

There came a low steady pounding on the door/wall, bits of stonework falling to the floor. The monsters had discovered our presence and were coming to pay us a courtesy call. How nice.

"Okay," I said, unfolding the wire stock of my Uzi. "We buy Jessica time the hard way. Formation number two. Routine nineteen."

"Ah, which one is that, comrade?" asked Tina.

Grimly, Patrika worked the bolt on her M-16 short carbine. "Just follow my lead, red."

"Da, tovarishch."

Quickly, we formed a semicircle before the door/wall. Knives were loosened, safeties clicked off, grenades prepped, spare ammo readied, wands polished, potions sipped, lotions poured and powders sprinkled. Tina even went so far as to draw a fake trapdoor on the floor with a piece of chalk. What the hey, it couldn't hurt.

The pounding increased and cracks began to appear in the door/wall. Suddenly, a hole was formed by the butting head of an iron golem. Taking careful aim, I lobbed a thermite grenade into the opening. Ken added a burst of .45 slugs. From the noise our gifts made, I do not believe that they were accepted in the true spirit they were given. Damn, and I had lost the receipts.

Raul gestured and a brick wall appeared in front of the hole in the door/wall. A black fist smashed through it without a moment's hesitation. In short order, another hole was formed and enlarged.

Pushing through the hole, a female centaur without skin shot lances of flame from her eyes. Raul met the attack with a golden ray from his staff and the fire changed to confetti. A ropy thing opened its mouth and George hurled a grenade straight in. There was a gulp and the stringy monster exploded. Even the other boojums seemed disgusted at the icky stuff dripping off them. I didn't think that I would ever eat spaghetti with tomato sauce again. Feh.

As the creatures started to charge, Tina waved her wand and an iron portcullis materialized in front of the monsters. Unable to stop itself quickly enough, a waspwoman clanged her two skulls hard on the metal bars and dropped.

Holding our positions, we fired in volleys, aiming for the small holes in the iron lattice. Mostly we succeeded, but ricochets zinged everywhere. Fortunately, our armor saved us from serious injury.

Screeching in protest, the metal was ripped/torn/beaten out of the way by hands/claws/tentacles. The first thing stepped free: a nasty customer resembling a human being whose entire body was covered with slavering mouths filled with sharp teeth.

"Banzai!" cried Mindy, and her hands jerked forward.

Silver-edged throwing stars sprouted from the forehead of the mouth man and he fell back, a chorus of screams. A wave of disorientation and dizziness swept over us then, but Connie clenched a fist to her heart in concentration and the feeling passed. Whew. I hate it when something tries to consume my soul. Just ruins my whole day.

Steadily, the Thompson kept firing a stream of mixed rounds, blowing chunks of monsters away. My Uzi sprayed a constant fusillade of 9mm Parabellums into the amassed hellspawn. Connie and the M-16 added controlled bursts of perfectly imbalanced 5.56mm tumblers to the barrage, and the chanting of the mages was barely audible over the yammering of George's big M-60 machine rifle, the ammo belt shrinking fast.

Lightning, explosions, snow, flame, deafening noise, utter silence, flying knives, bullets, bombs, grenades, steel, shells and spells. An Invisible Fist broke my nose and I spat out the blood that flowed into my mouth. The Thompson mysteriously jammed. Tina smacked it with her staff and the weapon was working again. Raul began to chant the word "tunafish." But it seemed to have less effect each time.

"Avon calling!" I bellowed.

Unexpectedly for the monsters, a Dutch door appeared in the corridor and we stopped firing. There was a momentary pause. Suspiciously, the female centaur worked the latch and swung aside the upper half of the split portal.

My team was waiting for this. We each dropped two grenades through the opening and slammed the door shut. As we stepped away, Donald made another stone wall.

The light fixtures in the command center rattled and chairs toppled over from the series of violent explosions. A section of the granite barrier cracked and fell away, and Many-Mouth Man poked his misshapen head through the hole.

"Jess, how's it coming?" I called, triggering a spurt of 9mms into the segmented face. Incredibly, he actually appeared uglier afterwards. Didn't think it was possible.

"Anybody got a twenty-five-amp transistor and some number fourteen wire?"

Uzi burst. "Don't think so!" returned Connie.

"Mindy, give me a shuriken!"

Without breaking stride, Ms. Jennings flipped her hand backwards and an oriental throwing star slammed into the desk an inch away from my wife's waiting fingers.

Tina thumped the floor with her short staff, and all of the uniforms of the dead guards rose to attention, loose bones rattling as castanets.

"Obey me!" she intoned in the Voice of Command. "Crew the sandbag nest and operate the guns!"

Moving to the embankment, the animated clothing crouched behind the weapons and did nothing.

"Fire!" Blanco roared.

They remained motionless.

It had been a nice try. But zombies can't do anything their master can't. And it was a good thing she didn't attempt that trick with Father Donaher present. Catholic priests take a dim view of zombies. It would have caused the most interesting of confrontations. Equivalent to checking your gas tank with a lit match.

"Charge!" she yelled in the Voice, and the dead guards rallied at the massed monsters, only to be vaingloriously annihilated once more.

Our mages appeared exhausted. Connie was pale, her hair a wild blond corona from the secondary static charges created by so much concentrated psionic outpourings. We were low on ammo and out of grenades. That was when the stone wall collapsed and in rushed the escaped prisoners. A trip wire made them pig-pile on top of each other. Raul then cast a sticky web to hold them there, and Tina added a poison-gas cloud. They started coughing, and the web started dissolving.

She said something short and biting in Russian.

I ignited the cloud with my pocket lighter, then twisted the top and tossed it at the struggling, burning group. One of Waspwoman's nastier heads went limp as her stinger and tail were blown off.

"Timex!" I cried. The team set our wristwatches to explode and stuffed them wherever we could reach and would do the most good. The result was pleasing, if brief.

Using her sword, Mindy cut the re-formed string demon into pieces, and the remaining boojums were upon us. Once more,

the ropy monster started to spin in place, reeling itself back
together.

With a scream, Ken dodged a stream of fire, leapt upon the
female centaur and ripped the creature's throat out with his teeth.
Yellow blood gushing from the hideous wound, the monster
staggered off to heal.

Wow. This guy made J. P. Withers seem like a sissy.

Steel blades snapped into position from both ends of Raul's
silver staff and he started wildly swinging. Bits of flesh and hide
went flying, then a blade snapped off as the mage hit something
invisible and very hard.

Snarling, Connie was firing her carbine one bullet at a time,
slowly retreating into the control room.

Biting a lip, Don formed an ethereal force blade in his free
hand and was thrusting and jabbing as best he could.

George and Tina were side by side. Renault was firing a .45
Army Colt pistol, and Blanco was in a boxer's crouch, punching
monsters with astonishing results. Then I noticed she was wearing velvet gloves. Through the visor of my helmet, the gloves
nearly pulsed with magic. Velvet gloves—iron fist?

Out of bullets, I drained the last of my Strength potion and
pulled a French police baton from my vest. With a snap, the
six-inch handle of telescoping steel rod extended to its full-meter
length and I started busting bones and scales with the rest and
best.

"Done!" cried Jessica.

Charging towards me, the stringy demon went stock-still and
toppled over limp as yarn. Brain Blasted, I was sure. What a
wife! She could cook too.

"Get the switch!" I yelled, going hand-to-hand-to-hand-to-
hand with Waspwoman. The goddamn hellgrammite was metamorphosing even as I smashed her mandibles. For the first time
in my life, I actually took pleasure in hitting a lady.

"Fast!" added Raul. He was cornered by a trio of blind, cack-
ling witches who had just joined the party. Necklaces of fresh
human eyes hung about their scrawny throats.

More monsters were arriving as the sounds of our battle spread
throughout the Facility.

Jess hitched her skirt and started for the office, with Patrika
running blockage. A pale, snaggle-toothed morlock tried to
snatch my wife, and the gypsy Healer slammed it aside in a

tackle worthy of any baseball center. Or some such sports analogy.

Dashing past the control dais, Jessica jerked to a halt and began to grapple with something invisible. Clothes were torn from her body, blood welling from countless cuts.

Throating a wild jungle yell, Ken grabbed the skinless centaur and hurtled the buxom beast straight through the Armorlite window of the office. I was impressed. The boojum crashed head-first into the wall above the switch and slid towards the floor, pulling the switch along after her. Click!

The lights dimmed, and instantly every thing was encased in a shimmering bubble of the brightest blue. Floating away, they pounded, howled and clawed in silent fury at the inside of the prismatic ball. Every prisoner, boojum and monster in Bangor-Maine—giant or microbe, visible or invisible, physical, ethereal or pure energy—was now being bodily hauled back to its waiting cell.

Raul bent over, trying to catch his breath. Mindy and Ken shook hands. I clutched my aching leg. George and Tina hugged each other. The twins did the same. Success!

"No," panted Jessica, slumping on the messy floor. "We're operating on battery power. Got no more than a few minutes at best." Patrika limped over to my wife.

Retracting his force blade, Donald opened a medical kit and Connie started repairs. "Can we fix the link to the main reactor?"

"I'm a telepath, not a nuclear scientist."

Leaning heavily on his staff, Raul said, "I can trickle a lightning bolt into the reserve power units. That might extend their service life."

"Go!" I barked weakly.

The mage got busy and lights flashed.

"Well?" I demanded.

"No good," he sighed, slumping into a chair. "If General MacAdams and his Phoenix team don't get here soon we're finished."

Without warning, a dazzling rainbow exploded in the room, and we were surrounded by a dozen hulking gray metal robots. Grimly, my team crowded together and raised our meager weapons for the last hurrah.

"Shakespeare," said a featureless golem with four silver stars on the shoulders.

"B-bacon," I managed to reply, happily watching a team of armored figures lug a portable generator over to the damaged power relay. "And, buddy, you just saved ours."

Yet one hour later, I knew it wasn't true.

This hadn't been an escape attempt.

It was a robbery.

7

We gathered in a small dark room. This time there were no jokes about popcorn, no silly buttons, no clever quips. This was business. My team was here to watch the tapes and films from the hidden security cameras showing what happened two hours ago to allow the worst escape, and second worst massacre, in Bureau history. And hopefully find out who the hell was behind it.

As usual, victory came at a price. A hundred guards and scientists were dead. Plus five of the students. And even worse, Don and Connie had requested permanent reassignment to office work. Apparently, Donald just couldn't take the grim reality of our work, and where baby brother went, sis had to follow. It was a shame. Constance Simon would have made a good field agent.

Settling ourselves in the cushioned chairs, I sat back and waited for the films to begin. There was a movie screen set at the front of the room, and behind us was a 16mm projector on a table filled with stacks of film cans.

As the senior field agents here, Gordon had assigned us the task of tracking down the who and finding out why. If he hadn't, I think we would have anyway and damn regulations.

"Ready when you are, Rosy," I said, steadying the clipboard in my lap for writing notes. Jess had an edemic memory, but I preferred to have my own info for studying.

What light there was dimmed. "Here we go," announced the bearded parson from the back of the room.

The screen lit to an aerial view of our arrival and meeting with Gil. Our subsequent journey through Bangor-Maine and then our Chicago boojum being hauled into the Holding Facility. From that point on, we paid real close attention.

As the last chunk of our boojum was hauled into the Facility, the monster re-formed and leapt towards the waiting guards. In midair it was caught and encased in a brilliant blue anti-magic bubble very similar to the fail-safe balls.

A guard with a hand-held control box floated the hairless lion-oid along the corridor past the flip-top wall, through the iron grate and to the scanner. It gave off no aura and no reading. They tried again, and then again. After conferring, a group of TechServe people boosted the scanner to maximum, even by-passed the safeties, and tried once more.

As Lumpy entered the scanning field, the arch registered solid black, laced with purple and green. The guards gasped, and there was a tremendous concussion. Now, in place of our boo-jum was a tall slim man, with a lantern jaw, slicked black hair with touches of gray at both temples. He was almost painfully distinguished and dressed in a formal tuxedo. What the hell?

However, what really caught our attention was the six-foot-long wizard's staff in his hands, made of glistening diamond. Not silver or gold with a diamond on top, but solid diamond. *Aye, carumba!* Not even Merlin had a diamond staff. This guy could eat Raul for a snack. No wonder he had been able to re-form after getting exploded into bits, and fool my sunglasses. What couldn't this guy do?

Boldly, our people jumped him, the staff pulsed once and only dust was in the air where six humans had just been. By this point, alarms were sounding, doors clanged shut and the tunnel stiffened. Then the boojum human waved his wand, it disap-peared and the video camera stopped.

Tina and Raul made gagging noises.

"His staff!"

"He destroyed his staff?"

Hmm, had to admit I had never heard of anybody ever doing it before. Not even when the mage's personal life was at stake.

With a ratcheting noise, the 16mm projector took over. It must have been minutes later, for monsters were everywhere. A boil-ing horde of hellspawn. The guards died in droves. Jessica had to turn away. The rest of us forced ourselves to watch. Infor-mation was more important than personal feelings. We would cry and mourn at a more appropriate moment.

Striding through the rampaging crowd came our mystery man. A few of the escaping prisoners tried to consume him, but Tux-edo Ted tossed tiny vials and blew 'em into pieces. Soon, he was an island of calm moving steadily through the boisterous crowd. Nothing was closer than ten feet to him, thus demon-strating the fact that supernaturals were not totally stupid.

The steps were extended on the curved walkway, and Mystery

Man skipped over mutilated human bodies while humming a tune. I was starting to really hate this guy. At the very bottom of the inclined ramp, level 84, Mr. Happy met with three prisoners, who obviously had been waiting for him.

"You are early," said an oriental gentleman in full kimono, hands inside sleeves. It was Rashamor, the vampire.

Impishly, the intruder grinned. "The fools were easier to trick than I had imagined."

"Up yours," growled George.

Tina added something appropriate in Russian.

While scribbling, I frowned. Rashamor Hoto was better known to the Bureau as Vampire X. Originally a regular vampire, he had been living in a small industrial Japanese village named Nagasaki towards the end of World War II.

Somehow surviving the atomic blast, Hoto was radically altered. Anybody who died within two miles of him—the precise blast radius of the Fat Man bomb—would become a vampire. A regular vampire, thank goodness. But that included anybody who died within that range: car accident victims, heart attacks, suicides, old age. Rashamor didn't have to have anything to do with their death. Merely being close was enough. Plus, all of the new vampires were his slaves, body, mind and soul. Before we finally destroyed his army and captured him, you could always find Hoto near the scene of any major accident. The bigger the better.

"Alert," I said into my new watch. "Code Ten. Rashamor Hoto is free. It is mandatory that everybody killed in today's escape have a wooden stake pounded into their hearts immediately. This is a priority notice!"

"Confirmed," said my timepiece. It sounded like Burton. "And already done. Geez, Alvarez, don't you think we know who we have in Holding?"

Good point. "Sorry."

"Better sorry than dead," reminded Raul.

Mindy ceased stropping a butterfly knife on a whetstone. "I think this is the very first time you have ever quoted a regulation."

A shrug. "Had to happen sometime."

With a word from Rosenberg, the film continued.

The second supernatural was Goshnar, a pulsating gelatinous mass with more mouths than brains. A genuine prehistoric pain in the ass, kill him and Goshnar would only be reborn somewhere else a minute later.

Goshnar made a guttural noise, and the mage responded in kind.

"Translation," I requested, pencil ready.

"Sorry, Ed," apologized my wife. "That language I don't know, and I can't read thoughts off a film."

Darn.

Stepping out of the shadows so it could be seen was a bipedal being of medium height and average build; a tan humanoid jumpsuit. The gloves and boots were a utility black, while the flattened ellipse helmet was a mirror that reflected nothing. Tanner.

The cryptic symbols on the front of its alien battlesuit of unknown origin seemed to vaguely resemble the earthly letters *TNR*, and thus it had been nicknamed Tanner. It had forcefields, a forceshield, laser beams, proton rays, disrupters, imploders, was superstrong and could fly. Tanner was always raiding military bases and NASA, trying to steal enough equipment to rebuild a warship to conquer this world and then construct an armada to return home and help win a war that we believed had been over a millennium ago. But try and convince him of that.

"Yes. Our. Plan. Has. Worked. Well," spoke Tanner. Each word was pronounced individually.

Undulating closer, Goshnar burped and gargled.

The mage seemed to take umbrage. "Not true! I was the person able to penetrate this base and disrupt their magical defenses, especially the ethereal bonds holding Tanner prisoner."

"And it took your wand to do it, scum," growled Horta.

"Yet," said a stiff artificial voice. "It. Was. I. Who. Then. Released. An. Electro. Magnetic. Pulse. That. Disrupted. Their. Primitive. Devices."

"However it was I," said the vampire, "who coordinated the escape. I, and only I, have communication with the outside world through a link to my only surviving slave."

Mentally, I tipped a hat to the creatures on the screen. Nothing I loved more than talkative monsters. Maybe if we listened long enough we could find out where Jimmy Hoffa was. I started to alert Base Command that Hoto had a slave alive, but Jessica stopped me.

They know, and it does not matter.

Why?

Watch.

Strolling along the strangely quiet walkway, the fearsome four went up to the access corridor, turned and entered the base again. But this time, they appeared in Storage. It was a slaughter.

"Are you sure there are no recording devices functioning?" asked Rashamor, wiping a trickle of blood from his red mouth. At his feet, a guard was groaning into death.

"Impossible," snorted the mage, straightening his hair with one of our combs. "Every magically powered machine is numb from my deudonic blast."

Deudonic, ah-ha! What the heck was that?

What a wizard staff is formed from.

"And. All. Electronic. Machines. Are. Deactivated. From. My. EM. Pulse," added Tanner, pushing buttons on his sleeve control panel.

That was correct, bozos. But they forget the basics. Next to each video camera in the walls, in case of failure, a spring-driven, mechanically operated, 16mm film camera went into operation. Nothing electric or magical about it. Simply chemical photography and a clockwork drive. TechServ strikes again! I must remember to send them a thank-you card.

Drooling and slurping loudly, Goshnar used a ropy pseudopod to remove a cleaned human skull from a smacking sub-mouth.

"Yes. Agreed." Tanner pointed a finger, a scintillating ray shot across the walkway and he vaporized an armored door the size of a bank vault. Calmly, they strolled inside. The camera shifted view.

Storage was a multilevel room, the center wide-open space. Metal catwalks zigzagged upward, leading to several platforms which ringed the outer wall. Made of wooden boards, boxes of every size and shape filled the place, with numbered stencils printed on the side to identify the crate. Only one was on the ground floor, in the center, behind a shimmering curtain of laser beams under a thick Armorlite dome.

But the lasers were deactivated from the EM pulse, and Mystery Man smashed open the Armorlite as if it were ordinary glass. Brushing aside the glistening shards, he ripped open the crate and hauled into view a book, which he promptly threw away.

Hitting a corner of the room, the volume exploded into thousands of tiny steel fléchettes. None of the monsters were hurt. Darn.

Outstretching a palm, Tanner disintegrated the solid metal block the fake book had been resting on. Now exposed was an identical volume, its bloodred cover seeming to pulse with some kind of a malevolent pseudo-life.

Mystery Man started to reach for the book, then recoiled.

"Ah," he hissed in annoyance. "There are additional protections. Would the three of you be so kind as to get me an obsidian blade from that crate by the door?"

"There's no obsidian blade in there," started George.

"This he knows," stated Tina.

Why, so the dirty bastard did.

"Ngarle. Burble," replied the monstrous blob, oozing to the crate. Tanner and Hoto followed, gingerly stepping over the slime trail on the floor. Extending another pseudopod, Goshnar easily lifted the unattached lid. Hoto and Tanner stepped close. Smiling, the mage turned around.

Knowing what to expect, we averted our vision.

When the screaming stopped, the lid fell shut and only wisps of writhing smoke hung in the air where the supernaturals had once been standing. And in the outside corridor was the mage. His clothes were smoking rags, he was horribly sunburned and blood seeped from both ears. But he was alive, and the Aztec Book of the Dead was neatly tucked under one blistered arm.

"Idiots," sneered the mage in a rude eulogy. "Why do you think the Bureau had the lid loose?"

Mystery Man was correct on that point. The Ark of the Covenant was nothing to fool around with. The story of how we obtained it would make a great movie by itself. The Ark serves the purpose of a lock on the room. If anybody departed without the proper ID, the lid of the crate flipped up and *zap!* Most of us wish we could use the Ark to exterminate our prisoners, but if anybody tried to deliberately use the Ark of the Covenant to murder—the Ark would turn on you. A trap was okay, but nothing else. Apparently, God was very strict on how you interpreted His Commandments.

Indeed, the holy relic was possibly the only lock that could hold some of the hellish objects in this room. And Mystery Man had beaten it. For the first time in years, I felt a touch of fear tighten my stomach. This guy was good.

Keeping a grip on the pulsating volume, the mage withdrew two small glass bottles from the inside pockets of his shredded tuxedo. Using his thumbs to pop off the corks, the oily vapor suspended in the air was promptly sucked into the vials like a genie returning to its lamp. What the hell? Laughing, Mystery

Man palmed the corks back into place. One bottle held about an inch of yellowish fluid, the other was half full of black and tan crystals. Hoto and Tanner?

Smiling contentedly, the mage flipped through the book, found a page, muttered, waved and vanished from sight. After a few seconds, the projector ratcheted to a stop, and the lights came on.

So the whole thing had been a damn trick, an insidious plan to steal a very special volume, the Aztec Book of the Dead, which contained every forbidden magical spell ever created. I would have been happier if he had stolen the nuclear bomb under the front crossbar. That we could have coped with. By just having the volume, the mage had been able to escape from the very heart of the Holding Facility.

"That's everything of importance," said Rosy, setting the projector for rewind. "The rest you know as participants."

"Thanks, Reverend."

"No problem, Ed."

"Conference," I called.

Rising and stretching, the gang pulled the chairs closer to review what we could gain from the films.

"Anybody recognize him?" I asked hopefully.

"Nope."

"Sorry."

"*Nyet.*"

"Negative, chief."

"Sir, no, sir."

"Anti-yes."

Oh well.

An amateur philologist, Jessica had analyzed the speech pattern of our new enemy and sadly declared that he studied with a speech therapist. Okay, that meant the mage originally had a highly distinctive accent. Something he wanted to hide. A lisp. Foreign, southern, Brooklyn. Maybe even a thick South Chicago accent, but we couldn't be sure.

"Did you examine those ears?" asked Raul. "He is a young man. That gray hair was phony."

"You mean hands," corrected Tina. "Gray hair, *da*, but no age spots. And wrists aren't wrinkled enough. He might use cream to remove the spots, but face-lift on wrists?"

Reflectively, I rubbed my broken nose. "A false face, eh? Then we can't circulate pictures of him taken off the film."

"Better try anyway," said George, resting a chin on the upright barrel of his M-60. "It might be his favorite face, and maybe he uses it often." To outward appearances, his chin was two feet in the air above a small banjo.

"Plus no scars or calluses. Not even softened ones on his hands," added Mindy. "This man has never done manual labor. And that tuxedo looked expensive."

But that didn't mean he was rich. Could have been a clerk in a video store. Or a CPA. And anybody can rent a tux.

"The tuxedo?" asked Ken, worrying his knuckles.

"Just a confusion factor to make witnesses focus on the suit, not him," explained Renault. "It's an old trick."

"Agreed," said Raul. "But a good one."

The end result was that Mystery Man covered his tracks well.

"It's not much to go on," I said, tallying my notes. "High probability that he is male. Caucasian. Approximately in his mid-thirties. Five feet ten, one hundred thirty pounds. Right-handed. Never did manual labor. Wizard."

"Not wizard," snapped Tina. "All chemist, beneath contempt!"

"An alchemist?" I translated.

A nod. "*Da!* Yes. Bottles used tell truth."

"But he had a diamond wizard's staff!" objected Ken.

"Which he destroyed to free the prisoners!" growled Raul, thumping his own staff on the floor in an angry tempo. "Any damn fool alchemist can concoct some brew to give them the full power of an adult wizard for twenty-four hours!"

"But," prompted Jess.

"It kills you afterwards. Total biological and spiritual burnout. Not even your ghost remains."

Whew. That was serious death.

Smiling, George threw his arms across the back of the chairs. "Then our problem is solved."

"*Nyet,*" stated Tina, slicing a hand through the air. Then she barked a phrase in Russian.

"He has the Aztec book," reminded Horta. "Just holding the volume will protect him from the ravages of his own potions."

I started juggling numbers in my head. From when the fake boojum first threw the police officer out the window, to our capturing him, to the escape . . .

We went through a time zone change, reminded Jess.

"Thanks. Whew. Twenty-three and a half hours."

George snorted. "A hell of a gamble."

"Which seems to indicate a desperate mage," said Ken.

Wizard staff banged on the floor. "Alchemist," retorted Horta. "He's no wizard!"

"Which is he did it why," garbled Christina, tugging on a lock of her long red hair.

"Explain, please," I requested, sharpening the point on my pencil. This promised to be a long session.

Raul started to speak twice. Nibbling on a nail, he finally got it out. "Using magic is a kick," he said. "A thrill. Better than any drug. Sometimes better than sex!"

"*Da,*" sighed Blanco sadly.

From Renault's expression, I think that particular problem of hers would soon be solved.

"And as an alchemist he could only nibble around the edges, getting a fleeting taste every now and then."

"Addictive," noted Mindy. "Similar to the adrenaline high of battle."

"You better believe it." He leaned forward, resting arms and closed hands on knees. "Do you know that in the history of the Bureau, eight wizards have lost their powers and all eight committed suicide?"

Our old pal Richard Anderson was not counted in that somber list. Anderson had retired with his powers and abilities intact, just unable to perform any major magic. That happened at his age. However, I was beginning to get the picture.

"So Mystery Man would have done anything, even gamble with true death, for a chance at real magic."

"No question."

"Great. So he's now an ultrapowerful nut."

"Unfortunately, yes."

"But why did he steal the gaseous remains of the other two supernaturals?" asked Ken. "But not Goshnar?"

"Good taste?" joked Renault snidely.

Tina snorted. "All chemist steal anything."

"So true," noted Raul. "They're infamous for being chemical and herbal pack rats."

The mention of food, slight as it was, made my stomach rumble, announcing that lunch had become an imperative. So I put the talk on hold and shooed the team out of the projection room. We walked along the branching corridors until finding a cafeteria. The smell of food quickened everybody's step. Half the tables were occupied, the others smashed. Apparently, fighting had taken place here also. Probably just some spectral chef furious over what they did to meat loaf at the Academy.

Noticing Patrika sitting alone at a table, I asked Jess to grab me anything fried on toast with onions, and ambled over to talk to the Healer.

"How have you been?" I asked, taking a chair. "Long time no see."

Wearily, Patrika raised her head as she spooned a good pound of sugar into her coffee mug. "Busy," she slurped. "Trying to repair the wounded and dying. I haven't been this busy since that 1990 earthquake in San Francisco."

"You were there?"

"My team stopped the giant beetle that caused it."

"Quoi?"

A shy smile. "I'm not a student," she confessed. "I'm a field agent from Team Angel in Los Angeles, here to be a ringer in the final exam. Open inappropriate doors, get captured, head in the wrong direction, that sort of stuff."

Wow. Burton was even sneakier than I had ever imagined.

"I have friends in Frisco," I said, offering the milk. It was refused. "Lucky a Bureau team was there."

"Yeah, lucky." The gypsy said the word as if it had a bad taste. "And every night in my dreams I hear the screams of the people who died in the quake. The civilians we couldn't save fast enough."

I said nothing. What was there to say? It was an agent's burden. You accepted it, went mad or quit.

Suddenly, Patrika touched my arm. "Ed, if you have no objections, I'd like to join your team for the duration."

"Eh? Why?"

"After having seen what this alchemist can do, he's gotta go down for the count. And I want to help."

Frankly, I was surprised. "That's kind of rough talk for a Healer."

"My powers may be benign," she snarled. "But not me!"

Major personal dichotomy. I thought about the suggestion. "What about your home team?"

She smiled. "I've already called Team Angel in Los Angeles and it's fine with Aki and Damon."

Damn. "Sorry, but I have to say no. Every field team the Bureau has is being temporarily assigned to the Facility until the damage can be repaired. Gordon has given Tunafish the job of getting Mystery Man. And besides, I'm getting Blanco and Sanders. Eight people is the most that I can handle. Any more and the tires on the RV will burst from the weight."

The Healer accepted that. Truth be told, I simply could not properly hold rein over nine Bureau-issue lunatics.

"Fair enough," she acknowledged with a weary smile.

Jessica was at our table with a trayload of food, so I stood. "Gotta go. Take care, Ms. . . . Say, what is your last name anyway?"

This seemed to embarrass her. "I am of gypsy heritage," she started as an explanation. "And we really don't use last names. Lineage is often a matter of opinion. I was going to use 'Gypsy,' but the TechServ random-name generator decided upon 'Ritter.' "

"Well then, take care, Pat Ritter. Call if you ever need help."

"Goodbye, Edwardo." She held out a hand and we shook.

A burning wave of warmth flowed over my entire body. I was no longer tired, the leg stopped hurting and my broken nose slammed into place.

"That's my way of letting you know what you're missing."

As I walked away, I ran fingers through my hair and scratched the outside of my brain. Goddamn. Maybe we should have kept her. Oh well.

The report from Technical Services arrived while we were still eating. That was fast, even for the gang at TechServ. Unfortunately, there wasn't much to go on. We had already gleaned the pertinent points. Caucasian male from America. Average height, average weight, right-handed. They had run a make on his fingerprints, but they didn't match against anything in the master file of the FBI. Not surprising.

It was too bad that he hadn't gone about barefoot. We caught more criminals from toeprints taken when they were born than we ever did from fingerprints. Too many cheap TV shows had taught crooks the value of wearing gloves.

After lunch, we retrieved Amigo from Base Command, had our broken windshield replaced, and my team headed for home. There were magical and scientific devices in our Chicago apartment that we could use to try and find Fink #1. With an amoral screwball loose holding the Aztec Book of the Dead, there was no telling what mischief he could be doing. Just reading the table of contents caused the sky to rain stones for a week. Which simply drove the U.S. Weather Bureau nuts trying to explain.

There was already a nice grave waiting for Mystery Man. It was the blast crater where Gil Lapin's jumpjet had crashed and burned with him trapped inside the wreckage.

Bureau 13 wanted this guy bad, and we were going to get him. Dead. Not alive.

8

Upon receiving our report, Horace Gordon contacted every government law enforcement agency. The FBI, CIA, Secret Service, DEA, Treasury Department, Army G2, Air Force Intelligence, Navy Security, SAC and NORAD each received a Hunt & Kill order on Mystery Man. An APB was issued to city, county and state police across the continent, including Canada and Mexico. His picture and fingerprints circulated via satellites and over wires. Our John Doe was listed as a homicidal maniac with rabies, heavily armed and totally insane. The police were strictly ordered not to even attempt an arrest. Just shoot the suspect and burn the body.

We highly doubted that any ordinary cop could bring in the alchemist, but their efforts couldn't hurt, and if somebody did manage to pull off a miracle kill, we'd put the person in charge of Bureau 13, just for being the luckiest sonofabitch on the face of the Earth.

Scowling at the tiny photo of Mystery Man on the clipboard, the traffic cop tore a ticket out of her summons book and handed it to George. The soldier's hands were knuckle-white on the steering wheel.

"Buddy," drawled the officer, "I don't care if you're FBI, CIA and Secret Service. Speed in Chicago, and you get a ticket!"

"Once again, the safety of humanity was in the capable hands of Bureau 13," announced Raul as the police officer walked back to her patrol car.

"Aw, shaddup," growled Renault, throwing the transmission into drive and easing off the berm at a stately 55 mph.

"Besides, you're still 412 to 2," added Jessica with a grin.

Although not telepathic, Mr. Renault's thoughts were plainly readable from the expression on his face. I was surprised he would talk that way about a lady in her presence.

Continuing on our way home, we actually obeyed the traffic

laws. It was a nice change. I had never known those green-brown blurs alongside the road were actually trees.

Taking the Wacker Avenue exit, we wiggled through the downtown traffic and took Dearborn Road until reaching a modest building in the middle of the block. Home. Our new members did not seem impressed with its innate grandeur, so I started my introductory spiel.

Since no field agent knows where our main headquarters is, each team operates independently. Everybody's home base has to be a fort, sanctuary, armory, supply dump, refueling station and information processing station. It makes for interesting structural designs. Once in Roanoke, Virginia, we had been forced to apprehend a demonically possessed Bureau mansion, and blasting our way into another agent's home base was not something I would ever like to have to do again. Their robotic lawn jockeys had damn near killed me. And to this day, Amigo will not go anywhere near a velvet painting of Elvis.

The six-story structure before us was an old warehouse converted into an apartment complex. And we did the conversion. The warehouse had an antique wrought-iron framework, which our mages polymorphed into chrome steel, then workers poured titanium wire reinforced concrete for the floors and walls. Afterwards, the outside of the building was hung with a foot of tough Italian marble, and we bricked the interior walls. The windows were three sheets thick: glass, Armorlite, Plexiglas. It never got cold in the winter. And for Chicago, that was saying something.

Every external door was wood sheeting over plate steel, cushioned with xytel plastic inserts and braced by four oversize hinges. The locks were Bureau specials. And the interior doors were six-inch-thick African ironwood. Termites broke teeth on the stuff.

Now, an apartment building in downtown Chicago which had no tenants would have caused talk. So we did rent out the lower floors, to folk like a family of deaf-mutes and a heavy metal rock band that liked to practice at odd hours. Nobody ever investigated any strange noises coming from our place.

Once, we had gotten a deadbeat, who refused to pay his rent and invited us to take him to court. Publicity is the last thing we wanted, so after a brief visit by some "friends" that Raul conjured at midnight, Mr. Deadbeat was gone by morning. Since then, we have had few problems.

Our team lives on the fifth floor. The fourth and sixth levels were jam-packed with cinder blocks, sensors, concertina wire, bear traps and Claymore mines: a safety sandwich, we called the layout. There was a heliport on the roof, but after what occurred to our last helicopter, the Bureau was rather loath to give us another. Hey, accidents happen. And personally, I think the new Statue of Liberty looks even better than the old one.

Now the students were impressed.

Narrowly missing a crunch between a Mack truck and a taxi, Renault drove the RV along an inclined ramp into our subterranean parking garage. Flipping a switch on the dashboard, the armored door rumbled into the ceiling, we entered and it noisily descended behind us.

To the left was the vehicle repair bay. To the right, parking spaces containing a sleek black sports coupe, a battered red pickup truck, a white limousine, a station wagon, a sleek speedboat dry-docked on a trailer hitch and a flock of bicycles. Every spot was filled but one. We took that.

"Others park here?" asked Ken, stooping to get out of the van. Both his and Blanco's suitcases were held in a single hand.

"Nope, they're ours," said George proudly, hefting his thirty-pound banjo from the RV. "Never can tell when you're going to need additional transportation."

"Of appropriate demeanor," added Mindy.

I pressed a button on my key chain, and a piece of the wall dissolved to expose a door. The team trundled inside.

In the lobby, there were two elevators: one for the tenants, another for us. Theirs went from ground level to the third floor. Ours went from the roof to the sub-subbasement where we kept a bomb shelter.

"There is a ghost there, no?" asked Tina. She had heard the gossip.

Adjusting the leash about Amigo's neck, Raul told her correct. "Old Pirate Pete, a buccaneer from the Spanish Main. He keeps ordering pizzas and stiffing the deliveryman."

"Why not exorcise the spirit?"

"He's crotchety, but the local kids love his antics during Halloween and Purim."

A fleeting smile. "A most valuable commodity, then."

"At least for PR purposes."

Silent, the elevator opened to our floor. For anybody else, it would have very loudly dinged. Our private lobby had a plush red carpet to help hide bloodstains, and a pleasing abstract wallpaper which disguised bullet holes with amazing success. A Japanese landscape triptych adorned the wall, and a couple of chairs offered hospitality to waiting guests. Of course, the chairs closed like a vise on the occupant when commanded.

While George and the students stood guard, Jessica slid the middle section of the triptych aside to peek into the apartment, I ran a security check, Raul performed a simple Sense Evil spell and Mindy got the mail.

"Apartment is clear."

"No physical intruders."

"Ethereal vibrations are harmonious."

"Our subscription to *TV Guide* has expired!"

After consoling my friend, I drew a pistol, unlocked the front door and eased it open with a foot.

The hallway was empty with the lights on. But then, we always leave the lights on. Day and night. George took point, with Mindy doing a cover sweep, and we entered the living room. Spreading out in a standard defensive pattern, we waited until Raul stuck his head into the aquarium and asked our fish for a status report.

"Is this really necessary?" asked Tina.

Mindy frowned. "Do you know what we found here once waiting for us?"

"No," replied the stolid Russian.

"Nobody else either. But it tried to eat the lot of us."

A pause. "Oh."

Raul surfaced, bone dry, but with a length of seaweed caught behind his ear. I decided not to tell him. "All clear," he announced, and everybody relaxed.

Dragging his leash, Amigo headed straight for the kitchen, and two seconds later his empty food bowl began to rattle against the refrigerator. As it was his turn, George shouldered his weapon and followed.

"Don't forget the sandbox," added Jennings.

The swinging kitchen doors cut off any possible retort.

Basically in a square format, the apartment had a fancy brick fireplace occupying the entire north wall of the living room, and set before it were three tremendous couches bracketing the hearth. The dining room, kitchen, pantry, laundry, armory and emergency exit were towards the east. Southward was a blank wall, behind which were Raul's magic library, our InfoNet computer, gymnasium and trophy room. And to the west was a door-lined corridor that led to our individual bedrooms. Only recently had we removed the dividing partition between Jessica's quarters and mine to form a honeymoon suite. Lord knows where we'd ever put a nursery.

A what?!

Oh, nothing, dear. Nothing. Smile.

"Only thing missing is a batpole," quipped Ken.

Wordless, Raul kicked a scuffed section of the baseboard, and a hidden panel swung out from the wall, exposing a slickly polished vertical pipe.

"But it only leads to the Jacuzzi," apologized the mage.

With a loud thump, Ken deposited the luggage on the floor. "What should we do first, sir?"

"Check the date," I said, striding to the library and flipping pages on our astrological calendar. Yep, the summer solstice was only two days away.

"So?" asked Ken when informed of this.

Taking a seat on a couch, Blanco crossed her long legs at the knee, her white silk dress hitching to a scandalous position. "Aztecs worshipped sun. Book is strongest at solar crossing."

The folding partition to the kitchen separated and George appeared. "This timing is too perfect," he said, popping the top on a beer can. "Stealing the book only days before its yearly power surge?"

"Never trust the obvious," remarked Raul, scratching at his green-draped ear. He extracted the seaweed and glared at me.

"Laying a false trail to mislead us?" suggested Ken. "When he actually plans on hiding for several months before using the book? While we exhaust ourselves running around in circles?"

"A possibility," I noted, starting to pace. "But I've never known any junkie who waited before hitting themselves with a fix. And Mystery Man is a junkie. A magic addict."

Getting a hanger from the closet, Jessica hung her holster and slid the taser into a recharging bracket. "Or perhaps," she postulated, "he believes that we'll never stop him quickly enough even if we do find him."

Now, that was an unpleasant thought.

Ceasing my walk to nowhere, I clapped hands for attention. "Okay, people, time is short, so let's divide into three groups. Jessica and I will do a nationwide scan of any unusual occurrences trying to form a pattern."

"Sounds good," acknowledged Ken.

"Raul and Blanco, as our resident mages, you'll hit the books. Try to find something, anything, on the contents of the damn Aztec manual. If we know what Mystery Man is doing, then we can outguess 'im and lay a trap. But we have got to know what the hell is going on!"

"I may have something on that," remarked Raul cryptically, rising to his feet and starting for the library. "Let's go, Blanco."

The Russian seemed mildly perturbed by our constant use of her last name, but there was a good reason. The Bureau lost recruits at a frightening rate, and calling new people by their last names helped us maintain a psychological distance, to lessen the pain when they died. It was a most unforgiving business we were in.

I went on. "George, Sanders and Mindy get the tough job. I want you three to try and concoct some kind of weapon we can use against the alchemist: containment, stun, disabilitating, confusion, anything. No holds barred. Got it?"

"Check." They headed for the arsenal on the other side of the kitchen. George had assisted in laying out the floor plans.

As I palmed the south wall, it broke apart to reveal our quietly humming InfoNet mainframe computer. The freestanding, cabinet-style, data processing units that composed the central core of the computer were staggered about in the room in the exact same order as the tissue folds of a human brain. For some reason it improved both speed and memory. What the hey, we'll use anything that works.

Reaching the main terminal, Jess took a seat at the fast-feed video monitor and set the dial to maximum speed. "Normal routine?" she asked. "I'll do radio, television and cable. You hit the magazines and newspapers?"

Typing away on a keyboard, I confirmed. " 'Sokay. But beside the usual things—bizarre robberies, mysterious deaths, that sort of stuff—be sure to watch for any rocky rainstorms."

"Gotcha."

We began.

As the team had been on the road for over a month, there was a ton of backlog to sift through. Luckily, it seemed to have been a fairly quiet summer in America. There was a report of cubist flying saucers in New Jersey. That was nothing. Probably just the Venusians again stealing more of our toxic waste, God bless 'em. But I made a note of it. The Loch Ness monster had been sighted by a drunk in Lake Ontario. Phooey. Nessie lived in the Bermuda Triangle these days. Elderly woman attacked by vampire in Atlanta, Georgia. The police already had the guy. Just a nut with a razor blade glued to his incisors.

Bunker #14 at the Picakinny Arsenal in Pennsylvania reports an unusually large shortage of weapons in storage. I wonder what was the normal shortage of weapons? The IBM research lab in Silicon Valley, California, hints that it was robbed early this morning, but refuses to divulge details for fear of making the company stock drop on the market. According to an FBI report on the matter, a twelve-ton steel door to the IBM vault appeared to have been removed by bare hands. I typed in a priority request for a copy of the fingerprints and got an immediate cross-reference to the prints of Mystery Man in the file of the Bureau. Might be a lead.

Indian ghost in mansion in Rhode Island scared an old man to death. Goshnar mugged and killed in Manhattan by street gang. So the blob had escaped! Giant robot spotted in Alaska—that was just the Pentagon's giant robot on another test run. The big mechanical jerk was terrified of toaster ovens for some reason. German U-boat sunk by Morman fisherman in the Great Salt Lake. Hmm. Goshnar killed in Philadelphia by a convention of science fiction fans. A tornado stole a farmhouse in Kansas—again? Goshnar run over by an ice cream vendor's truck in Mississippi. When will he ever learn? Amelia Earhart's luggage arrived at Midway Airport, Gate A-4. Well, it's about time. Man arrested in Reno for cheating at casino. Gambler declares he wasn't cheating, but simply knows what numbers and cards will win. Psychic? A possible recruit. I annexed it for headquarters. A weeping Goshnar surrenders to Bureau team in Los Angeles.

Werewolves in Texas are actually just big wolves. I put a maybe by that. Satanic cult in Delaware had a gunfight with the local police. The cult lost. Hurrah for our side. Axe murderer about to be fried in the electric chair in North Dakota swore he would return from the grave to seek revenge. Then a special notice appeared saying that the Bureau team, Roger's Rangers, had stolen the body, burned it to ash and sealed the remains, upside down, in cement. Way to go, Rangers! Time travelers in Toronto, vegetarian vampires in Vermont, moon men in Memphis, poltergeist penguins in Panama, hellhounds in Hollywood—how had anybody noticed?—and smooth, sexy, slinky, silky, succulent, succubi slayers in Seattle. Sigh. Groan. Eye drops. Coffee.

Sorting, sifting, searching, the hours swiftly passed. Tons of data deluged us, with Jess and I heroically struggling to separate grain from chaff. So much of this input was the result of drugs, hoaxes or just plain lack of common sense. Where the heck was the real bad guy? I was starting to feel like an overworked private investigator again. Digging through mounds of rotting garbage to find that single crumpled theatre receipt that blows the lid off a million-dollar art smuggling ring. Ah, the good old days.

No daydreaming. Get back to work.

Slave driver.

It was dark outside when the intercom announced dinner. Listlessly, we shuffled into the dining room and fell upon the food like purple fungus from Betelgeuse. By unanimous decision, the meal was quiet. I could almost hear the mental wheels grinding.

During dessert, I decided to give the aching brains a rest and lead the conversation off on a tangent. Always a favorite subject, we discussed initiations into the Bureau: my bloody rescue, George's heroic stance in the jungles of Vietnam, Raul's rather explosive discovery that he had been a mage his entire adult life, Mindy's hilarious tale of derring-do at the World's Fair, and how Jessica had boldly stridden into a Bureau 13 divisional headquarters having found the covert organization all by her telepathic self.

In awkward stages, Tina recounted how she became a mage during a command performance of *Brigadoonski*, the disastrous aftereffects and her subsequent defection. I knew that the KGB secretly had a nameless antisupernatural section, but they indiscriminately killed nonhumans and had absolutely none on their staff.

Rather prissy of them, in my opinion.

Embarrassed, Lieutenant Colonel Sanders refused to divulge his story, saying it was Alpha-coded and not privy for general disbursement. Sorry. Given the sign from me, Jess tried a soft read on the man, but she got a flat nothing. Another natural telepathic block, same as Englehart. She said it was like trying to read a rock or an animal. Oh well. When I next got the chance, I'd slip some truth serum into his tapioca.

After piling the dishes in the sink, I ordered my yawning team to call it a night. Sleepy minds made mistakes, which we could not afford. Blanco and Sanders got our two spare bedrooms. I activated the alarm system, turned on the automatic defenses, set the scanning perimeters for the computer and went to bed with my wife. Sleep came fast, but troubled dreams disturbed my rest.

And four hours later, it happened.

9

With a shout, I tumbled to the floor, blankets wrapped about my feet and Magnum in hand.

"What? Who? Where?" I demanded at the darkness, in my perfect impersonation of a frightened cub reporter. The noise sounded again. It was the red alert Klaxon from the InfoNet computer.

'Let's go,'' said Jess, pulling a robe on over her flannel night-shirt and grabbing a taser from the bed table.

Dashing through the living room, I easily avoided the strategically placed hassock which seemed to love shins, and placed my palm against the south wall. Silently, the wall parted. Hitting either side of the opening, we listened for a second, then I charged in as Jess kept me covered.

Nattily attired in woolen longjohns and fluffy bunny slippers, Raul was standing impatiently in front of our top-secret laser printer. His hands were hovering above the controls, almost touching the switches, but not quite. Horta knew better. Our printer could use its beam of condensed light for more things than just printing.

Suddenly appearing behind us was George, sporting an Uzi machine pistol and wearing striped pajama bottoms. Next came Tina, her wooden staff at the ready, and tastefully draped in a matching striped pajama top. So they were collaborating already, eh?

Leaping into the middle of the room, Ken landed on tiptoes, dead silent and absolutely stark naked except for his Thompson .45 machine gun and a bowie knife. I admire a man who has his priorities straight.

The whining ceased, and blank paper scrolled from the top of the printer. Ripping the top sheet free, I reached into my boxer shorts and retrieved my Bureau commission booklet. Pressing the federal ID against the paper, words began to form.

"What does it say?" demanded Mindy, lowering her sword.

Wearing only skimpy red lace panties, she was most distracting and disgustingly wide awake.

"It's an event chain," I told them. "A school bus crashed into a tree outside of Huntsville, Alabama, at noon. Thirty passengers were killed. All of the bodies have been reported stolen from the city morgue around ten P.M. Huntsville, Alabama, blood bank robbed of thirty gallons around midnight. Huntsville, Alabama, farmer reports a herd of cattle drained of blood by flock of bats just prior to dawn."

"We have a bingo!" announced Mindy, donning the robe Jessica offered her.

Amigo waddled into the room, yawned loudly at us for disturbing his rest and waddled out again.

"How could the crash victims have become vampires?" said Renault, puzzled. "Hoto is dead."

"Theoretically," I sternly corrected. "And then maybe Mystery Man was able to reconstitute the vampire like mutant orange juice. However, it's a hot lead, so I'll do a recon."

Hesitantly, Ken raised his hand for permission to speak. Lord, give me strength.

"This isn't grammar school, Sanders," I chastised. "Talk already, dude."

"Sir, if Hoto has been brought back, then perhaps the TNR device is also functioning again. And if I remember correctly from the casebooks, the alien machine habitually monitors all radio broadcasts and telephone lines listening for enemy communications. So if you do find them, how will you notify us?"

"Take Jessica along?" suggested Blanco. "Comrade telepath can contact team here in Chicago."

"Not practical," said Jess patiently. "This may be a lead, a diversion or a trap. Two are enough to find out which. If there's trouble, they will call for help."

I added, "Plus, if it is a diversion and a real situation occurs elsewhere, how will the team contact us, to tell where the actual danger is?"

The Russian mage had to chew that over for a moment, then accepted the cold logic. Communications in battle were always a tricky matter. Most important things were. Cellular phones helped, but anyone could tap/jam/trace those transmissions. Even short coded phrases were dangerous.

"Ah, excuse me, sir. But how *will* you contact us?" asked Ken again.

"We'll send a postcard."

Blink. "Sir?"

Quickly, I explained. A magic postcard was a plain white paper rectangle, soaked in liquid magic for months. When ready, you simply address the perfectly ordinary-seeming postcard to whoever should receive the message and the card disappears, to reappear in the recipient's hand. But everything had to be perfect for it to work, and bad penmanship counted against you. Expensive and tricky to operate, we usually reserve the postcards for emergency correspondence or belated birthdays.

"How many are available?" asked George.

"None," yawned Raul, his bunny slippers copying the motion. "I printed a fresh batch last month, but they're not dry yet."

"None? As in zero?"

"Yep."

Oh swell. So much for that idea. I chewed a lip in thought. "Okay, then we do it the old-fashioned way. Jess, please telepathically contact either Raul or me every hour on the hour."

"I'll link with just you," she said after a moment. "We have a much closer rapport."

Ain't it the truth.

"This could be a trap, Ed," noted Horta. "Whoever this guy is, he knows the Bureau is hot for his ass. And he tricked us once with the animal disguise."

Yeah, and it still galled me that we had personally hauled the murdering bastard exactly where he wanted to go. Well, we would soon correct that mistake. At the end of a gun.

"And then he turned on the very monsters who had summoned him for aid," noted Jess.

"Okay, okay. He's a lying, amoral, backstabbing fink who loves traps," I agreed. "Fine. Let's use that to our advantage. Raul, you up for burning some rope?"

Three delighted grins. "You betcham, Red Ryder!"

"And us," said George, placing an arm about Tina's dappled curves.

"Sorry, chum. You're a top-notch gunner, but as a spy you make a fine demolitions expert. And as for Ms. Blanco, burning a rope is no job for a newcomer. Besides, your Russian accent would cause too much notice down South."

Renault accepted the rebuke with what grace he could. Tina seemed confused.

"Accent, *da*," she agreed. "But what rope is it that you will burn?"

"I'll explain in the kitchen," said Mindy, taking the tall redhead by the arm. "Come on, let's start the coffee."

"Bless you," yawned Horta and company.

I added my own benedictions. "The rest of you stay here and continue the work. We may need every gimmick you can think of to take this guy. And just in case this isn't a mistake, but actually is a trap or a lead, be ready for a teleport and full unrestricted combat."

"Done."

"Sir, yes, sir."

"Of course, dear."

"Lock and load, chief."

Returning to our bedroom, I quickly showered, shaved and dressed in black shoes, black socks, black pants, light blue shirt, dark blue sweater, black tie and tweed sports jacket. Glancing in the mirror, I resembled a badly disguised undercover police officer. Just the effect I wanted.

Jessica already had the armoire open, and I chose my assortment of supplies. In blatant combat situations, Bureau agents could wear full body armor, ride tanks and carry bazookas. But operating in suburban Doo-dah-ville, such paraphernalia only caused undue attention and frightened the horses.

Sliding on my double shoulder holster, I checked the loads on both of my .357 Magnums, and made damn sure I had extra speedloaders, one of them filled exclusively with wooden bullets. Swiss Army knife, Bureau sunglasses, unbreakable pocket comb, EM scanner, flame-retardant handkerchief, FBI ID, wallet, keys, a thousand in cash for bribes, Visa, MasterCard, American Express, pocket cassette recorder, mini-camera, four fountain pens, a pack of cigarettes and a signet ring. Yep, I was ready for war.

I hate burning a rope, sent Jess.

It's my turn for recon duty, darling.

Well, be extra careful. Tanner and Hoto are dangerous enough by themselves. If Lumpy has brought them back, the four of 'em could be a match for the whole Bureau.

The four? I blinked. *Oh yes, the Aztec book. But without an operative, it's relatively harmless.*

So is a subcritical mass of plutonium. Jess gave me a kiss.

I returned the lip service. "Worry worm."

"Wife," she replied.

Raul was waiting for me in the library. The mage had changed clothes and was wearing sneakers, denims and a red flannel shirt. I was surprised he lacked a straw hat and wasn't munching on a weed. His arms were tanned brown, his neck was red and his chest a pasty white. He looked Southern with a capital *S*. Perfect. We were sure to go unnoticed.

On a hunch, I gave him a glance through my sunglasses. Ah-ha, damn near every inch of his body rippled with green auras.

"You wearing anything that isn't magic?" I asked.

"Socks, shorts and smile."

"Where's your staff?"

"In my socks and shorts."

Of course. How foolish of me.

Pulling a massive volume prominently marked "A" from the packed library shelves, George laid our travel journal on a walnut table. Raul started flipping through a book of photographs. A mage had to see location of where to teleport, so we had an immense library of full-color photographs of most every major city in North America, and a few overseas. It had really saved our butts when we tackled the riddle of the Seven Doors.

"Birmingham is the closest we have," called the mage. "About a hundred miles away. No, wait! Here's a postcard of the Huntsville sports arena!"

Accepting a mug of Morning Thunder tea from Tina, I drained the brew straight. My eyes popped open and I shivered to full consciousness. Nothing magical about it. Just enough hard caffeine to burn a hole in asbestos. Panting, I thanked her.

"Good enough. We'll take a cab or buy a car. Whichever is faster. Let's boogie."

Mindy handed us a bag of sandwiches, and I kissed Jessica goodbye. Then the team stepped clear as Raul began gesticulating. There was a flash, and we were suddenly standing on a corner near a streetlamp, a mailbox and the Dixieland Photo Supply store. Dawn was just tinting the skyline above the Huntsville sports arena.

Stepping onto Jefferson Boulevard, I whistled for a cab.

Paying off the happy cabdriver, Raul and I entered the Our Lady of Mercy Hospital, where the sole survivor of the bus crash was recuperating. Our FBI badges and serious expressions got us past the nurse at the reception desk and the doctor on duty in the critical ward. Apparently, Sam McGinty, the driver of the bus, wasn't expected to see noon.

Badgering and blustering, I got us ten minutes alone with the unconscious man. A nurse demanded to know why the federal police wanted to see a dying patient, and Raul told her it was to measure his feet. That confused her long enough for us to gain entry to his room.

There were six other patients in this ward, none of them appearing any too good, but all with human auras. Our man was by the window. The chart on the wall was indecipherable doctorese, but Horta and I had come equipped with common sense. This guy was a mess. Both legs were in casts, arms suspended from a ceiling harness, and he was wrapped head to toe in more bandages than Billy-Bob. A clear-plastic oxygen tent covered his head and clusters of drip bags were attached to his arms and neck. A beeping monitor on a nearby table registered heartbeat and pulse. The poor slob had more wires running into him than a cheap radio receiver.

The door had no lock, so I slipped a chair under the handle to guarantee us a modicum of privacy. Meanwhile, Raul slid the curtains closed around the bed and pulled his staff into view from his pants. I joined him in the middle of a mumble and the mage bathed the dying man with a soft white light. Gently, the monitors started registering stable life-signs and McGinty stirred. Taking a ragged breath, our only witness moaned and opened his eyes.

"Wha . . . ?" he asked as we removed the clear-plastic tent.

Raul crouched so he would be at face level with the man. In the cab ride over, I had lost the coin toss which decided who would be bad cop to the good cop. I still think we should have done best two out of three.

"You're all right, Sam," said the mage in soothing tones. "This is a hospital, and you're fine. A little banged up, but you will live."

McGinty used a full minute to digest that information. "Who . . . are you?" he finally asked.

Brusquely, I flashed my badge and he registered the usual surprise and respect that we always get from southerners.

"Am . . . I under arrest?"

"Not yet," I growled in my official patented tough-guy voice. "Not unless you don't cooperate with the government fully in this serious matter."

"How . . . can I he'p ya, Officer?" he croaked softly.

"Sam, can you tell us what happened?" said Raul, tucking the top part of his commission booklet into a shirt pocket so the badge would always be in sight. A psychological inducement to help us maintain mental authority over the civilian.

"Y'all mean the crash?"

"Yes."

Visibly, the driver tried to think fast. "Why, a . . . skunk . . . yeah, a skunk ran in front of the bus, and I swerved to avoid hittin' the thing and hit a tree," McGinty lied with a straight face. "Don't remember much after that."

"You are an excellent poker player," complimented Raul. "But we stopped at the Huntsville police station before coming here and saw the wreck. That vehicle was cut in half like it ran straight into a horizontal buzz saw."

Nothing. " 'Fraid I dun' know what yewr talkin' about, sir."

"Yet the ends of the cut were slightly slagged. Molten!" I snapped. "McGinty, you know what a laser beam is?"

The expression on his face said that he did. Mystery Man had probably used a Disintegration spell or a tightly controlled lightning bolt, but either one would resemble a laser beam to the uninformed.

"Well, enemy agents of a foreign country have stolen a working military prototype of a laser rifle from"—frantically, I struggled to remember the local army base, failed and took a wild stab in the dark—"Fort Washington. The Pentagon wants it returned."

"America needs that weapon, Sam," added Raul.

"Was it the commies?" asked the man, registering shock.

Lying was part of the job. "Exactly."

"Well, shoot," he said, patriotic resolve strengthening his voice. "I didn't wanna tell the truth for feared of going to the loony bin. But if it's for my country . . ."

"We know most of the story, Sam," said Raul. "Just tell us what you saw. Everything. The tiniest detail could be important."

A hanging arm attempted to move. Then McGinty scrunched his face in concentration. "It was Thursday, 'bout noon, and I was driving a load over to Sayerton when I spotted this here kook astanding on the berm. Sure caught my attention, 'cause he was wearing a kimono, with a fishbowl on his head."

The world went very still. I could hear my own breathing and the subtle machine noises of the monitors.

"Did the fishbowl resemble a space suit helmet?" asked Raul, having trouble with the words.

"Yep," said Sam. "Jus' like in the movies. Well, this guy shifted the book under his arm, then pointed a finger at me, and a white light shot out of his hand and hit the front of the bus. 'It 'er like a bar of white-hot steel. But there weren't no shock or even a bump. I jus' sailed along straight on through 'til the gas tank 'ploded." He ruefully smiled. "I kin remember seeing the bottom half of the bus go arcing over the cornfield as the top flipped onto the roadway."

"The space suit was wearing a kimono?" I asked to make damn sure I was hearing this correctly. "And was carrying a book?"

"A great big red book?" asked Raul in a small voice.

"That's the one." McGinty gave a shrug. "Know it sounds coon, but it's gospel. By the way, how is the team doing? Any of the boys going to make it?"

"The team?" I queried, my mind elsewhere.

A puzzled nod. "The football team. The boys I was hauling over to Sayerton for summer training." Suddenly, McGinty became very suspicious. "Iffen you're cops, why don't you know 'bout the Huntsville Pumas? Shoot, they won just about every game they ever played. Our boys be famous!"

I cleared my throat. "Now, don't you worry about them, Sam—"

The bus driver's eyes went wide, and he began to struggle.

"Holy shit! Y'all not the feds! Yer the commies! Help! Help! 'nemy agents! Spies! Help!"

Fast, I clapped a hand over the injured man's mouth, and pulling his staff from under the bed, Horta tapped the patient on the head. With a sigh, McGinty went limp and started to snore. Oh hell. And everything had been going so well.

"Ed, how soon till Jess contacts you?" asked Raul, dematerializing his staff. That way it was invisible, but constantly in his grasp and ready for use.

I glanced at my wristwatch. "Forty minutes."

"Too damn long."

"Agreed. Let's scram."

"What's going on in there?" shouted a voice from the outside corridor. The handle and chair began to rattle. "Open this door!"

Crossing the room, I kicked the chair out from under the handle. Immediately, the door slammed aside and a gang of orderlies rushed in, toppling over each other. Nimbly, we squeezed by the squirming bodies, running past a shocked flock of doctors and nurses.

Taking a side corridor, I tipped over a gurney full of bedpans in our wake to hinder pursuit and make enough racket to wake the dead. Or undead. We wanted Mystery Man to attack us, but not here. A hospital was no place for open combat. We would be at too much of a disadvantage trying not to hurt the surrounding patients. Raul and I had to get out of here fast.

"Hey, you!" cried a man in a hospital security uniform. "Stop!"

Raul flicked a hand and the man toppled asleep. We hit the fire escape doors at full speed. The alarm rang once, my belt buckle vibrated and the bell went silent. We did not want the police in on this matter.

"A football team," said Raul with meaning as we danced down the emergency stairs. "Young, muscular men in the absolute prime of physical health."

"It's a ready-made army," I added. Sliding along the banister, I went from one landing to the next. I knew that I shouldn't, but old habits die hard.

"And apparently, Mystery Man did more than capture the vaporous remains of Hoto and Tanner to hide their disappearance. He drank them and absorbed their powers!"

Moving past the lobby level, we continued on to the basement, which was packed with laundry carts, gigantic industrial washing machines and two orderlies already snoozing. How nice.

"Is that possible?" I asked. "To drink a person?"

"Shit, yes! But so dangerous no sane person would even attempt such an act!"

"Sane is not a word I use in the same sentence with Mystery Man. But did he get all of their abilities, or only parts?"

"Parts, most likely. But I wouldn't lay book on it."

"Book. Ha."

"Sorry."

Wrapping plastic sacks about ourselves, Raul and I exited by the never-ever-guarded garbage chute. It was a short slide, but a smelly one. Depositing the bags in a trash compactor, Raul changed our appearance into that of the pair of sleeping orderlies in the basement, and with exaggerated casualness we strolled through the parking lot, searching for a car to steal. The legal owner would be compensated later, and we had to get out of here quickly. Taxis were even more dangerous than staying at the hospital. We needed an isolated phone and open combat stretch in case Mystery Man hit us early. One vehicle in particular caught our attention, so we headed that way.

"So an insane alchemist, with the most powerful book of evil magic in existence, has absorbed the abilities of a mutant vampire and is wearing an alien battlesuit," muttered Raul softly as we walked along the lines of parked cars. "Ed, this is big. Really big."

"And extremely bad," I added as we reached the car, an old luxury sedan with racing tires. Nondescript and powerful. It was tailor-made for our needs. Couldn't be better.

Coming close, I noted the keys were still in the ignition. Hold it. This car was just a bit too perfect. My sunglasses said the area was clear, so I reached for my pocket EM scanner.

"But what is the lunatic bastard planning to do tomorrow night?" snorted the mage, scratching at his neck. "What?"

As I pointed my scanner at the sedan, the meter instantly hit the red line. That car was rigged to blow!

"There's a knot in the rope," I whispered, reaching for Raul's arm. But at the sound of my voice, the sedan flipped into the air on a strident column of flame and the concussion blast of the explosion smashed us to the rough pavement.

Dazed, I lay sprawled on the ground, hurting in every part of my body not directly covered by torso armor. My ears rang with a painful silence. But vaguely through the acrid smoke, I could dimly perceive a score of car trunk lids pop open, and out climbed a squad of men in bedraggled football uniforms. Large beefy young men whose long sharp vampire fangs shone unnaturally clean and white. Moving fast, they advanced upon us.

In broad daylight.

10

Rolling to my knees, I snapped off a fast twelve rounds with both Magnums. One undead burst into dust, another clutched a wounded arm and a third was grazed in the throat from the wooden bullets. But my 66 Magnum was only loaded with silver and steel, so the other three vampires just recoiled from the impact of the bullets.

Retreating, the undead formed a circle as Raul and I went back-to-back in a standard two-man defensive position. I reloaded as Horta materialized his staff, its silver length weakly pulsating with power. This was the first chance I ever had of seeing a vampire in broad daylight. That is, for longer than thirty seconds. I had no damn idea how they were doing this unpleasant miracle. Suntan lotion from the planet Krypton? And there had been a trap within the trap. My respect, and hatred, for Mystery Man went up another notch. He was good enough to be one of ours.

Happily, at this hour of the morning, the parking lot was deserted of people, sans us. Awkward but functional combat room. However, our plan had been to detect the trap, summon aid and then go into it, burning our way up their rope of command until we found the top knot. But then, these were only high school kids. Vampires or not, how tough could they be?

"R-47-12!" cried a slim vampire crouching low behind the line of his fellow undead, the fingertips of one hand resting lightly on the ground. "Hut! Hut! Hut!"

Hopefully, I glanced at Raul.

"Basketball is my game," apologized the tall man.

Great. And I knew as much about football as I do that game with the stick and a diamond. It appeared that I was about to witness the effectiveness of secret fight codes from the wrong side. Hoo boy.

"Hut one! Hut two!"

The front four dropped back and two others took off for the

sides in a flanking maneuver, while the rest charged. There was only a single factor in our favor. These athletes had been taught to fight in a game. We were trained to kill.

Sidestepping a rushing Puma, I pumped two rounds into his head as a distraction, his protective helmet shattering into pieces under the booming impact of the Magnum slugs. Which is how it should be. As he yanked off the chin strap, I moved in close and stabbed him in the chest with a fountain pen. He jerked aside as I snapped off the cap.

Thick acrid smoke started pouring from his chest, and the undead monster began screaming as four fluid ounces of hydrofluoric acid dissolved everything it touched.

Hydrofluoric acid is about the nastiest stuff in the world. It dissolved anything with a carbon atom in its molecular construction, and violently exploded even the most mild of flammables. The damn stuff could even eat stainless steel and glass! Nothing could safely hold the acid for very long. Which was why I had filled my pen just prior to departing.

With a sizzling hole in his torso big enough to drive through, vampire Bubba crumpled to the ground extremely dead. At least that weakness they still had. Fine.

Reaching inside my shirt, I pulled out a cross, and as I am Catholic it was hot with power. The vampires sneered in hatred and from out of nowhere a football smashed into my hand with stinging force, sending the cross flying away into the weeds surrounding the parking lot. Lost for good. Raul got the same treatment with a plastic squirt gun filled with holy water. These guys had pinpoint accuracy with that pointy leather thing. No wonder the Pumas held the state championship. But I was a crack shot and their remaining two footballs got deflated the .357 Magnum way.

But now it was hand-to-hand, with them having the advantage. This was the middle of the night for me, and after a two-thousand-mile teleport, Raul was not exactly brimming with magic.

Running round a truck, Horta made ready to punch a vampire. The burly undead smiled contemptuously and spread his arms invitingly. But as the mage drove his fist forward, there was a flash and the entire limb turned into dark wood. The vampire could only gasp as the living stake rammed into his heart and he exploded into ash. Three down.

Hmm, only the vampires killed with wood turned into dust. I filed that information away for future usage.

"Tunafish!" cried Raul, holding his staff aloft, and I blinked as a burst of blinding light filled the parking lot. They didn't appear to notice. These guys must have some sort of protection against light.

"Hut fourteen!" answered the slim undead.

Feinting with my right, I slammed a left into another suck fiend and felt my signet ring jerk. Inside the nifty device was a coiled-spring steel rosette of razor blades that snapped into action whenever it hit something hard. Like a head.

Vampire Lad recoiled in pain as half his countenance was torn off. Roaring in fury, he lunged and slipped on his own face. Using my full weight and all my strength, I dropped, ramming my knee into his back. Above the noise and confusion, I clearly heard his spine crack and that was the end for him.

Lightning and thunder said Raul was cutting loose. Turning, I rolled across the hood of an import, managed to stuff my pack of cigarettes down the numbered shirt of a Huntsville Puma and slapped it with my pistol. His chest burst into flames, arms and legs jerked stiff with an electric stun charge, his scream was recorded and then he exploded.

A beating inhuman heart skittered across the parking lot to stop under a car. Tracking on the gas tank lid, I pumped six rounds in a cluster about the locked flap. The vampire was beneath the vehicle scrambling for his vital organ when the fuel tank detonated. The blast hurled the car into the air to crash down again on the half-a-brain fullback. He staggered into view a flaming humanoid torch, and I let him have my derringer. The one trigger fired all four of the .22-caliber barrels, and he was hit with a cold iron slug, a silver round, a soft-lead dumdum and a blessed wooden bullet.

Poof. Ash. Wind.

As I put my last reload into the Magnums, the slim vampire called "Hut" a few more times and the remaining five hit us from every side.

Firing both .357 Magnums in a steady barrage, I tossed the pistols at the kids when the guns became empty. Kicking a vampire in the throat, I buried my knife into the ear of another and was brutally tackled to the ground. I butted one in the groin, stabbed another with the awl of my Swiss Army knife and got an elbow in the teeth. Blood filled my mouth and I started to choke.

"Manhattan Project!" yelled Raul.

And despite the fact that I was drowning on my own blood, and that there were three snarling vampires fighting each other for the privilege of biting my tender neck, I smiled and tried to bury myself deeper underneath them.

Suddenly, there was a searing burst of light, deafening thunder boomed, the ground shook and a heat flash singed me even through the mass of limp corpses piled on top.

As I struggled free from the stunned undead, I could see Raul standing on a bull's-eye of macadam surrounded by a steaming blast crater. The mage was smiling, and removing rubber plugs from both ears. Body Boom was something a mage did only when none—repeat, none—of his pals were nearby.

A truck with real wood siding gave us the necessary tools and we started to stake the stunned undead when I stopped. Ah, I was about to be brilliant.

"Ra . . ." I hawked and spit blood. "Raul, we can still burn this rope. Have you enough magic to do a full illusion?"

His woebegone expression said no. Guess a personal nuclear blast took a lot out of a guy.

I paused to spit again. "Okay, can you polymorph two of these yahoos into duplicates of us?"

Tilting his head, the mage listened to his staff, which was feebly flickering with magic. "Just barely, if I drain my belt and shoes. But I'll manage. It's a great idea. And fresh bodies does facilitate matters."

Gathering my pistols, I next retrieved knives and hacked the unconscious vampires to pieces, scattering the body parts and dusty ash around so it would not be immediately obvious just how many corpses were present. Hidden inside their clothing, I found a small electrical device of unknown design. I postulated that the machine was a modified form of Tanner's forceshield, some massively weaker version built to protect the vampires from sunlight. A neat trick, that, and one I had not even contemplated. Thank goodness, Mystery Man hadn't trusted his slaves enough to give them full-power forceshields. Or else Raul and I would be on our way to the dentist for a cleaning and sharpening.

Meanwhile, the wizard mumbled in his secret language and then used his staff to smite two of the football players who were the closest to our sizes. Every little bit helps. Rippling with colored lights, the cold flesh melted and re-formed into mirror images of us, clothes, guns and everything. Then we tore accessories off a few cars and sprinkled the debris around the blast crater so it would seem a car had exploded, instead of Mr. Horta. When satisfied, we hid in the relatively undamaged trunk of a Buick Roadmaster and waited.

Fire engines and police sirens were sounding in the distance when the slim vampire who had been shouting orders finally roused. He hissed his displeasure at the carnage, then smiled in fiendish delight when he spotted ''us'' lying limp on the ground.

It was rather disquieting to watch him drink our blood, rip out our throats, smash our skulls and throw the brains away. Then he cracked open our chests and ate the hearts. Although disgusted, I had to admire his efficiency. Now, that was what I called dead.

When finished, the vampire went to a foreign compact, removed his helmet and drove off. When he was far enough away, Raul and I scrambled out of hiding and into a cherry '62 Corvette. I used to own a similar model and could hot-wire this sweetheart in my sleep. Plus, it was a lot faster than the dinky fuel-efficient compact. And having only one car to tail our quarry, that extra speed could be an important factor.

''We have been seriously underestimating our foe,'' muttered Raul, collapsing his staff to a size that would fit inside the dimensions of the 'Vet and laying it across his knees. ''McGinty was probably primed with some potion to flip out if questioned, making us run from the hospital and into their trap.''

Shifting gears and leaving the hospital behind, I mumbled agreement, a line of red drool flowing down my cheek. Noticing, Horta pulled a button from his shirt, made a fist and punched me in the jaw. When the stinging faded, so did the pain and blood. My mouth felt fine. Gingerly, I tested my teeth. They were solidly attached once more. That was some button.

''Thanks,'' I said, wiping off the spittle with a handkerchief.

He winked. ''No problem. So what now? We follow our quarterback until he leads us to Mystery Man, then we call in the troops?''

''Natch. Which brings up an interesting question. How do we contact the team in Chicago? You can't teleport a fly, and our radios only have a two-kilometer range.''

''The telephone?'' suggested Horta. ''No, we don't dare. If

Mystery Man has the abilities of Vampire X, then he also has the powers of Tanner. He could be tapping the entire Alabama phone system waiting for us to try such an act. Jess?''

A shrug. ''It's not time, but I'll try.''

JESSICA! I screamed inside my head. *JESSICA! IT'S ED! CAN YOU HEAR ME, BABE? THERE'S TROUBLE! HELP, JESS, HELP!*

No answer. My telepathic wife must not be thinking of me at this exact instant. And by when the hour mark came, we might be too far away from Huntsville for Jessica to focus on me. Damn, damn, damn! So close, yet so far.

''No good,'' I reported, my temples throbbing. Whew, even trying was a bit of a strain.

Raul rubbed his chin. ''How do we contact a secret agency? An interesting problem.''

''Got an interesting answer?''

''Cogitating, Ed. Ruminating.''

''Swell. Tell me when you start to think, okay?''

''As a great man once said, natch.''

Keeping a careful watch on our Judas goat, I maintained a discreet distance behind him as he turned onto the highway and headed north. Ah, this shouldn't take too long.

But we were wrong again.

It soon became obvious that Mystery Man was much too smart to lay a trap for us at his own front door. Our vampire drove on through the day and into the night, stopping only for gas. I guess the blood he had consumed in the parking lot was tiding him over. Hospital food is supposed to be good for you. Ha.

Alabama, Tennessee and into Kentucky. Raul and I took turns driving and sleeping. The sandwiches Mindy had given us came in extremely useful. And at one stop for fuel, I stole a box of .38-caliber ammunition from the desk of an attendant. Well, stole is perhaps the wrong word, as I did leave behind a hundred dollars in cash for a $24.95 box of bullets.

As befitting a mage, Raul was surprised to discover that .38 ammunition would fit a .357 gun. Politely, I started to explain the difference between a normal and Magnum round, but stopped when he yawned and attempted to turn on the radio. I can take a hint.

Later, when he took over the driving again, I used my knife and pistol butt to painstakingly cut a pattern into each of the soft-lead slugs. They were now incredibly illegal, and delightfully deadly, dumdums. Not having a proper workshop, there was always the chance of doing a bad slice, which when I triggered the round would jam and explode my gun. But that was a chance I would have to take. It was better than being totally unarmed.

"If only we knew what the bastard was planning," I said aloud, after successfully dodging a radar trap.

"The kid?"

"No, Mystery Man. Destroy the world? Conquer it? Or something too fiendish to contemplate? Some hideous act we haven't even thought of yet."

Raul made a diplomatic cough. Then another.

"Okay, talk," I sighed.

"Well," said the mage, "when Tina and I were perusing my file copy of the Aztec book—"

"Your what?" I interrupted, almost losing control of the car.

"My file copy," he repeated. "When we originally captured the volume, I made a photostat of every page."

Furious, I could only glare at him. Mages! "But isn't even a copy dangerous to read?"

"Not a copy," stated Horta. "It would be similar to trying to put electrical current into a photograph of a radio. Nothing happens. The book itself does the conjure."

"Meaning any damn fool can operate it."

"Yep."

"Hardly good news."

"Anyway," Raul went on, "if Mystery Man was an ordinary guy who became an alchemist, and then risked death to become a wizard for one day to get his mitts on this book, I decided to search for the other end of the spectrum, what spell, conjure, whatever, would give him the most power. Permanently make him a real wizard."

"And?"

"You won't like it."

"I'm braced."

A drumroll sounded from nowhere. "I think he's going for the World Mage spell."

Rimshot. Cymbal crash.

I groaned. The World Mage spell. It had never been fully successful, but the last time anybody got the foul conjure even partially functioning, in 1871, the newly formed Bureau waged a brutal war that burned old Chicago to the ground in their effort to kill the caster. Mrs. O'Leary and her demonic cow had been tough customers to beat.

"Okay," I said, rallying to the task. "The bigger the spell, the more limitations."

Raul lifted a finger. "One, it has to be performed within the boundaries of the kingdom he stole it from."

"We're not a kingdom," I reminded him.

"Magically this country is," he stated. "Science obeys the letter of law. Magic follows the intent."

Okay, I bought that. "Continue."

Another finger. "Two, it has to be on property he has legal access to."

Interesting. "And three?" I prompted.

The hand closed and dropped. "There is no three."

"None?"

"Nope."

Hoo boy.

Deep in thought, we tooled on through the picturesque mountains of Kentucky. Semi-tractor trailers passed us regularly, and I expertly used them as protective coverage between us and the compact. Twice already Horta had changed the color of our car, added a roof luggage rack and even made the whole damn thing invisible for a while. Three near collisions later, we stopped utilizing that ploy.

I had tried following our young killer by using my sunglasses to keep track of his evil black aura, but had nearly lost our quarry when we started to tag along after a sports compact full of lawyers.

Afterwards, we kept to sight and skill. Nothing fancy.

Night had fallen once more when our quarry pulled off Interstate 70 and into Saddle Brook, just south of the Ohio River still in Kentucky. On the other bank of the river was the pleasant industrial town of Cincinnati. Despite its nickname, Cin was an ultra-squeaky-clean place. Vulgar language in front of ladies was not permitted, pornographic magazines like *The Physicians Medical Journal* were not allowed to be sold, and once the locals had tried to edit the word "Hell" out of the Bible.

However, Saddle Brook was where the people from Cincinnati went to remember what a good time was. The streets were lined with massage parlors, adult-book stores, strip joints—both male and female—gay bars, biker taverns, saloons and twenty-four-

hour liquor supermarkets. Drug deals took place with total lack
of regard for police or witnesses. Every window had iron grilles,
every door was triple-locked. And we passed an all-night gun
store. It kinda made me feel homesick for South Chicago. I
wished we had the chance to stop so I could get some proper
ammo. But our marathon vampire sailed on past, and I waved
bye-bye to the boxes of semi-steel-jacketed, hollow-point, Magnum Express Supremes. They went in like a finger, came out
like a fist. Now, that was a proper bullet.

Everywhere, prostitutes jostled whores and streetwalkers, their
outfits more garish and hair more colors than anything I had ever
seen before in this dimension. Weaving through the heavy traffic,
I started to explain the technical differences between the types
to Raul when the mage told me he already knew. Maybe my
buddy did at that. Horta was from New York. And no Boy Scout.

We both gave a groan of relief as the Compact Kid pulled into
the parking lot of La Petite Court, a combination motel, strip
joint, nude mud wrestling parlor and topless bar. It was not
much more than a carnal amusement park, where the rides
charged by the quarter hour.

The teenage terror chose the strip joint and left the vehicle
unlocked. He wasn't coming back. Bingo. He also had changed
into street clothes somewhere along the way.

"'Base of operations or relay point," postulated Raul, his attention momentarily distracted by a buxom young lady with the
most amazing ability to defy gravity.

I glanced at my watch. Six hours till midnight and the equi-
nox. "Let's find out," I said, parking the car and saying goodbye. In this neighborhood, an unattended Corvette wouldn't last
ten minutes.

"We'll need a disguise," stated Raul, climbing from the front
seat. "Especially since he's seen our faces. Not to mention
snacked on our hearts. I've recharged quite a bit in the last
eighteen hours. Want me to do some magic?"

"Honey, I can do you magic," boasted a platinum-blond Oriental in low-cut lavender spandex and fake mink stole.

We tendered our apologies for the misconception, discreetly
moved on and lowered our goddamn voices.

"Better save it," I decided, testing the draw on my Magnums.
"Let's do this the normal way."

Glancing at the human stew swirling around us, I chose my
first customer. A bone-skinny man dressed in leather and smok-

ing a cigarette in a sequined holder. In my opinion, he had on far too much mascara.

"How much for the leather jacket?" I asked.

The question amused him. "Just the jacket, or me in it?" he countered.

"Ah, just the jacket."

"Two hundred bucks."

I flashed cash. "One hundred."

"Done!" We exchanged goods.

"Excuse me, miss," addressed Raul to a mature woman in fringed vest, miniskirt and dirty white boots. "I wish to purchase your vest. How much?"

Red lips snapped juicy gum. Her bountiful jewelry must have weighed almost as much as she did. "Forty dollars."

"Twenty-five, and toss in the gloves."

"You get it, handsome," said the lady, jingling as she removed the garment. Nothing but flesh was underneath. This place was worse than Hong Kong.

"And an extra ten for the crucifix."

She glanced downward at her ample breasts. "I got one of those? Okay, sure."

Nobody else seemed promising, except a biker gang lounging on the corner, so I tried there next. Not every motorcycle rider was a thrill-kill nutcase. Many were very decent people, who simply enjoyed the freedom of the road. Peaceful, law-abiding folk.

"Nice hogs," I complimented as an opener. "My friend and I need some clothes to change our looks. And fast. Wanna sell?"

For some reason this seemed to vastly interest them.

"And what you offering, Mr. Money?" asked a bald fat boy, snapping a switchblade into life. His cronies chuckled and displayed more lethal ironmongery.

Okay. So much for doing it the nice way. I drew both of the .357 Magnums and let 'em have a good look. "I'm offering a half ounce of hot lead apiece. Any takers?"

Heads shook no, then yes. Then no again.

Impatiently, I gestured towards the alley. The question was so complex, it might take them a week to figure an answer.

"Move," I commanded, and they hustled into the darkness.

Five minutes and six low-grade Sleep spells later, a punk rocker and a hippie strode into the strip joint. Once we were past the front door and the photograph-lined hallway, the music, laughter, noise, lights, smoke and smell formed a tangible atmosphere that threatened to overload the senses. I pocketed my Bureau sunglasses. They were useless in here.

The place was a standard bump-and-grind establishment. Small tables were clustered around an equally small stage backed by a tremendous mirror. On the runway was a pair of skinny, semi-clad women dancing listlessly to the hottest rock tunes. A disco ball hanging from the black ceiling scattered light dots in a vain attempt to generate excitement. Hostesses in lingerie loitered near every table, hoping to find a lonely drunk who wished their company—at fifty bucks a drink. Pitiful. My bachelor party had started in a place such as this. I was bored then, and I was bored now. None of the women were pretty or could dance, and there were probably more diseases floating about in this dump than a military virus factory.

Separating, I grabbed a vacant stool at the bar, while Raul took a table. We each ordered drinks. Mandatory in a place such as this, or else the burly bouncer let you sample his knuckle sandwich. Watching our adolescent undead, I noted that the boy seemed much too intense to be reporting a victory to the boss. In the rear of my brain, I was starting to get a terrible suspicion that this was not the end of the line, but merely a pit stop. Our quarterback was going to feed.

JESSICA!

Silence.

Over in a dark corner, Dracula Jr. was chatting with an almost pretty young hostess in a satin lace teddy, spiked-heel shoes and not much else. He smiled. She shook her head no. He grabbed her wrist. She looked him in the eyes, paused and then woodenly nodded yes. Hell and damnation! The bastard was here for blood.

Shuffling through the crowd, the high-schooler escorted her into a back room. We rose to follow, but they promptly appeared and she was pulling on a coat. Keeping his face towards the wall, Horta sauntered around behind them and rejoined me at the bar.

"What now?" asked the mage.

I took a sip of my drink and spit it back into the glass. Yuck! My mother made better tequila than this slop. "Continue to follow. This vampire is our only lead."

Just then, a greasy man in leather walked up to Raul and made the most astonishing suggestion. Unperturbed, Horta snorted his disdain, and the man departed pouting. Wearing an earring did not mean you were gay. Ask any pirate.

"And at what point do we stop him from killing the girl?" queried Horta.

Sadly, I had known this question was coming and was braced for the response. Five hours thirty minutes till the World Mage spell. And if it was successful, humanity would be facing a god. An actual, grade A, full-fledged god. There was little choice as to what we had to do.

"We don't stop him," I said honestly, feeling weary to my very soul. "In fact, I hope he kills her as soon as possible. Her death may be our only chance."

Raul's jaw sagged.

11

Then his chin snapped shut. "What?" demanded Raul past clenched teeth.

"This may be our sole hope of ever finding Mystery Man," I explained coldly. "Look, we're not dealing with a pro, but a high school kid. He just won the big game and wants to party. This is his celebration. Afterwards, he'll report to the boss."

The mage had trouble speaking. "This is totally unacceptable."

"Friend, don't make me pull rank."

He snorted. "Screw you, and the regulations you rode in on. The whole purpose of the Bureau is to protect people from just this kind of danger, not put parsley behind their ears and ring a dinner bell!"

Our conversation was starting to draw unwanted attention, so we moved to another corner where we could still keep watch. A hostess came over, and we shooed her away by ordering more drinks.

Scrutinizing our boy through a curtained window, we saw him and the girl walk across the parking lot, over to the motel section, and enter a room. Only minutes remaining in which to act. If we were going to. And we weren't.

"Ed, please!" implored the mage.

I sighed. "No."

"But we have to do something!"

"You got any ideas?"

"Damn straight," growled Horta. "We snatch the boob and wring the information out of him. Better to torture a monster than let an innocent get killed."

"Wrong," I told him. "Because anything the slave vampire knows, Rashamor knows. I mean, Mystery Man should know."

"But he may not!"

Lifting a wrist, I displayed my watch. "Can we take that chance?"

Raul's face underwent a wide variety of expressions, none of them pleasant, until at last, he accepted the awful truth.

"Come on," I said, standing. "Let's go." Tossing a few bills onto the table, I started shoving my way through the drunk, leering crowd. The waitress moved in fast to get the cash before a patron did. Before joining me, Raul downed his drink and then mine. For once, I said nothing to stop him. All mages drink. Horta just a bit more than the rest. But for good reasons.

A short talk and surreptitious money exchange with the reception clerk of the motel got Raul and me the room with our lucky number on it, which just happened to be next to Vampire Boy and his unwilling date. Inside, we dimmed the lights and Raul produced a peeper pen. Sheathed in Teflon-coated surgical steel, you could easily shove it into almost any wall, and the needle tip made only a minuscule hole in the other side. Inside the pen, a prism and lens assembly gave a wide-angle view of what was happening in the next room. There wasn't a PI in the civilized world that didn't have one, or would admit that they did.

Braced, I took the first look. "Goddamn it, we're behind a picture!"

Moving the peeper a foot to the right, gauging the location of the picture from the position of the portrait in our room, we managed to get a clear view this time.

It wasn't pretty.

Pert breasts sticking up from a ripped lace bra, the girl was spread-eagled on the bed, hands and legs tied to the four corners with torn sheets, panties dangling off an ankle. He was stark naked, his lean body pumping hard. But suddenly he stopped, and an expression of raw terror crossed her face. She started to struggle wildly. The boy laughed, and buried his mouth onto her neck. The girl went stiff, her fingers clawing at the air.

"Is he . . ." said Raul, his hands twisting on the silver staff. "Yes, I can see it in your face."

An agent's burden, I told myself.

"Want me to take a turn?" the mage hesitantly offered.

"No!" I snapped. And after a moment, added, "Thank you."

He accepted that. And so I watched, God help me, I watched him kill her. I wanted to shut my eyes, to close my ears to her faint, barely audible screams. Desperately, I wanted to burst in there before it was too late and kill the freaking sonofabitch. Raul was correct. Our job was to save lives. Yet three billion lives rested upon our inaction. But was the world worth this? Was the life of one useless stripper worth the rest of humanity?

Morally? No.

Tactically? Yes.

So I did my job and did not glance away. If I was to be responsible for her death, I would watch. To know what she went through, so I could carry the memory to my grave. I would not be a coward. And yet, deep down inside my guts, for the first time, I hated being a Bureau 13 agent.

Eventually, he finished and rose from the mutilated corpse.

As I removed the pen from the wall and handed it to Raul, the mage took hold of my shoulders and forced me to face him.

"Maybe he'll make her an undead also," offered the wizard. "Then the Bureau can recruit her and train the girl to handle the difficulties of being a vampire. But she can still have a full life. And a really long one!"

The words were torn from my throat. "He ate her heart."

Raul slumped. She was dead for keeps. There would be no graveyard resurrection.

Silent, we moved to the window, parted the thin curtains and watched as the young butcher departed the room, carefully closing and locking the door. Hands in pockets, the monster headed for the streets. Showtime.

We followed. Using a standard two-man rotation, we trailed the murderer to the nicer section of town and then over the Covington Bridge into south Cincinnati. Quickly, Raul and I modified our disguises as much as possible, into something a bit more respectable. Our boy stopped to take a leak on the Tyler David monument at the Fifth Street traffic circle and then moved off into the shadows of a nearby alley.

Waiting a minute just to be careful, Raul and I tagged along. Traffic was sparse, and the footsteps of distant pedestrians echoed strangely in the still night air.

And sure enough, from the alley came a trickle of smoke that disappeared down a metal grating by the curb and into a storm drain.

"Go," I softly commanded. "I'll call the team."

"How?"

"Go!"

He paused. "Good luck."

"Thanks, buddy. You too."

"Bread crumbs," he replied, producing a jar of petroleum jelly. Glumly, I nodded. Then swirling an imaginary cape about himself, Raul vanished.

Anger and hatred fueling my resolve, I headed for a liquor store. Time was of the essence. I had to get drunk fast.

For more reasons than one.

Returning to Saddle Brook, finding a liquor store doing business this late at night was no problem. Using cash, I purchased six bottles of Everclear and a pint of whiskey. Moving a few blocks away from the store, I prepared for my new role in a garbage-strewn alley. Holding my nose, I forced myself to drink half of the whiskey and placed the rest aside for later.

Next, I removed every Bureau-issue article and piece of identification I had on me. Sunglasses, ID booklet, signet ring, lighter, body armor, false tooth filled with Untruth Serum, wallet, keys, unbreakable pocket comb, my last fountain pen, shoulder holster, extra ammo, knife, derringer, handkerchief, belt buckle and wristwatch.

Spreading my flame-retardant cloth on the bottom of a metal trash can, I dumped my possessions on top and then poured in the Everclear. At 99% pure grain alcohol, the liquor was highly flammable. Setting my watch and cigarette lighter for self-destruct, I grabbed the whiskey bottle and retreated. I barely made it to the street when the trash can thunderously detonated. The alley was filled with flame and shrapnel, illuminating the whole neighborhood and rattling windows for blocks. Fleetingly, I saw the pocket comb zoom by, chip a brick wall and zing off into the night. I guess it really was unbreakable.

Lights came on in a dozen places, and I quickly dumped the rest of the whiskey over my clothing and pocketed the bottle.

"Ya-hoo!" I cried, triggering a Magnum and shattering two store windows. Alarms began clanging. "Yippee! I'm on Earth again! Hurrah!" Two more booming rounds punctuated my goofy expressions of joy.

Needless to say, even in Saddle Brook, a police car soon rolled by to investigate. I had been rationing my bullets, and only three were remaining when they arrived. Parking a half block away, the cops advanced in regulation one-on-one formation, guns drawn. Good lads. Please, please, consider me dangerous. I shot out another streetlamp and pissed in my pants. The things I do for America.

"Now, put down the gun, fella," said the officer, approaching steadily. His voice was low and soothing, calm and even. He was very good at this. Must handle a lot of drunks.

"You can't arrest me," I snarled, and hiccupped. "I'm from Mars!"

The officer smiled. "Why, me too! Buddy! Neighbor!"

Damn, this guy was really good. I thought fast. "You're no buddy of mine," I slurred, weaving drunkenly on my feet. That part was not altogether an act. The cheap booze mixed with no food in eight hours was hitting me hard. I didn't dare try any more marksman shooting. I might kill somebody. "You're a thul sucking biggle-fargul!"

"Naw," he denied, coming ever closer. "That's my partner. He also smokes and fizzle gorps!"

As much as he was messing up my scheme, I had to admire his total professionalism.

"A fizzle gorp!" I drooled, waving the Magnums overhead. "Da Earth-loving scum. Let's go shoot him in the spleen!"

"But those guns won't work on Earth folk," said my buddy, nearly within arm's reach. "Here, use mine." He held out a revolver that I knew must be empty.

"Look out!" I screamed, firing my last two shots in the air. "He's gonna spur-tune!"

Tossing my weapons away, I dizzily reached for the offered gun. It was immediately withdrawn and somebody tripped me from behind. Down I went, flat on my face, and the cops piled on top. My arms were yanked behind my back, and I heard metallic clickings.

"Shut up, ya loony," snarled somebody. "And don't give us any more crap!"

That was my cue to roll over and bellow into their faces, "*But I'm from Mars! Mars! Mars! Mars!* You can't arrest me! I gotta get back to my spaceship or die!"

The cuffs clicked with brutal force, and I was roughly hauled erect. I loudly burped in one officer's face while the other attempted to frisk me.

"Whew, what breath," said one, holding his nose.

"Don't touch me there," I screamed again at the top of my lungs. "That'll kill a Martian! And I'm from Mars! Mars! I gotta get back to my ship and go home to Mars!"

"And where the fuck is your ship, Darth Vader?" demanded

the first officer, grabbing a fistful of my collar, neatly cutting off my air and greatly restricting movement. "On the moon?"

About time he asked. "Bangor, Maine," I said, attempting to vomit or fart.

Surprised, the second officer smiled in spite of himself. "Bangor, Maine?"

Screeching, I struggled futilely against the cuffs. "No human can say that word! Only another Martian like me! Bangor, Maine! Bangor, Maine! Argh . . . !"

Charging, I butted one cop in the stomach, then attempted to spin around and kick the other, but I fell down with a thump. Ouch. Then the patrolmen moved in and I gave them the best fight I could under the conditions. Kicking, biting, spitting, clawing, and constantly shouting over and over again that I was a Martian on my way to Bangor, Maine.

The Saddle Brook police actually accepted my behavior for a lot longer than I ever would have. But finally, bleeding, sore, dirty and half deaf from my raw-throated screams, they pulled out the nightsticks and did a little tap dance on my head, using Morse code to politely inform me that it was nappy time.

As I was pounded into a red haze of pain, I tried once more to shout out my home world and goal. I had to be the most memorable arrest these two ever made. It was imperative!

The fate of the world depended upon it.

And personally, revenge for a skinny blonde girl whose name I didn't even know.

12

Reeking of disinfectant, I was languishing in my cell, nursing a severe headache from both the bad booze and the beating the cops gave me, when I noticed a thick black line form on the exterior cinder-block wall.

About six feet off the concrete floor, the line steadily progressed in both directions until it was three feet in length, then the ends did a sharp angle downward and extended to the floor. With a creak, the rectangle swung aside and Mindy stepped in through the hole.

"Hi, Ed," she whispered. Beyond the doorway, I could see a wooded park with our RV from Chicago looming in the shadows underneath a nearby copse of trees.

I raised a finger. "Shush. Not so loud."

She nodded, and the snoring of the other forty inmates of the drunk tank resumed their normal singsong buzz-sawing. Personally, I did not believe that saturation bombing by the U.S. Air Force could wake these guys. But I was playing it safe.

"What's the story?" Jennings asked sotto voce. "Do you want to be rescued?"

"Believe it," I said softly, forcing myself to stand. "We've found Mystery Man."

"Great! Where's Raul?" Her voice had unaccustomed emotion.

"Heading smack into the lion's den, but leaving a bread crumb trail for us to follow."

"Then let's go."

"Yowsa."

As we stepped through the magical portal, the wall closed and sealed. Climbing into the van, I kissed my wife hello, and we drove off into the night.

"Cincinnati, downtown," I told the front of the van.

A hooded video monitor in the dashboard changed from displaying a street map of Saddle Brook to a grid of the neighboring city.

"Faith and begorra, will we be wanting city hall or the wee police station?" asked a redheaded bear of a man behind the steering wheel. Wearing a flowing black cossack and track shoes, the Irish goliath had a string of rosary beads dangling from the holstered Bible at his hip and a massive gold crucifix hung about his neck.

"Donaher!" I cried, and then held my head in both hands and pressed hard, trying to force the pieces back together again.

George and Ken helped me to the couch, then Tina knelt before me and drew apart the top of the leather medical bag, producing an assortment of items. She poured an envelope full of blue powder into a jelly jar containing a yellow liquid, and the mixture turned green. What a surprise. But then it went purple, brown, red, frothy white and clear.

She shoved the jar into my hands. "Drink!"

Hoping it was fast-acting poison, I chugged the brew down, and *wham*! I was a new man. Headache, pain, tiredness—gone, gone, gone. I felt fit and ready to do battle.

"What is that stuff?" I asked, licking the rim before returning the glass container.

"Old family recipe," said Tina, wiping off the jar with a disposable antiseptic clothette.

"Okay. But what is it made of?"

"Old families."

I laughed. Then paused. Nyah.

Moving to the rear of the RV, I rummaged about in a locker until I found some respectable and less odious clothes. In my personal box, I obtained duplicate personal effects, and another FBI ID commission booklet. Going to the weapons locker, I got a watch, more body armor, a new double shoulder holster and my spare set of Magnums. Ultra-lightweight 42 in the left, combat model 66 in the right. I grabbed a fistful of pens, filled my pockets with speedloaders and added an HE grenade for luck.

"Perfect!" I exclaimed.

Timidly, Jessica handed me a breath mint. "Not quite yet, dearest."

Properly chastised, I sucked and munched. Cheap whiskey did that to a man. And lack of food. So I raided the stash of military K rations we always keep on board. It was like chewing a shoe, and just as tasty. Briefly, I wondered if the Mexican Army had field rations more fitting a soldier about to do battle.

"Did my message get to you?" I asked after swallowing. "Or did you locate me some other way?"

"When the InfoNet computer rattled off a report of a drunk with two Magnums claiming that he was from Mars and on his way to Bangor, Maine, we knew it had to be you."

"Why didn't you try and contact me?" I asked the wife. With the halogen streetlights illuminating her from behind, my bride was even more lovely than ever.

"I did," she replied, blushing. "But in Huntsville. This place is a thousand miles off target."

True enough. Moving to the co-driver's seat, I checked the map on the monitor and showed Donaher where we wanted to go.

"By the way, how did your . . . er, sabbatical end?" I asked the priest.

Father Donaher scowled, then smiled. "I actually made it into the throne room this time, before they discovered it was me, and threw me out." The priest lowered his voice. "Faith, Ed. Satan is a lot larger than I had ever imagined."

"How big?" I asked curiously.

"Texas is what comes to mind."

Wow. *Mucho grande*.

"What will the police do when they discover that your finger-prints are those of an FBI agent?" asked Sanders. The huge M-60 machine rifle he held in both hands appeared to be a child's toy. Ken Sanders was the only human being I had ever met that made Father Michael Xavier Donaher seem small. With these two protean behemoths tagging along, it was going to be difficult remaining inconspicuous.

"The Bureau will not identify the prints of any agent in jail," I explained. "How would the folks at HQ know if a field agent is going under cover as a criminal and wants to be in jail? They only ID the fingerprints off a dead Bureau agent. And I'm not missing until roll is taken in the morning."

"Besides, there is a number we can call to get us out of jail on anything but a murder one charge," said Renault.

"What is?" asked Tina.

"1-8-0-0-B-U-R-E-A-U-1-3."

She quickly counted. "But this is too long. American phone numbers only have seven integers. *Da?*"

"Not ours," said George, smiling and patting a shapely knee.

As we turned onto Fifth Street, I brought the team up to date on the current situation. Parking the RV by a meter at the curb,

Donaher took change to feed the municipal quarter-eater as the rest of us prepped for underground warfare.

Wading boots were the first thing we wanted, but there were only two pairs. Blanco fixed that by having Mindy slice the boots into rubbery shreds and then magically repairing the pieces into seven whole sets of boots. Now, that was a useful trick. Wonder if she could do it with money? Hmm.

We also took gloves, flashlights, bug-repellent, gas masks and magnesium underwater flares. Plus an ultraviolet lantern.

After emptying the weapons locker, Jessica was carrying an Uzi machine pistol with a bulbous silencer on the barrel, and a pouch of clips over a shoulder. Rare indeed was the fight when my lovely telepath went deliberately armed with lethal weapons. On her back was a canister and pressure tank assembly, with a holstered pistol at the end of a segmented hose. Tina, George and Ken had similar tanks. Each was color-coded differently.

"Okay, what did you guys come up with?"

Jessica spoke. "Mine is a possible stun. It squirts a combination of MSG and DMSO, with a stabilizing agent."

Hmm. MSG, monosodium glutamate, was a flavor enhancer used in cheap food. It boosted waning tastes by stimulating the nerve endings of the tongue. It also gave terrible headaches and swollen joints to many people sensitive to the stuff. Occasionally even unconsciousness. And it would cause these symptoms in anybody who got a massive dose.

DMSO, which stood for something or other, I forget, was a by-product of making paper. Considered useless for decades, the bizarre garlic-tasting chemical had only one known function. It could permeate the entire human body in less than a second. I once participated in a demonstration, where I put my finger into a beaker of the stuff and tasted garlic in my mouth. My mouth tasted what my finger was in. Incredible, but generally useless. Mixing the two was brilliant. Instant liquid headache. I liked it.

The tanks on Tina's back were frosty cold, and wisps of escaping vapor spurted from a release valve on top. The hose was heavily insulated, as was the pistol.

"Liquid nitrogen," she stated proudly, adjusting her thick gloves. They went to her elbows. "Intense cold can crystallize steel, making brittle as glass. What does to flesh is painful to watch. And my magic in no way hinders operation of device."

I heartily approved. Let's see Mystery Man beat that!

"Ken?" I asked.

"Nothing special," rumbled the man mountain. "Just ninety-nine percent pure, concentrated hydrofluoric acid."

Gasping, I took a step back. Concentrated? Wow! And he was carrying maybe fifty gallons. "You're a brave man, Mr. Sanders."

"Thank you, sir."

Shy and quiet as always, George had a satchel charge of C4 plastique, a pouch of grenades, and was sporting the usual M-60, plus a backpack jammed full of rolled ammo links. A new feature was the tiny black box clipped under the pitted maw of the long ventilated barrel, a short-range microwave beamer.

"It gives a thirty-second emission that cooks a man solid as a potato," he explained with a fiendish grin. Mr. Renault enjoyed our line of work just a tad too much.

Father Donaher was carrying the usual flamethrower, his favorite weapon for general combat, and a sawed-off double-barrel shotgun rode in a holster at his hip. Mindy had a triple quiver of arrows on her back, her ever-present sword slung at the waist, and a bandolier of wooden knives across her chest.

Donning combat armor over my street clothes, I put a .44 AutoMag at my hip, a derringer in my boot, checked the action on an assault rifle and kissed it hello. A combination M-79 machine gun and M-16 40mm grenade launcher, this handy little deathdealer had gotten me out of more tight squeezes than even the friendliest of lubricants.

A mixed clip of 5.56mm ammo went into the M-16 machine gun, and a bandolier of 40mm grenades went across my chest. A thermite shell was thumbed into the underbarrel-slung launcher.

And everybody was wearing a cross.

It was an odd fact, but since Count Dracula, the very first vampire, was Catholic, and violently allergic to garlic and white roses, all of the subsequent vampires created by his biting people and their biting people, and so on, have the exact same weaknesses.

"Should we alert the locals to the possibility of a terrorist attack?" asked Mindy, preparing a haversack of magical supplies for Raul. "So they'll have the ambulances, fire department and such ready."

"Negative," I stated. "For the same reasons I couldn't call you over the phone or radio. If the Tanner part of Mystery Man is listening, it'd blow the whole show."

Leaving Amigo to guard the van, we moved individually out

of the side door of the vehicle and into the dank alley. When the street was clear to both binoculars and sunglasses, the team scampered into the road, Ken thumbed up the manhole cover and we quickly climbed down a steel ladder. The eighty-pound manhole cover was replaced with gentle fingertip pressure.

We descended past the electrical service duct, beyond the massive water pipes and finally into the sewer. Almost immediately, we were glad we had brought along the gas masks. The murky water swirled with stuff best left unmentioned, and more poured from the open pipes set along the curved brick wall. Slime was on everything.

The bread crumbs that Raul was going to leave were smears of petroleum jelly. Ultraviolet light infused the material with an unearthly blue glow. It was an age-old trick. The jelly was waterproof and barely visible, even in direct daylight. But it made for perfect tracking in the dark.

Only it wasn't dark. The damn brick-lined tunnel was brilliantly illuminated by wire-encased light bulbs set every few meters in the ceiling.

"Cut a power cable?" asked Mindy, proffering her sword.

Ken raised a mauled fist. "Smash them, sir?"

"Unscrew the bulbs?" asked Donaher.

That I approved. It would be mildly suspicious, but much less so than seeing seven heavily armed people marching your way.

"Get hard, people," I ordered, and my command was answered by a chorus of metallic clicks. "Silent penetration, one-meter spread, Mindy on point, Ken get the bulbs, Donaher on flank."

Turning the ultraviolet lantern to maximum power and minimum aperture, I scanned the walls at chest level. Then remembered that it was our Belgium basketball player doing the writing and tried a bit higher. I found an arrow marker, barely discernible, on the wall pointing northward, upriver. Below it was scrawled, "evil man this way. ugh. tonto."

With Jennings prominently in front, I sloshed along behind Sanders. Constantly checking the bricks, I soon found another jelly smear which read, 'clothespin!' And since tiny sniffs of the city sewer's ambiance were reaching my nose in spite of the gas mask, I heartily agreed with the sentiment.

Approaching another ladder a half block later, I found more writing on the wall. An arrow pointed upward, accompanied by the word 'beats me, chief.'

"It's a blind entrance to throw off pursuit," I explained to the massed troops. In essence, all we had done was cross the street. My opinion of Mystery Man was going higher and higher. This guy was good enough to be a spy.

We followed the trail of greasy markers up to the street and into another alley. Stout doors backed the rear of stores, each boasting heavy padlocks and signs announcing the name of the electronic alarm service used. This close to the Saddle Brook border, I guess it was necessary. The alley lamps were easily disposed of by the simple process of Sanders flicking a knife upward, cutting a wire and then catching the knife as it fell. Masked by darkness, we proceeded. The glowing markers got lower and lower, until they stopped at the delivery entrance of a modest two-story building. No sign. Nearby, sitting on top of a cardboard box, was a small gray-striped tomcat.

"Hello," said the animal in a tiny but recognizable voice.

Silent, Ken continued on along the alley killing more lamps. Good man. Made it appear that the whole block had suffered a power outage.

I kept my assault rifle level. "The quality of mercy is not strained."

"Ah . . . oh hell, I forget the answer code," meowed the feline.

Instantly, Jessica tasered the beast. Stunned, it fell off the box and into the big hand of Michael Donaher, which closed about the soft neck. George put a silenced pistol barrel into its cute snout, Jennings placed a knife blade against the fuzzy-wuzzy throat.

"Pax!" the kitty whimpered around the .45 muzzle. "My name is Raul Horta, Thursday is my night to feed the lizard, I once turned Jimmy Winslow into a frog and our subscription to *TV Guide* has expired."

"More," I demanded. "And better."

The kitty squirmed uncomfortably. "Okay, okay. My real name is Sir Marnix Charlemagne Saxe-Coburg, and I'm the bastard son of Leopold III, the rightful King of Belgium!"

We relaxed, and everybody released our absentminded pal. Wiping sweat from his furry brow, the cat leapt straight up, the body blurring and growing into Raul Horta. He was still disguised as a punk rocker.

"Report," I said, doffing the gas mask.

"They're inside," said the mage, taking the haversack from Mindy. Turning the rigid canvas satchel upside down over his head, the supplies tumbled out and Raul was now shaved, showered, shampooed, wearing fresh clothes, combat armor, dripping with bags and pouches and had a silver-inlaid flask in his grip. He took a quick swallow and slid the container inside his clothes. One must forgive dethroned aristocracy the minor eccentricity.

"Who exactly?" asked Jessica, scowling at the building. I knew how much she wanted to do a mind probe, but that would have been as bad as trying the radio, firing off a flare gun or just plain shouting that we were here.

"The football team and some sushi chef."

"Hoto's surviving slave."

"Probably. But not MM himself?"

"Nope."

"So what do we do now, sir?" asked a wall of blackness the size and shape of Ken.

I took the vacated box for a seat. "We wait until Mystery Man arrives and then blow him to bits."

"As simple as that?"

George shrugged. "Yep. It's ninety minutes till the solstice. And his gang is here. He'll show."

"And if he does not?"

"We lose," I said bluntly.

There was an awkward moment of silence.

"Status?" asked Mindy, removing her encumbering boots.

Grimly, I worked the bolt on my machine gun. "I officially declare this situation a Mad Dog alert. There is no order of attack. Anybody with even a wild chance of getting Mystery Man, go for the kill. And that includes if one of us is in the way and will die also. Do it anyway."

"Why?" demanded Donaher hotly.

And we explained about the World Mage spell.

As the group digested that unsettling information, I pulled Raul aside.

"A favor," I asked softly. "We kill Mystery Man. But afterwards, I want the football player."

While Raul considered the request, I checked the load in my .44 AutoMag pistol. Silver-jacketed wooden bullets, soaked in holy water with an explosive garlic center.

"Agreed," said the mage.

"Thanks," I said, slamming the clip shut. "I owe you."

"No," he said in a voice of stone. "You owe her."

Steadfast, I looked at my friend. "Agreed. But if I die, you get him for me?"

"With pleasure, pal."

What are you two talking about? asked Jess.

The matter is privacy-sealed, I thought in tight control. *Just like birthday gifts. None of your damn business.*

She gave me a hard stare, then Raul.

Later, I promised her.

Though unhappy, Jessica didn't push.

"Ed, how about a routine eight?" asked Renault.

I returned to business. "Sounds good. Groups of two, one-on-one coverage. Simultaneous strike. Donaher and Blanco into the cellar. Raul and Mindy take the alley on the left. Jessica and Sanders, the gas station to the right. George stays here, I'm on the roof."

"Affirmative, sir."

"Done."

"Check."

"Roger wilco, chief."

"But what about the front door?" queried Sanders, stepping protectively close to my wife. The tiny Oriental smiled in kindly amusement at the gesture. Him protect her?

"He has to get in somehow," noted the priest pragmatically as he minutely adjusted the pre-burner on his flamethrower. "Why should we make it difficult for him to enter an ambush?"

The point was well taken. As the team moved silent into the night, I started climbing a rusty fire escape. Judiciously, I eased my shoes down on the outermost sides of the metal steps. Reaching the roof, I chose a pool of shadow by the maze of pipes constituting an antique air conditioner. This was almost always a good place to hide. PIs learn the damnedest things from the criminals we catch, get drunk with and sometimes date.

I had just comfortably positioned myself when I heard the flapping of leathery wings. Turning, I found myself face-to-face with Mystery Man changing from a bat into a kimono-draped battlesuit holding a pulsating red leather book.

"Sonofabitch!" we cried in unison.

13

Kimono flapping, Mystery Man gestured, and I pumped a 40mm grenade into his belly. The shell went straight through the battlesuit and exploded against a brick chimney flue. His own body acted as a shield to protect me from ceramic splinters, but I staggered under the explosion, wildly fired my M-16 at a figure I could not properly see. Not that such had ever stopped me before.

Running out of ammo, I drew the AutoMag as Mystery Man heaved a bottle at me. Impulsively, I fired and the glass container shattered, the contents forming gaseous scissors which snipped and cut at the point of impact. Mentally, I thanked George for making me practice all those nights at the target range.

Taking aim, I triggered two more thundering rounds at MM as he shifted into multiple images and shimmied downward into the building. Slamming in a fresh clip, I noticed that my shoulder was bleeding from a nasty laser wound. The energy ray had penetrated combat and body armor, but the puckered hole wasn't very deep, and the intense heat of the laser had cauterized the muscles so there was no immediate bleeding. The pain was minor, so I decided to ignore it for the present. After the battle, I'd whack myself with some astringent lotion, sulfur powder, Healing potion, pizza and beer. An Alvarez cure-all special.

Suddenly, I heard a rustling of leaves that grew in volume and tempo until I recognized it as millions of leathery wings beating frantically. Uh-oh. Reloading the M-79, I noted that the stars were being blotted out by swarms of bats. And from the increasing barks and howls, it seemed as if every dog in Ohio were coming our way. Mystery Man was pulling no punches. We were about to get hit with the full unbridled fury of a vampire.

Ignoring the rooftop door as far too obvious a death trap, I trained my M-16 on the roof itself and spent four clips chewing a circular pattern into the tar and tile. With the sound of splintering wood, the round path fell and crashed to the floor below.

Peeking in, I saw the jagged circle had landed next to a large
desk, but the rest of the office was empty. Damn.

Grabbing the edge of the hole, I lowered myself and dropped
the last couple of feet. Just then, some bats flew into the room
and I machine-gunned them in flight. But it took another whole
clip. Nimble little buggers. Two minutes into the fight and I was
already in danger of running out of ammunition. NG. Gotta
stopper that hole, and fast.

Rummaging in my pouch, I found two Willy Peter grenades.
Pulling the pins, I tossed them upward and onto the roof. In a
dull thump, the two white-phosphorus bombs spewed fiery blos-
soms, and a zillion bats screeched in annoyance. A rain of fire
and dead fluttering bodies sprinkled through the opening, as I
added a 40mm shotgun shell to the woes of my aerial attackers.
That'll teach 'em to mess with the Bureau. Back to the belfrey,
guys!

Thumbing in a fresh shell, I did a quick check of the office. The
walls were covered with sports posters of football players, and
three framed ticket stubs. For the World Series, I guess. Sports
was not my hobby. But it explained how he chose the Pumas.
Dozens of metal-framework shelves were jammed full of books
and papers, and the massive mahogany desk was overflowing
with the same. A wall-spanning counter was neatly arrayed with
mailing supplies, scale, postage meter, bales of string, boxes of
manila and padded envelopes. And a small vault supported a
tiny refrigerator. Oh, how I wanted to get into that safe, but it
would have to wait till later. Murder first, then pillage.

Putting a burst of the 5.56mm tumblers through the sole door,
and the wall on both sides, I kicked the portal aside. Nothing
but empty corridor. Faintly from below, I could hear shattering
glass, wild animal howls and Mike Donaher intoning a deadly
blessing. Ataway, Father!

Moving fast past book-filled alcoves and a hundred file cabinets, I reached the stairs. Down below the yammering and chat-
tering of machine guns, explosions, the crackling of lightning
and strange screams. But there was also the high-pitched whine
of laser beams, and I knew the football team was fighting back.

Shooting the door of a utility closet off its hinges, I climbed on
top of the makeshift sled and slid down the steps in a bumping,
jostling journey of four seconds. D-d-damn! F-f-forgot t-t-to
r-r-remove kn-kn-knob!

Reaching the main floor scrambled but alive, I tumbled away

from the door, rolled to my feet and glanced about, but MM was nowhere to be seen. However, everybody else was here. Football players jumped from wall to wall, hissing and firing brilliant light rays from their hands. Bullets riddled bookcases and pages went flying in high-velocity military editing. Posters were ripped, crystals smashed, kilometers of slick brown audio tape arced into the air from unwinding cassettes, the door to the lavatory was gone completely, display tables were overturned and I had no idea which side was winning.

Stumbling out of the hallway came George with an alligator firmly attached to his armored leg. An inhabitant of the local sewer, most likely. I had always known people should never flush those things down the toilet. At point-blank range, Renault was pumping .45 slugs into the reptile's body, but it seemed to have no effect. Taking aim, I placed a 40mm grenade into the soft skin of the alligator's pale belly, and the beast went to pieces. Prying the bodiless head from his leg with a bowie knife, George nodded his thanks. I gave a salute with my rifle and then butt-stroked a screaming senior in the face. Fanged teeth went flying. Years ago, TechServ had replaced the plastic shoulder rests on Bureau rifles with old-fashioned, but deadlier, wood stocks. With internal steel bracings, of course.

A long metal barrel shattered a window, and watery fluid splashed upon a pair of the undead. Crying in unbearable torment, the vampires melted into a puddle on the floor that was probably going to be hell to clean. Beyond the jagged glass, I saw Jessica. Guess she had forgotten to inform me that the stabilizing agent in her MSG/DMSO concoction was holy water. But the secret ingredient was not hidden from the vampire connoisseurs.

Amid the ruin of the occult-book store, Mindy was sword-to-sword with the demonic sushi chef, both opponents moving with blurring speed. A football player stumbled close and his body fell apart. The clothing of the beefy player was in tatters, exposing coaxial cables lining his arms and legs. Great. Cyborg vampires. For this I graduated college?

Sparks flying, the two martial artists swirled in a flashing whirlwind of clanging steel. A jade statue of Kali got a rude lobotomy, Buddha received an instant diet and a bookcase was cleaved in twain. I tried for a shot, but it was impossible. The two master swordfighters were going round and round each other like debating lawyers paid by the hour. A display case of crystal pyramids showed them inverted for a moment, before the two crashed though the front window and into the street. Neither slowed, nor missed a stroke. Silent in their concentration, the deadly duel raged back and forth along the sidewalk, a lamppost was cut in half and toppled to the ground, flattening a Yugo and just missing our van. The fire hydrant had its top removed and white water geysered into the air. Somehow the mailbox survived, but then, disturbing one of those was a federal offense punishable by three to five.

Suddenly, the sagging front door to the store was kicked open and in strode a police officer, his pistol drawn.

"What the freaking hell is going on here!" demanded the cop.

"Go home!" bellowed Raul in his Voice of Command, struggling with four vampires.

Turning on his heel, the officer holstered his gun, and whistling a tune, ambled casually away.

Brocade curtains parted, and Donaher came backing out of the cellar, hosing the floor, walls and ceiling with his flamethrower. Wriggling through the inferno of jellied gasoline was a horde of rats and cockroaches, the dark bodies barely discernible through the boiling orange flames. As the big priest cleared the jamb, Tina shouted and the walls slammed together, sealing the doorway shut. Two seconds later the flamethrower sputtered and died. Whew. In comedy, sex and war, timing was all-important.

Firing his shotgun at an approaching linebacker, Donaher slapped the release buckle on his chest harness and the empty tanks thudded to the floor. Turning, he shoved his Bible into the snarling mouth of another vampire and its head burst into flames. Blind, the undead pointed its laser beam wildly, slagging a candle counter, annihilating a hundred packs of tarot cards, wounding Jessica in the knee and beheading another vampire before it died. I appreciated the assistance.

A shimmering light beam lashed out at Raul, who dodged and sent a barrage of spiked ice balls into the group of undead. His lightning bolts crackled over their forceshields, and their laser beams were reflected off his ethereal hand barrier. Since the fight appeared to be going nowhere, I pulled the pin from a grenade without removing the bomb from my pouch, let the strap slip off my shoulder and tossed the whole thing behind the chesthigh book rack. One football player, faster or smarter than the rest, tried to leap clear, but the resulting multiblasts tore the lot of them into bloody gobbets and sent the cash register into the ceiling. Coins and bills sprinkled downward in a fantasy rain of monetary gain.

Moving through the chaos and death, my M-16 spraying hot lead and silver at anything not a member of my team, I continued to ruthlessly search for MM. Twice I was hit in the chest by laser beams, chunks of my combat armor puffing into nothingness and clothes catching fire, but the body armor held and I used a holy-water pistol to extinguish the blaze. These guys' lasers had nowhere near the power of their bastard boss.

A pair of the undead had gotten the drop on Donaher and pinned the big priest behind a flipped-over table. I started to assist when Blanco appeared and grabbed them by the arms. Instantly their lasers winked out. Grinning in triumph, Donaher rose and squirted each monster smack in the face with his pistol. As they clawed at melting features, Tina froze one solid with liquid nitrogen and the priest garroted his with a rosary. Ouch. I couldn't even imagine what his penitence would be for that.

Personally, I was impressed. It was the finest example of making your disability into an asset that I had ever seen. Using the jamming factor of a mage to neutralize an enemy's weapon was going into the handbook, surrounded by stars, asterisks, exclamation points, underlines, italicized and in bold type. Helvetica, maybe.

The tumultuous donnybrook spilled into the back room of the store and Raul and I both spotted our quarterback at the same moment. He was struggling with the fire escape door trying to get out. A coward as well as a murderer. Gesturing, Horta set the killer's clothes ablaze and I blew off his head with a 40mm shell. Then the mage disintegrated the legs of the vampire and I emptied a full clip into his spine. The monster's hands feebly clawed the air in a ghastly reminiscent manner. The next thing I knew, I was pounding the demon with my rifle stock and only ceased when Raul pulled me off the pulped oozing mass of very dead flesh.

Catching my breath, Raul and I shook hands and rejoined the battle. For some reason, I felt much better now. Pounds lighter. And cleaner.

The ventilated barrel of the big M-60 machine rifle bent, Ken was whirling the colossal weapon about him in the manner of a Viking war hammer when three football players blindsided the Bureau giant. But he didn't fall. Sinking their teeth into his clothes, one broke fangs on body armor, and the other two jerked away spitting. Eh? Our super-duper soldier boy must have drunk some holy water just prior to the battle. Actually, I'm surprised it worked. But what else could have caused that weird reaction? Garlic after-shave?

Dodging laser beams and the falling cash register, Ken threw aside the M-60 and unlimbered his hydrofluoric spray gun. A drop of the acid steamed into his hand, but the wound healed even as I watched. Wow. However, the two vampires, the floor they stood on, a chair, a rack of astrological charts and anything nearby hissingly dissolved. A section of the terrazzo floor gave way, but merely sagged low and didn't break through to the cellar.

The cellar. Hmm.

"Where's Mystery Man?" I screamed above the turmoil.

"Basement!" answered Donaher.

"You sure?"

"Yes!"

"Bad?"

"I'm up here, ain't I?"

True enough. "Little Big Horn!" I screamed, and my team pulled into a defense arc, our rumps to the wall. The vampires took the opportunity to regroup and lick their many wounds. Black fumes from a hundred small fires made seeing difficult. And a ceiling-mounted smoke alarm was keening loudly until I put a .44 silencer into the noisy distraction.

"Roarke's Drift!" I bellowed.

We stopped firing and the vampires formed a neat attack line. What putzes. God, I hoped none of them was a history major.

"R-14-9! Hut! Hut! Hut!"

As the idiots charged, the shorter members of my team dropped to a knee and raised their weapons. The taller members stood close and leveled theirs. In unison, we cut loose with everything we had. The noise was almost deafening, but somehow the death screams of the collegiate vampires came through loud and clear. Incredibly, they harmonized. A football team glee club? Huntsville must be a really weird town.

"Cease fire!" I bellowed, waving smoke away from my face with an aching arm.

Only carnage and conflagration filled the store. Burning books were everywhere, whole cases sheets of fire. On one shelf, a slim volume with tooled-leather binding and gold-leaf pages hopped to the floor and tried to scamper to freedom. Tina snatched the runaway and tucked it into her blouse. Sheesh! I hope it bit her and raised a welt. Sometimes wizards have no common sense at all.

Faintly from overhead, my helmet detected high-pitched stridulations and leathery rustlings. My rooftop fire must have expired and the bats were rushing in. Time to move.

"Floor?" I asked Donaher fast.

His face said no. "Too high a drop."

"Then it's the door!" cried George, and blew away the wall with a LAW rocket. We charged through the smoking hole and down the stairs.

"Sanders and Blanco on point! George does cleanup, and watch the freaking ceiling!"

The basement was dark, we roughed a couple of flares and tossed them about. Briefly, I had a glimpse of a new furnace, old water heater, melted plastic window decorations, hundreds of burned rodent corpses, a charred ladder, an ajar manhole cover, and that was when the rats hit us, a squeaking squalid tidal wave of dirty diseased teeth supported by mindless hunger.

The bitter blue spray of Blanco's liquid nitrogen froze dozens into crystal states. Unlimbering his hydrofluoric acid spray gun, Ken dissolved hundreds, the melting bodies spewing noise and hate.

Invisible, Renault's microwave beamer spoke its thirty-second charge, baking more of the furry freaks solid. But another wave swarmed over the first, the second, the third, fourth, until an ocean of the snarling rodents filled the floor. A living carpet of snapping death.

"Musketeers!" hollered Sanders.

We closed ranks, with everybody protecting everybody. I had been just about to yell the same myself.

The cockroaches crawled over us, but were merely an annoyance, as their bites only stung. But I made damn sure not one got inside the breech of my weapon. Stomping rats, I stabbed Jessica in the back with my knife, the blade rebounding off her body armor as it speared a rodent. Mentally, she thanked me and shot another off my boot. Ken crushed a rat in his gloved hand, and George sprayed four off of Tina's helmet. Good grouping!

Gritting her teeth, Jessica clenched both hands into fists and stared at the boisterous horde. Half of the rat bastards went stiff and keeled over dead from the Brain Blast. Donaher bounced a

Willy Peter grenade into the manhole, and in a strident flash, the flow of rodents slowed noticeably. The Pied Piper of Hamlin had nothing on us. A flute? Piffle. Gimme good ol' army-issue antipersonnel grenades any day.

Hooting a roar, Raul was wrestling with an alligator, and two swamp monsters waddled at Tina. Reaching over my shoulder, I grabbed a LAW from George, prepped the tube and aimed real freaking careful in both directions. I pulled the trigger, and a lance of flame shot from the front, the rocket annihilating the oncoming two enemy suitcases. Plus, the backblast blew the head off the angry swamp denizen trying to consume my buddy. Raul's helmet was discolored, his visors cracked and flak jacket charred to black flakes, but he was alive. Merely smoking mad.

Barking dogs poured down the stairs and a river of bats flowed along the ceiling, knocking off a hailstorm of cockroaches. Boldly stepping forward, Blanco sprayed the contents of her canister on the sagging hole in the wall. Working her way from the top, she formed an impenetrable seal of supercold ice. Several dogs and bats had been caught midway in the barrier, their bodies cleanly snapping in half as they struggled to get free. Yuck.

A low hum filled the building, and I checked the furnace. Nope. Off. Then a brackish light began flickering from underneath a door in the far wall, illuminating the inverted pentagram on the riveted metal panel.

"Charge!" I screamed, and we advanced into the cellar stomping, crushing, shooting, and burning our way across the dim-lit basement.

Reaching the door, Blanco shouted something unintelligible and a stonework wall materialized, cutting the basement in half. Then her wooden wand went limp in her hand. Tenderly, she slid the dowel into a special holster at her hip and snapped a protective flap firmly into place. One mage drained. But it only took us a couple of seconds to kill the handful of rats, dogs, bats and insects that were on our side of the barrier. I hated acing the dogs, innocent animals summoned to their deaths by the vampire part of Mystery Man. But I took great delight in rubbing out the rest. Bats were only rats with wings, rats were only cockroaches on steroids, and what big-city dweller didn't hate cockroaches?

Using powders and potions, the mages disengaged the magical seal on the metal door, George removed the detonator switch for the explosives hidden under the floor, Jessica cut the wires feed-

ing straight electrical current to the latch, I picked the lock and
Ken ripped the door off its hinges and then threw it ahead of us
as a rude calling card. George typed our signature with the .30
rifle rounds of his M-60. Hello, it's us!

Inside was a totally ruined alchemist's laboratory. Both walls
lined with smashed· jars, broken beakers and cracked retorts,
seconds ago filled with every conceivable color and manner of
substance: dust, gels, liquids, mud, hair, fur, spices, canned
goods, bones, blood, brains. Most of it was on the floor, or
slowly headed that way. A complex array of destroyed pestles
and mortars, steaming beakers, dripping tubing, glass spirals
and boiling retorts filled a workbench alongside a totally undamaged microwave oven. Astrological charts adorned the wall,
and a poster of the human anatomy was situated prominently
above a coroner's dissection table. There was a ten-foot-tall spice
rack, a case of antique books and even a medieval anvil and
hearth with bellows.

It was a fairly standard mad-wizard laboratory. I wondered
where Igor, the hunchbacked, semi-human assistant, was?

Amid the decimation was the mandatory black iron caldron
set in the middle of a freaking great pentagram, its shining lines
thick silver rods embedded into the flagstone floor. And a duplicate pentagram was sunk into the concrete ceiling. Behind the
bubbling caldron stood Mystery Man, reading aloud from the
Aztec Book of the Dead, his words forming visible symbols in
the air which dropped into the caldron with tiny rainbow
splashes. He appeared exactly as he had at the Holding Facility,
except there was no gray at his temples. And no tux.

"Abraham Lincoln!" I cried. "To the max!"

And the team cut loose with everything we had. But neither
our physical nor magical weapons could penetrate the shimmering forceshield Mystery Man had erected about the pentagram.
From top to bottom, and side to side, we probed for a weak
spot, an entrance; the ricochets and rebounds destroyed the rest
of the room in vainglorious fury.

"The floor!" shouted Jessica, and we tried there, but again
our weapons failed to undercut the pentagram and topple our
foe. The silver lines were actually slabs of the precious metal
which seemed to descend forever. Damnation, there had to be a
way to stop him! Death spell? Earthquake? IRS audit?

Unperturbed by our attack, Mystery Man continued to drone
on, occasionally gesturing, or pouring into the caldron tiny vials

of colored fluid taken from a bulky vest under his kimono. A brisk wind began to build in the basement, and I felt a painful tingle of static electricity crackle across my skin. I didn't need my sunglasses to tell me that this was the blackest sorcery: major-league magic and totally evil. Scratching wildly, Raul popped the top of a bottle of calamine lotion and poured it inside his body armor.

"How close is he to completing the World Mage spell?" demanded George, determinedly firing irregular bursts at the alchemist.

"*Nyet!*" spat Tina, scowling.

Thumbing in my last shell, I dropped the bandolier. "It's not the World Mage spell?" I asked, puzzled.

"*Da.*"

"Then what is it?" asked Jessica.

With difficulty, Raul swallowed. "He's doing the Big Drain!"

I went icy calm. The Big Drain. Oh no. Even worse than the World Mage spell, the Big Drain was an insane effort to siphon off all of the magic from the entire planet and store it in a single living person. The World Mage spell we could fight, had fought successfully once. But if the Drain worked, humanity wouldn't have enough magic remaining to light a candle in hell. We would be totally helpless, and MM could do with the world as he willed. The very notion of Mystery Man as ruler of the planet was like eating glass. Impossible to swallow.

A small vortex of force started to form above the caldron, tendrils of misty fog masked the floor and the wind buffeting us became a miniature storm, with tiny raindrops and small lightning bolts crashing around us.

"How long?" demanded Donaher, wet hands ramming fresh shells into his shotgun with grim intentions.

"We got about one minute," shouted Raul over the screaming winds.

I wiped rain from my face. "And then?"

The Russian mage moved a finger across her throat.

Hoo boy. "Okay! Hit 'im again!" I ordered.

LAW and HAFLA rockets impacted on the magical barrier to vanish without a trace. Silver throwing stars bounced off. Bullets musically ricocheted. Arrows splintered. Streams of acid, MSG/DMSO and liquid nitrogen pooled about the pentagram, forming a crude moat of biochemical death.

"*DIE!*" throated Jessica, fisting each temple.

Incredibly, the man actually faltered for a second, then went on reading and chanting. Limp, my wife slumped to the floor, gasping and heaving for breath. It had been a good try.

Mystery Man was double his original size. The caldron had sunk into the floor to become a yawning pit from which fiery tongues of raw ethereal power lashed upward into his body. With each lambent energy whip, his smile grew and his voice became louder and more purposeful. He was already tapping the natural magical resources of our mother planet herself; after that would come the monsters, the people and absolute victory.

We were in a full-scale hurricane by now and had to hold on to each other to keep our footing. Bits of glassware and books swirled madly around, going faster and faster to the ever-increasing tempo of the building maelstrom. We stood on the eve of the apocalypse. The hour of doom.

"Bureau!" I shouted into my watch. "Condition Alpha Four! Repeat! Alpha Four! Request immediate tactical nuclear strike on Cincinnati! Immediate nuclear strike on Cincinnati! Respond!"

Static. I hadn't thought the radio could penetrate the swirling holocaust of unearthly forces bombarding us to reach the van parked just outside on the street. Okay, Alvarez, here was your big chance to justify the trust the American people have placed in the Bureau. Think, damn it, think!

"Raul, what are the limitations on the spell again?"

He repeated the operational parameters, and I got a goofy idea. It was insane. Moronic. But it was my only remaining ace, and I hoped MM couldn't trump it.

"This is the FBI!" I shouted above the roaring hurricane, and flipped open my commission booklet to show my badge. "I am Federal Agent Edwardo Alvarez. You are under arrest for over a hundred counts of murder, arson, attempted murder and inciting a riot!"

My team gave expressions of total bewilderment, and the enemy alchemist only laughed in delight. Thirty seconds.

I swallowed. Here goes nothing. "As a duly authorized law enforcement agent of the Justice Department of the United States Government, I hereby confiscate this workshop, impound that book and declare this store a sealed criminal scene, closed to all but authorized police officials!"

With a thunderclap, the book slammed shut and the winds died.

Caught by surprise, my team took a full second to reorient themselves. Alchemist Al had no such lapse.

Even as the magical boundary of the pentagram faded away, I sprayed him with my M-16, the bullets punching a line of holes in his kimono. Screaming in pain, the baby mage raised an arm high, crushed a vial in his fist and vanished from sight—about one heartbeat ahead of a staggering barrage of bullets, arrows, lightning bolts, missiles, grenades, Fire Lance, Ice Storm, Death spell, Sleep spell, microwaves and every other assorted death-dealer the rest of my grim teammates possessed.

The rear cinder-block wall disappeared under the fusillade, a mountain of dirt poured in and a section of the burning building crashed down around us. Bitterly, I cursed as we headed for the stairs. We had failed. Failed! Oh, we had stopped Laughing Boy for the moment. But he was still free and had—wristwatch—fifty-eight minutes to conquer the world. And we didn't even know his name yet. Or where he would go next.

Fifty-seven minutes till doomsday.

14

"Okay, everybody search for clues!" I ordered above the crackle of the flames and rumble of tumbling masonry. "We've got to know where this asshole went!"

Forcing our way out of the windswept laboratory, my team squeezed past the ruin of the door, kicking aside mounds of dead rodents. With a fingersnap, Tina made the stonework wall ahead of us vanish. I raised an eyebrow. Guess canceling that spell didn't require any magic. We crossed the basement to clamber up the rickety staircase. Lying on their backs in the flames, cockroaches burst like popcorn, and Jessica tripped on a blackened alligator. Even dead, those things were dangerous. The ice wall at the top of the stairs was easy to breach, as the flames had already softened the material tremendously. A few machine-gun bursts and the frozen air shattered into a pretty snowstorm, the white flakes vaporizing before they hit the floor. On the other side were a thousand smoking corpses, human and non, but the animal army was gone. When Mystery Man had fled, so had his influence.

The heat was almost unbearable as we reached the store, so Raul formed a tiny rain cloud over us, its cooling downpour giving much-needed protection from the inferno we nervously stood in.

"Jessica, where did Mystery Man discuss the matter most frequently?" asked Donaher urgently, loosening the starched white collar of his cossack.

Gamely, the telepath closed her eyes and slowly rotated, once, twice, paused, then jerked her head upward. "Second story . . . somewhere."

"His private office!" I cried, remembering the desk and vault. "Triple time, harch!"

The stairs were gone, so we tilted a relatively undamaged bookcase against the charred wall, the sturdy shelves serving as temporary rungs. Tainting the thick smoke filling the store was the porkish smell of roasting human flesh. As horrible as it sounds, it made me both nauseous and hungry.

On point, I went first. Reaching the upper story, I stood erect and checked for danger with gun at the ready. The place was ablaze: shelves held neat lines of burning books, piles and stacks of paperbacks flared with sputtering flames from the ignited glue in their perfect bindings, the green metal file cabinets had warped from the intense heat spilling their contents to the fire, the linoleum tiles on the floor were melting, embers filled the air and fried bats littered the place, making it resemble the aftereffects of a truly Homeric Halloween party. My dead football player was only smoking bones and discolored metal endoskeleton.

Grabbing a fire extinguisher from the wall, I hosed us a foamy zone of safety to the next room. The floor tiles were sticky but passable. In the office, the updraft from the hole in the roof fed the flames as a bellows, making it hotter and even more difficult to breathe.

At the desk, Raul tapped the bedraggled piece of office furniture with his silver staff, making the wood ring. "Speak!" intoned the mage. "Tell us what you know of your master's plans should failure come here. *Speak!*"

Muted groans and creaks came from the battered piece of mahogany. ". . . go into self-publishing . . . maybe become an author . . ."

"*No!* Speak of your master's plans concerning the book of magic he has recently obtained!" corrected the angry wizard.

". . . no fail . . . was impossible . . ."

So the arrogant fool firmly believed that he would have succeeded. There was no contingency plan. Maybe we had won. With twenty or so U.S. Army tumblers in your chest, almost anybody would be wearing grass for a hat.

But could we chance it? No.

"Find the safe!" I bellowed, sweat stinging my eyes.

"Here!" cried Jessica, pushing over a stack of UFO magazines with the barrel of her Uzi. Then Mindy kicked off the tiny refrigerator.

Stepping close, I inquisitively touched the stout metal box of the safe with a finger, but immediately jerked away. My skin was a glossy white. Boy, was that going to hurt.

Using our helmets, we formed a bucket brigade from the bathroom, conveying endless amounts of tap water which we splashed upon the safe, each sizzling into steam upon contact. But even with Raul's rainstorm, we were clearly fighting a losing battle. And now the floor was growing uncomfortably hot to stand on even through our boots. Soon this place would reach critical tinderbox temperatures and explode.

Yet we kept on. The contents of that safe might be our only chance of tracking Mystery Man. Fifty-three minutes. Soon the water only bubbled instead of steamed, and Ken tucked the safe under one mighty arm. What a man. Sprinting for the east wall, George blasted us an exit and we painfully jumped over the alley to the lower roof of the gas station. Gas station? Oh swell.

Just then the bookstore roof gave a mighty creak and collapsed. Spiraling gouts of red and orange flame formed a volcano into the sky, spewing an endless supply of embers and ash over the sleeping Cincinnati.

Dropping to the cooler back alley, we found Mindy still engaged in furious combat with Bruce Lee, Jr., their swords clanging audibly above the oncoming fire engine bells and police sirens.

"Alli-alli-oxen-free!" I shouted through cupped hands.

Reluctantly, Mindy broke and ran. Grinning in triumph, the vampire started after her and we cut him to ribbons with our weapons.

"Wow," panted Jennings as she joined us near a dumpster. "He was really good." Her sweaty body was trembling with near exhaustion.

"Well, now he's really dead," snapped George, prying aside the manhole cover.

Sojourning through the smelly sewer, we surfaced on the other side of the street and took refuge in our van. Effecting repairs, we watched as police, fire engines and a helicopter arrived on the scene, hordes of reporters pushing their way through a growing crowd of civilians. Guess this was big news for Cin.

After bandaging my finger, I obtained gloves and a stethoscope from the equipment locker and got busy with the safe.

"Ed, what's taking so long?" asked Mike after a whole minute.

Spin left, spin right, jiggle-jiggle. "It's an excellent model," I irritably snapped. "Top of the line. Even an expert yegg, a master safecracker, would have a tough job opening this box."

Pushing me aside, George slapped a lump of C4 plastique onto the dial, pressed a button on the wired battery pack in his hand, and with a subdued bang, the door jumped ajar.

"Usually," I corrected myself, both hands busy digging into the massed papers. I passed them on to Jessica, who memorized each with a glance.

"Deed, tax receipts, insurance forms, nothing but formal business papers. Ah!" she cried in delight. "His name is Wilson C. LaRue!"

"Sure?" asked Mindy, draining a quart of that nasty-tasting sports drink which is supposed to be good for you.

"Passport photograph matches the face we saw on the guy in the pentagram."

"Never heard of him," stated Raul, glancing at the picture.

As if that meant anything. Ninety percent of the bad guys we fight are unknowns. The rest are major historical figures.

"Raul, Blanco, how long do we have before LaRue can perform the conjure again?" asked Father Donaher, sliding a new clean collar about his neck. As always, when dealing with vampires, his collar was steel-lined.

Tina shrugged and turned to Horta. This must be out of her league.

"Normally, it should take a person a couple of hours to recover from the systemic shock of having the spell disrupted," stated Raul, scratching at a bite on his cheek. "But as Mystery Man is in actuality three people, we had better operate on the assumption that it will only take him . . . say, forty minutes."

Giving Mr. LaRue twenty minutes to try and conquer the world once more. And we were down ten minutes already, leaving only thirty minutes for us to search the entire continental United States and locate/kill this crazy bastard.

Going to the computer terminal, I annexed the telephone modem and dialed 1-8-0-0-B-U-R-E-A-U-1-3. It was time to bring in the big guns. There was a hum, a click and then nothing.

I tried again, and got the same.

As we murmured among ourselves, Raul and Tina held a fast conference.

"When LaRue started the Big Drain, he caused major disruptions in the ethereal dimension," said Horta.

"First things to go would be highest magiks," added Blanco.

"Like pocket universes," postulated Jess.

They nodded.

So the Bureau was trapped in another dimension. Oh swell. We were totally alone on this one, with literally everything riding on our decisions. I sighed. So be it. Because unlike LaRue,

I had a contingency. That was how we kept winning against the monsters. Usually.

Rummaging in my locker, I unearthed a codebook given to me years ago by the President as a reward, and dialed a number so secret, I couldn't even let the rest of the team see what it was.

"CIA Information Center," said a calm female voice from the monitor. There was no picture. "How can I help you, Mr. Alvarez?"

Impressive. My mouth started to ask a hundred questions, but we were in a hurry. "This is a Priority One request. There is nothing more important."

"Accepted. Go."

"I need a full personal readout on a Wilson C. LaRue. Most importantly, any land or property that he has legal access to."

There came the faint sound of tapping.

"Working," said the voice. "Wilson Charles LaRue, the only child of Brian and Wilma LaRue. Father was professional magician—stage name 'The Amazing LaRue.' Mother a carnival tarot reader—'Wondrous Wilma.' Both deceased. Wilson was born in Dayton, Ohio, October 23, 1948, Dayton General Hospital. Graduated from Cambridge Elementary School 1964, Dayton High School 1968. No criminal record. Served four years in the U.S. Navy stationed at Fort Hamilton as an assistant librarian. Discharged with honor. Currently a member of the naval reserve. Owns and operates an occult-book store in Cincinnati, Ohio, 435 North Eighth Street. LaRue Books. Owns a 1989 red Toyota Corolla, vanity license plate: Matthew Adam George Ink Charles. Has leased post office box 666 for his mail-order business at the main branch of the Cincinnati post office. Rents a ten-by-six storage locker at You-Store-It, Mulberry Drive, Cincinnati. Contents unknown. Had a safety-deposit box at People's Federal Bank. Lease expired and he withdrew the contents eight days ago. Rents with an option to buy a house, 2842 West Morris Avenue." A pause. "No other listed properties in either the IRS, state land registry, post office, FBI, Federal Banking Reserve, Justice Department, Pentagon or CIA computer files."

She hadn't listed the Bureau. But then, that was because we didn't exist. "You sure that's everything?"

"Are there any other questions?"

Damn! "No. Thanks."

"Good luck." And the line went dead.

The unremarkable story on an ordinary man living an unspecial life. The safety-deposit box was where he probably kept the cash receipts from his business. Raul had already said that buying the ingredients for the alchemist spell would cost a small fortune. The occult-book business was a natural after learning what his parents used to do fcr a living. Apparently, Wilson had simply gotten his hands on the wrong book, one that contained real alchemical potions. And the rest is a sad story of power addiction and murder.

"Three places to search," noted Sanders with a frown. "Sir, split up into smaller teams?"

"Faith, lad, we're not sure that we can take this guy as a group," countered Donaher. "Smaller teams is just asking for a disaster."

"We've got to hit him as a unit," agreed Mindy. "But where? At which location?"

"All of them," I answered, buckling my seat belt. "Renault, do your stuff!"

Jumping behind the wheel, George hit the gas, and I swear to God that our fourteen-ton van did a wheelie pulling away from the curb.

"Sir . . . ah, Ed," said Tina hesitantly as we rocketed through the empty streets. "Might not LaRue have another legal name?"

"Explain," I demanded.

"In Russia, actors can have stage name, and it is their second legal name. Your John Wayne could write checks under that pseudonym, but born name was Marion M. Morrison."

"No good," I countered. "Everybody's name is listed with the IRS. If he had another, we'd know it."

"A question, sir?" asked Ken, scratching an armpit.

"Yeah?"

"Since LaRue has absorbed the powers of Tanner and Rashamor Hoto, might it be possible that he has some nebulous legal claim on their property?"

Seven jaws sagged.

"Jesus H. Tap Dancing Christ!" I cried. "Yes!"

Donaher smacked me on the head and I apologized.

Scrambling for the phone, I punched redial. Tanner was an alien machine, and thus of highly questionable legal status, so it couldn't own any property. However, Rashamor Hoto was filthy rich.

"Negative," I announced, replacing the receiver. "Hoto has been in our custody for ten years and thus has been declared legally dead. As a foreign national, his property has been confiscated by the Japanese government and resold."

As Jessica loaded her taser, and Raul consulted his crystal ball, Mindy ripped open a jumbo bag of dried fruit snacks. Instantly, Amigo was by her side, forked tongue lagging, scaled tail wagging.

"You know, I didn't see any coffins in that store," said Ken.

Father Donaher dismissed that idea. "A vampire needs a dirt-filled coffin to rest in when they're not in their homeland. An American vampire—in America—can sleep at the Holiday Inn with impunity."

"Fascinating."

"Makes 'em a bitch to find," munched Mindy.

Ain't it the truth.

We hit the storage place first. *Nada*. Just old furniture and mementoes of his parents. Family photos, pressed flowers in albums, a big box of eight-track tapes. Guess everybody had some of those around somewhere gathering dust. As the team took its leave, Donaher blessed the metal cubicle, Tina spot-welded the door shut and then Jessica sealed it as a criminal scene. Just in case Wilson did a surprise return.

Twenty-four minutes to go.

The post office box was empty. LaRue had not shrunk himself to an inch in height and hidden inside. But I sealed it anyway. We were leaving nothing to chance.

There remained his house, and eighteen minutes.

The neighborhood was quiet and clean, as most were in Cincinnati. His house was a two-story Cape Cod with bricking, a white picket fence and smiling lawn jockey. His car was parked in front, but my sunglasses, binoculars, radar and infrared thermal scan showed the vehicle unoccupied.

Parking on the corner, I spotted a group of young adults singing in the backyard of a neighboring house. At midnight? They didn't sound drunk.

Rabbinical students from Hebrew Union College, sent Jessica. Great. The innocent bystanders were also highly trained observers and just over the fence of a possible major battle. On the other hand, we might be able to use the seminary students to aid us against LaRue and his unholy slaves. Vampires and Jews had never gotten along too well.

The yard directly behind LaRue's home was empty, just grass, and the house on the right had an aboveground swimming pool full of water. An inflatable raft and a purple unicorn floated serenely in the calm chlorine. Mentally, I logged the position of the pool. It might come in handy.

"Suggestions?" I asked.

"Blow the place to tinder with the Amsterdam missiles in the launching pod of the van," offered Ken eagerly.

Renault grinned approval. He would.

"We go in," I stated. "But silent." I knew Christina was drained. "Raul, how's the magic?"

Bending an ear, the mage listened to his staff, obviously not pleased with the answer. "One, maybe two, major spells, then I'm kaput."

"Dome of Silence?" asked Donaher.

I nodded.

"Done," said Horta, gesturing, his staff leaving sparkle trails in the air. Tongue between lips, Tina hastily scribbled notes into her mostly blank book of spells.

Totally silent to any outside observer, we exited the RV and dashed across the street, pausing only to slap a "criminal evidence" sticker on the car before scampering up the front walk and kicking down the front door to the house. Instantly, our weapons—hell, everything metal on us—began to grow warm, hot, hotter, scalding!

"Huey, Dewey and Louie!" cried George, firing the M-60.

On the floor, I grabbed a puzzled Sanders by the arm and yanked him down with the rest of us who had ducked.

Steadily firing, George rotated in a neat circle, the .30 rifle bullets chewing a path of destruction along both walls. Then he flipped the flame-spitting muzzle upward and executed a vertical loop, getting a wall, the ceiling, and the floor.

In a searing spray of sparks, something under the floorboards shorted and our weapons cooled with astonishing speed.

"How did you know?" asked Donaher, rising and dusting off his pants.

"Induction fields have a short range," calmly stated George, unwrapping a fresh beef stick with one hand. "Didn't know where it was, but it had to be close."

Just then the chandelier released from the ceiling and crashed onto the spot we had vacated. Sanders frowned, and the rest of us chuckled. Geez, was it that old a trick?

"Suggestions?" I asked, watching the closet. That should be the next problem spot.

Even as I spoke, the door began to silently swing open. In a smooth move, Mindy drew her sword and plunged it into the door and whatever was on the other side. There came a soft whispery gasp of pain and the door closed.

"LaRue has been here," reported Jessica, releasing her forehead. "But he is gone now."

Raul and Tina agreed.

Damn, missed him by minutes. "Okay, but what did he do while he was here? Grab a book? Make a call? Get supplies?"

"Leave," she replied succinctly.

So much for that.

"But what about these traps?" asked Sanders.

Mindy informed him, "They're not traps. This is where LaRue lives. What we've encountered are simply his home defenses."

Softly in the living room, a telephone began to dial 411 entirely by itself. Before the police could be contacted, I pumped a .44 slug into the jingling Ameche. "Great for burglars, but laughable against us."

I glanced at my watch, 11:29. In sixteen minutes the world would be his to play with, and the game would not be fun for anybody else. Blink. Now fifteen minutes.

Priestly robes billowing about his legs, Donaher started to pace. "Okay. LaRue didn't stay here because he knew we could do the same thing again to him."

Thoughtfully, I rubbed fist to chin. "Then he must have gone someplace where we can't confiscate his property. Ideally, it would be a location where we have no authority."

"With no psychological data about him, we lack any way to postulate his possible modus operandi."

"He use disguise," contributed Tina.

"True," I noted. "But he also exhibits extreme intelligence and thus is unlikely to repeat a gimmick."

"Anything to go on from the robbery across the country?"

"Nope. Straight smash-and-grab runs. No finesse."

"That's not like him."

"Exactly," I agreed. "This time we are dealing with a highly motivated, intelligent enemy, who has at his resources magic and technology equal to our own.''

George tapped my shoulder. ''Ed, did I ever make that request for transfer to Clerical?''

''Sorry, it was refused. Not enough people in Clerical to process the form.''

Fourteen minutes.

On a hunch, I went to the kitchen telephone and hit the button for automatic redial. With any luck . . .

''Pizza-Pizza!'' sang out a happy voice. ''Today's special is a medium double pepperoni with anchovies for ten ninety-nine. What is your order, please?''

Sounded good, but I hung up. ''Jess, any other phones in the house?''

''No.''

''Car?''

''No.''

Double damn! LaRue knew we were hot on his trail, and how we had last beaten him. Was there any place he had legal access to where we couldn't pull the same trick twice? What did he have that we didn't? Son of a stage magician . . . a union hall? Carnival? Nyah. Bookstore owner . . . ABA convention? Librarian for the—

''Navy!'' I cried aloud.

Renault and Sanders understood at once. ''He's a member of the naval reserves! Federal agents have no authority on military bases unless they are in direct pursuit of a known felon, or they get authorization from the base CO!''

''Technical,'' muttered Raul. ''And vague. But maybe good enough for magic. Maybe.''

''We play the cards we're dealt,'' I said. If I was wrong, it meant the end of civilization. I tried not to think about that.

''Jessica, where was he stationed in the navy?'' I asked. ''That should be the only location he has actual legal access to. A reservist would have to be assigned to any other base, and register with the commanding officer.''

''Fort Hamilton,'' she replied instantly. ''But his discharge papers placed him on the U.S.S. *Intrepid*.''

''George?'' I snapped.

He shrugged. ''Beats me. I'm army.''

''The U.S.S. *Intrepid* is a World War II aircraft carrier permanently docked in the Hudson River off Manhattan,'' rattled off Father Donaher. "Moored near Forty-second Street. The vessel has been converted into a naval museum. Perfect place to find a librarian."

"How the hell do you know about the ship?" demanded Mindy.

Wryly, the big priest grinned. "I'm originally from Brooklyn. And, faith, what New Yorker doesn't know about the *Intrepid*? Sweet Mary, the ship is bigger than the GWB!"

Whatever that was. "Raul?"

"I'm on emergency reserves," said the mage wearily. "Only one medium spell remaining."

Medium, eh? Darn. "Okay," I decided. "Then forget the van and just take us to Chicago."

Ken was scandalized. "Sir, we retreat?"

"Hell no," I said, hefting my nearly empty assault rifle. "We attack!"

15

"But not naked," I amended sternly.

Faces brightened as understanding came.

While George did the legal mumbo jumbo with his FBI badge sealing the place as a crime scene, Raul drew a circle about us, chanting constantly. When Renault was done, Horta gestured and we were back in our Chicago living room.

Nine minutes to go.

"Blanco, with me!" cried Horta, stumbling towards his magic laboratory.

"I'll get the Healing potions," said Jessica, going for our small medical theatre.

"Armory," I cried, and we stumbled off towards the kitchen. Not even George stopped to get a snack. There are priorities.

Two minutes later, everybody gathered in the living room, re-armed to the max, and the broken pieces of our armor hastily replaced. We had a set of liquid nitrogen tanks for Tina, and another for Raul. Mindy was dressed in her ninja outfit of solid black, and I had a four-barrel HAFLA bazooka, plus my combo backpack. There was a spare liquid delivery system for Jess, filled with MSG/DMSO, but as a fillip we added every deadly poison we had in stock: arsenic, curare, potassium cyanide, strychnine, manticore venom and pure quill heroin. We had wisely omitted a dose of LSD, as this guy was crazy enough to begin with. No sense priming the pump when the well was already overflowing.

Plus, each of us was carrying two satchel charges of high-explosive C4 plastique. This wasn't Bureau HQ with miniature A-bombs, laser pistols or molecular disrupter wands available. But it was the very best we had on hand, and we were going for a kill.

Marching into view, George and Sanders had replaced their dinky M-60 machine rifles with bulky backpacks which cushioned shoulder hooks, a chest harness and hip supports to distribute its awesome weight. From the top of the ammo pack snaked a flexible, enclosed feed link that connected to the top of a squat, bulky rifle with a gaping pitted maw.

The weapon was a Masterson assault cannon. Designed by some mad genius at the Pentagon, the ammo packs held 18,000 caseless rounds of 20mm, armor-piercing, high-explosive mini-shells. Because they were almost too destructive to control, the Bureau had absolutely prohibited their use outside of an officially declared war.

"And where the hell did you get those?" I demanded.

"Got a friend in Ordnance," replied George, adjusting the waist strap. "You pissed?"

"Hell no! I wish you had four more of them!"

"What about regulations?"

"Screw 'em. They can fire us later."

My wife was waiting for us with jugs of Healing potion. In scandalous waste we poured the magic elixir over us. Exhaustion disappeared, wounds closed, burns healed, hair was replaced.

The potion was beyond price. Money could not buy any. You had to make it painstakingly, drop by drop, from blood, sweat and tears. Just like in the song. This little improvisational show was totally exhausting our ten-year accumulation of emergency reserves. If we lived through tonight, we would be without magical healing for months—years! If we lived. Big if. Between the Healing potion and the Strength elixir, in the morning we were going to be hospitalized for weeks.

But then, that was what an emergency reserve was for. And if this wasn't an emergency, then Noah Webster had changed the definition. Heck, I guess it was war. George was safe.

Tina came from the lab, her eyes rimmed with fatigue shadows, but her wood wand was rigid again, full of power. A moment later Raul walked into view, with a meager foot-and-a-half-long stainless-steel wand in his clenched hand.

"This is twice I've been reduced a level for fast recharge," he snarled, grabbing a jug and pouring the contents over his head, the burns and bleeding wounds washing away as common dirt. "The Bureau owes me big for this."

I acknowledged the debt. "Horace Gordon himself will put a gold star on your permanent record card."

"Oh, golly gee, really? Swell. Give me the travel book!" snapped Raul. Then for a moment, he seemed pained, and Tina went faint. George gave her a candy bar. Poor kids must be near exhaustion from all the magic they were casting.

Without looking, Jessica opened the "N" volume to the correct page and handed it to him. Flipping through "New York," the mage stared hard at the tiny photograph of the warship. Whatdayaknow, the naval museum was a tourist attraction!

"Remarkable clarity," he murmured in approval.

As he started to cast the Teleport spell, I had a flash thought that I certainly hoped the picture was taken from the shore, and not from a helicopter.

. . . and we stepped in the dark shadows of the elevated Henry Hudson Parkway in Manhattan. Before us loomed the mighty majestic outline of the *Intrepid*. Behind my team stretched the endless neon vista of Forty-second Street.

Longer than two city blocks, and tall as a skyscraper, the navy warship dwarfed the nearby office buildings and hotels into insignificance. Viewed edgewise, the massive vessel resembled an inverted metal mountain, with a small building set on top—the control island, i.e. bridge to us common folk. Truly awe-inspiring, the seemingly endless expanse of the ship was highlighted by a thousand lights strung along its colossal sides, spotlighting the control island and bristling on the shore parking lot. A hundred assorted planes filled the flight deck of the floating city, yet the parking lot was empty. Thank God for small favors.

"What kind of armament does that thing carry?" queried George, his face a mixture of fear and respect.

"The *Intrepid* was an Essex class carrier," said Ken, his eyes nearly closed. "She has four sets of twin five-inch cannons mounted two on the forecastle, two aftercastle. There are twenty-four forty-millimeter rapid-fire mini-cannons set in tandem all over the vessel, and some hundred quadruple fifty-caliber machine-gun nests."

I whistled. No wonder we had won the war.

He continued. "Modern aircraft carriers also have Phalanx antimissile cannons, nuclear missiles, Tomahawk antifort missiles, Amsterdam Mark IV all-purpose missiles, antisatellite missiles, antisubmarine missiles, antitorpedo missiles, antimissile missiles and anti-antimissile missiles."

A breath. "Normally, the *Intrepid* would carry some one hundred planes of assorted design: bombers, fighters, reconnaissance, rescue helicopters. However, in museum format, it also has an additional forty planes, of varying age and condition, on display. Corsairs, Hellcats, Delta Daggers, Bell & Howell gunships, Ashanti attack helicopters, AWACS, Harrier jumpjets and so on.''

"Armor?'' asked Donaher in a small hopeful voice.

"The landing deck top is made of twelve-inch-thick layered teakwood, coated with a special nonskid, fire-retardant chemical composition, but it can still be ignited with sufficient thermite or napalm.''

"Yes!'' cried Mindy, raising a fist.

"Under the flight deck is the hangar deck with an eighteen-inch-thick steel alloy flooring. The hull itself is thirty-six-inch layers of multiple types of military armor, backed by decompartmentalized U-frames and two-ton H-brackets.''

"Three *feet* of solid armor?''

A nod. "Yes. She's an old ship.''

Hoo boy. "How many levels are there?'' asked Jess, gazing at the titanic vessel as if trying to guess for herself.

"Fifteen,'' replied Sanders. "Eight below the flight deck and seven on the command island; from Crash Control to the crow's nest beneath the radar antennas. Eight hundred and twenty feet long, it can carry a crew of thirty-five hundred.''

"Worthy of the Soviet fleet!'' said Tina with a touch of patriotism creeping into her voice. Expelled for being a mage or not, home was in your heart, not under your feet.

"And how do you know all this?'' I asked. "Ex-navy?''

Lieutenant Colonel Sanders pointed a muscular finger towards the distant blackness. "There's a small sign giving the pertinent details over there by the ticket booth.''

I tried not to show my astonishment. He could read a sign in the dark at over two hundred feet away?

"However,'' added Jessica slowly. "There are only thirty guards on duty tonight.''

"Are they alive?'' asked George.

"I'm not sure,'' hedged my wife. "I sense life, but not exactly in any form I am familiar with.''

"Cocooned? Metamorphosing? Possessed?'' asked Donaher, concerned. "Zombies? Protestants?''

"Yes. No. I don't know!'' Jess seemed uneasy. "I can only say that the guards are conscious. And hostile.''

Checking the safety, I worked the bolt on the M-16. "Then

we have to count the sailors as dead men controlled by LaRue and kill them on sight.''

This stratagem sat well with nobody. Reality rarely did.

As I scanned the foredeck of the gigantic vessel, I noticed one of the jet fighters bend a wing to scratch its prow. Aw shit.

"It's the exhibits that you sense, Jess," I told her. "The planes are animate. Especially the jet fighters."

"Annoying," said George confidently. "But as this is a museum, none of them have any ammo for their guns."

Grandly, I gestured. "Then you go first."

"Ah, perhaps tomorrow?"

Five minutes to go. How could we get on without being noticed? The carpeted gangplank was extended, the sixty feet of roped-off ramp well enough lit to read a book of regulations by. Ha. It made me laugh. Ah, we could just shrink down to mice size and run on board!

No. The gangplank and anchor chains have rat-proof baffles and sensors, sent Jessica. *Ditto the mooring lines and power cables.*

Good security. Too damn good. Phooey on the navy.

"Jess, can't you get a reading on LaRue?"

She shook her head. "Impossible. His mind is so jumbled between the alchemical potions, his new magic, the mixed personalities and the influence of the book that he is nothing but telepathic hash. His thoughts blend into the background murmur of the city."

Boy, this guy was tough to find. Hmm, we could turn invisible and fly in past the planes. Wasteful of magic and extremely dangerous, between the sensors of the *Intrepid* and all those warplanes, we would almost certainly be caught. Make a magic door in the hull? No, too thick. Use a Meld? No, too many people. This was infuriating! Bureau 13 headquarters was situated somewhere in New York City. But if I used my wristwatch, the Tanner part of LaRue would know instantly. Briefly, I weighed surprise against a direct mass attack. We couldn't summon help once he started the spell, since all lines of magical communications would go down. What the hell, let's go for the gold. Sigh. It would be nice to watch a battle from the sidelines for once.

Stroking my necktie, I produced a quarter and handed it to Donaher. "We're gonna need an air strike. Father, go find a public phone and call the local FBI office. Tell them we have a terrorist team on board the *Intrepid* with biological weapons. Request an immediate bombardment. Blow the ship out of the water. The code is . . . ah . . . um, oh heck . . .''

"Faith, I know the proper code," said the priest, and he became one with the shadows. Eh?

Mindy has been tutoring him, supplied my wife.

Ah, that explained it.

A minute later, Mike reappeared.

"No good," panted Donaher, breathless from his run. "Apparently, the phone system is down."

"A la Tanner LaRue," snorted Mindy.

Then to hell with security. I activated my watch. "Alert! This is a Priority One call. The situation is Alpha Four, repeat, Alpha Four! Respond, please!"

Static answered me. Not even a carrier wave signal. What the hell. It had been worth a try.

With obvious intent, George primed the action on his Masterson, its bulky backpack making him resemble Donaher in the dark. "There's a bank nearby. Want me to rudely summon the cops?"

"Against this guy?" I retorted. "No. We got to take him ourselves."

"We did not fare too well last time," reminded Ken, his hands moving restlessly along the encased feeder belt to his Masterson assault cannon in a kind of military rosary.

On the port railing, the Harrier sharply whistled, and a French Saber, a Delta Dagger and a Spitfire joined it at the gunwales. Something old, something new, something borrowed and something blue. The four fighters watched the dock with particular intent. My radio broadcast had been heard.

I glanced at my watch. Sweet Jesus! Time was ticking away, no assistance from either the Bureau or standard military was possible and I still had no idea how to get on board the ship without dying—a prime prerequisite for us.

"Sanders, what else is on that bulletin board sign?" asked Father Donaher curiously.

He gazed in the proper direction. "The times the museum is open to the public, prices for admission, a simplified sketch of the carrier and several photographs."

"Of?"

"The first captain, two major battles in the South Pacific and some interior shots."

"Interior!" breathed Mindy. "Sanders, you dolt!"

The man mountain was confused. "What did I do?"

Rummaging in his haversack of munitions, George produced a set of night binoculars and gave them to Raul. Frantically, the mage studied the distance sign.

"With a photograph, we can teleport inside, bypassing the defenses!"

In shame, Ken hung his head. "Oh. Yes. Sorry."

"No problem, kid," I said, watching an assault helicopter lift into view off the flight deck. "That's why you're still a student and not out on your own yet." Two more gunships swiftly followed. Briefly, I wondered if my insurance premiums were fully paid.

"Well, Mr. Wizard?" asked Donaher.

Minutely rotating the dial, the mage fine-adjusted the focus. "I think . . . no, that's . . . yes! The engine room!"

Just then a dozen planes launched from the carrier. A cumbersome double-prop Bell & Howell helicopter, a bulky Grumman Hellcat, a Curtis two-man Helldiver, two Corsairs, a sleek Harrier jumpjet, a squat Spitfire and a Japanese Zero. Half of them were antiques, propeller-driven logs made of wood and cloth. Yet, massed together, the assemblage of airplanes had sufficient firepower to level west Manhattan. But only if LaRue had taken the time to conjure them ammunition.

He had.

Banking sharply in the starry sky, the Harrier angled for an attack run and the street exploded, chunks of macadam jumping into the air. Parked cars fireballed in a steady progression of violent detonations, the stout wire fence about the carrier was torn to pieces and massive chunks of concrete were torn from the parkway overhead. Boulders of roadway crashed into the street before us. Helpless, I gritted my teeth and cursed. Freaking jet was firing blind! Probably thought we were invisible. An off-duty taxicab turned the corner and was promptly annihilated. More civilians were dying!

I was going to kill LaRue with my bare hands! Twice! And then do it again!

"Raul, teleport us now!" I shouted as metal decks and walls appeared around us.

In the muted rumble of the house-size engines surrounding us, the mage rested an arm casually on an operating fuel pump the size of a watermelon. "Gosh, what a swell idea."

Ruefully, I forced a grin. "Sorry."

A simple catwalk led straight down the middle of the twelve towering gas turbines which filled the engine room with their throbbing presence. The air was pungent with the oily smell of diesel fuel and hot metal, tainted with the bitter stink of ozone. Steam pipes capable of conveying a whale joined collector reservoirs above us in a soaring archway of leviathan plumbing. Power transformers that could have electrified a city crackled inside safety cages made of industrial-gauge insulated wire. Bigger-than-a-buffalo bus bars glowed from the ionization effect of the tremendous voltage passing through them to the drive motors below. I could not even begin to calculate how much pressure these furnaces had to generate in order to push the giant turbines which supplied the staggering electrical current needed to power the behemoth motors which moved a ship as big as the *Intrepid*.

Passing a workstation of controls and tools, we prepped for battle and started for the oval steel door set in the metal bulkhead.

Hatchway, supplied Jess.

Thank you, O fount of wisdom.

'Sokay.

"Kill on sight," I reminded them. "No dicking around." And the thick hatch slammed in our faces, its spoked-wheel handle spinning to latch and dog the lock shut.

"Red alert," said a calm voice over a PA speaker set in the ceiling. "Intruders in the engine room."

Donaher muttered something in Latin, and it didn't sound like a blessing to me.

"How could they have found us so fast?" demanded Mindy, sword in hands. A rainbow of colors played along the deadly curved length. When she got nervous, it did also.

"The ship told him," said Jess softly, both arms wrapped round her chest.

"Eh?" I spun about. "What was that?"

"The ship," she repeated. "It's alive. Same as the planes."

I broke four regulations by shouting, "The whole freaking aircraft carrier is sentient!?"

In response, the lights dimmed. The titanic engines revved to thundering fury. An intake valve snapped open, and billowing clouds of hot exhaust fumes from the diesel engines spewed forth gentle as a summer breeze from hell.

Coughing and hacking, we retreated from the noxious fumes as a distant humming made itself felt in the perforated metal deck.

The harsh vibration was augmented by a crackle of sheet lightning and the howl of rising winds.

Wilson LaRue had started the spell again.

16

Half blind from the deadly exhaust vomiting from the hundred giant diesel turbines, we took refuge in a clear area with nothing overhead but bare ceiling. We had some rough idea of what to expect, having fought living houses before. But an animate warship? This was an experience I would have gladly denied myself. Suddenly, a transfer to Clerical didn't sound like such a bad career move.

The PA speaker continued to bleat a warning until Mindy sliced it off the wall with her sword. Lifting the face shields of our helmets, we tied handkerchiefs over our noses and mouths to get a bit of respite. But we had to move fast or die of plain old-fashioned asphyxiation. Crude but effective.

Retaining bolts spinning by themselves, a huge tool rack fell from a bulkhead and almost crushed Raul, but he jumped out of the way. A pipe burst, spraying Donaher in the back with scalding steam. His cassock dissolved, and Mike gave a howl, but his body armor held and the priest lived. Wiggling like a canvas snake, a fire hose tried to strangle Jessica. She gutted it with her pocketknife. The spring assembly on a pump snapped free and nearly succeeded in punching a hole through my helmet. A rolling chair rammed Tina's leg, cracking her shin armor, and a supply cabinet door slammed open, nearly succeeding in swatting Sanders flat. I pumped a few rounds into a trash can that seemed to be loitering suspiciously near us, and Raul cast a Seal spell on a wooden locker full of power tools. Dancing chain saws we did not need.

Steam spurted from joints at irregular intervals, keeping us hopping. The exhaust fumes grew thick enough to chew. Raw fuel got George in the face mask and dripped onto his weapon. Donaher washed the highly flammable fluid off the Masterson with his holy-water pistol. Smart move.

Unexpectedly, at every corner and crevice, sparks jumped from deck to wall, and our hair began to stick straight out from our heads. I guess a few trillion volts were being shunted through the floor. Our shoes were insulated against such an old attack, but if we even fleetingly touched anything made of metal directly connected to the ship with our bare skin—*poof!* Instant barbecued agent. Retirement option #37, if I remember correctly.

Nobody was stupid enough to try and shoot the vessel. Bullets would simply ricochet off the metal walls and might finish the job the carrier was so valiantly trying to do. We had plenty of explosives and two primed mages, but so what? How the hell do you kill a 250,000-ton ship? Stab it with the Eiffel Tower?

The noise of air vents sucking in and exhaust pipes blowing out sounded like breathing, and that gave me an idea. If magic followed the intent, not the letter, and the ship was alive, then it had a heart equivalent. I glanced around at the turbines and engines towering above us. Here most likely. Yeah. The bridge would be the brain, radar its eyes and the fuel tanks its stomach.

"Gloves!" I cried, pulling on my kid-leather beauties.

Ken grabbed a pair of engineer's gloves from a worktable and wrestled them on, George produced electrical mittens and Tina donned her velvet/iron slammers over her insulated lab gloves. Together, the four of us managed to pry the cover off a fuel vapor exchange unit. Normally, this piece of machinery trapped rising fuel vapors and condensed them for return to storage. But I had a different function in mind.

"Jess, whack it!"

Shoving the nozzle of her spray gun down the pipe, she triggered the spray. In seconds, a loud knocking sounded from all around us. Rapidly, it grew in volume and tempo. The engines revved to overload, and the lights began flashing insanely. The vessel rocked from side to side as if in a storm on the high seas, and we slipped and slid on the rough floor fighting to keep our footing on the deadly electrified deck. Jessica lost her balance, and Mindy kicked my wife upright. Wrapping her armored legs tight around the big fuel pipe, Jess shoved the spray gun in deeper and locked the trigger into position.

Klaxons rang, sirens howled, alarms buzzed, the hatch slammed open and shut. Every valve in the place was spinning wildly. On the control board, switches flipped, buttons rose and depressed, dials turned, yet every meter hit the red line and went beyond. In rattling fury, the entire cubic mile of navy property gave a mighty shiver, decks buckling and walls cracking. Then the vessel went still, and in faltering stages, the engines slowed to a halt, the lights gradually dimmed and went out.

Darkness and peace engulfed us.

A second later, the battery lights came on, illuminating hatchways, control panels and not much more. But it was an automatic programmed response. The ship was dead.

The MSG and DMSO couldn't have done much, but there was enough assorted poison in that mixture to kill an army battalion of rabid rhinos. Just about the correct amount for a sentient aircraft carrier.

Then again, maybe the ship was only stunned.

"Triple time, harch," I whispered. "George and Sanders on point. Donaher and Blanco take the rear. One-meter spread. Silent. Stop for nothing."

As the team got into order, Jess removed her empty tanks and set them in a utility closet. Not used in the manner planned, the poison spray had still saved our butts. Lucky we had it along. I had thought of two other ways to kill the ship, but each had been more chancy and dangerous than the other. Besides, I didn't have an atomic bomb or a cucumber on me.

Now the humming of the siphon vortex was clearly audible, and both our mages began sliding across the floor sideways. I smiled. As LaRue drained the world of magic, at close range the spell was sucking in our mages. We could find LaRue easy as floating with the currents of a river. Just had to do it fast.

Sprinting down the dim main corridor, Donaher tried a running exorcism, to no avail. Either LaRue was too powerful for him, unlikely, or else alchemy had been used to animate the warplanes. Nothing the Catholic priest could do about that.

Bypassing a freight ramp, Raul and Tina angled to the right, and we followed. Mastersons at the ready, Sanders and Renault covered each other as they swept constantly forward, searching for danger, or LaRue.

The team went up a level to Storage, then on to Ammunition. It was empty. Damn. I had possessed a fleeting hope of blowing the ship to smithereens with its own explosives. Sleeping quarters came next. As we broached an intersection with stairs and an elevator, Ken and George jerked to a halt. A raised hand with fingers upright stopped the rest of us, and a closed fist made us gather together. Creeping forward, I peeked round the corner to see what they had spotted.

Silver and sleek, a Harrier jumpjet was stalking along the

corridor, its delta wings held flat to its fuselage like the wings
of a bird. The wheeled landing gear was extending and contracting in a gross pantomime of walking. The British jet fighter
nearly filled the passageway, it was so big. And close behind
was a stubby yellow Corsair and a tiger-striped Hellcat.

"This is bad," said George, prepping the Masterson.

"How so?" I asked, checking the load on my Magnum 66.
The small-caliber tumblers of the M-16 and the wooden bullets
of the .44 AutoMag wouldn't scratch the paint of a Harrier.

"Most of these planes are incredibly easy to destroy," he
explained. "Especially the jet fighter. A single HE round into
the main turbine and they'll tear themselves apart to explode."

Ken raised an eyebrow. "Sounds great."

"We're in a steel corridor," said Renault, tapping the wall
with a knuckle. "When a plane detonates, the debris will go
fore and aft."

"Like a shotgun blast," said Donaher.

Tina added, "With us sitting in muzzle."

"Great. Well, we have to shoot to protect ourselves. So, any
suggestions?"

"Fire and duck?"

That was hardly a masterful strategy whose clever feints and
ploys would leave the enemy gasping in shock, but it sounded
faintly plausible. Our armor could take a lot of punishment. And
our options were severely limited.

"What the hey. Pass the word."

But then, suddenly feeling extremely clever, I turned and
ripped the cover off an air vent. With the infrared visor of my
helmet, I could see razor-sharp metal plates studding the vent-
way along its whole length. I stood and frowned. Damn navy
efficiency! They probably had barbed bars in the bilge, spikes
in the sewage pipes, daggers in the drains and forked flails in
the flues. I know I would. But then, I'm paranoid.

"The currents go this way!" shouted Raul, and we happily
ran away. Discretion and valor, yep, that's us.

The dim lights worked for us, making it difficult for the warplanes to spot their targets. At least, for the older planes. The
Harrier and the Ashanti helicopter had chemical/thermal scan-
ners and infrared viewers better than what we had in our van.
And if the planes thought of using their sonic guidance systems,
they'd have us in a minute.

Just then a small red missile on a column of flame and smoke shot by the end of the corridor we were in. A moment later, another turned to curve into our passageway. Holy Hannah, a heat seeker!

From the waist, I fired my 40mm shell hoping for a lucky shot and Donaher triggered his flamethrower attempting to prematurely detonate the warhead. Frantically, Raul threw a fistful of coins, and a steel wall appeared directly in front of us. Mike cut the flames. One second later, the wall violently exploded, the concussion hurling us brutally to the floor. Flames cooked the air from our lungs and shrapnel pounded us mercilessly.

Lying limp on the deck, I ached in every part of my body. But I was alive. Technically, at least. My clothes were black with blood, the stains spreading. Frightened, I grabbed my neck but apparently my anti-vampire collar had deflected most of the fléchettes.

Crawling on hands and knees, Blanco gathered some blood from everybody on a strip torn from her uniform. Then neatly tearing the cloth into eight pieces, she breathed heavily upon them and stared with visible force.

"Go!" she bellowed in a Voice of Command. "Rise and run until you die!"

Obediently, the drops of our blood stood tall, and exact duplicates of the team dashed away down the far corridor. A barrage of yammering machine guns, rapid-fire cannons and explosions greeted their appearance. Gradually, the sound of battle faded into the distance.

"Nice . . . move," moaned Raul, using his staff to lever himself erect.

"Thanks," she croaked. "You also."

Assisting each other to stand, we shambled along, still following the current. En route, the team effected repairs as best we could. Wearily, Jessica dropped some of her combat armor to lessen her weight load. Lithe and beautiful, my wife was nót a muscle-bound samurai like Mindy and had limits.

Going up a dark staircase, we moved silent as possible along a main-access corridor, then took a branch hallway and went north. The ethereal flow was becoming thicker, almost visibly dense. Tendrils and streamers of wispy fireworks flowing swiftly onward, ever forward.

At an intersection, we hid in a map room as a lumbering French Saber interceptor moved past us. It was so close, I could read the serial numbers stenciled on the missiles tucked under the clipped delta wings, and the museum plate attached to the white-striped fuselage. The brass square detailed the noble craft's history, evolution and attributes. Unfortunately, the plate did not list any known weaknesses. An oversight, surely.

And there was nobody in the pilot or copilot's seat.

Where were the guards?

Silent, Renault proffered his Masterson, but I shook my head vehemently no. Whether by alchemy or the magic of the Aztec book, these planes were fueled and brimming with armament. When one died, they would let the whole world know. At a range of two feet away, the resulting blast could make us go permanently deaf.

Try again, bucko, sent Jess. *They'd be mopping us off the walls with a sponge. If even that!*

True, but I'm an optimist.

The river of magic took us further into the great ship, and eventually we had to loop our belts through those of the mages to keep them from being physically hauled into the air by the powerful eddies of concentrated magic.

Tagging along after our human kites, we were pulled past a corner only to find half a dozen warplanes waiting for us. Even as the team frantically scampered back round the corner, the massed fighters opened with gun and cannon. With propellers spinning, it was like staring into the mouth of an angry garbage disposal full of firecrackers.

"We must be close to LaRue," noted Donaher, peeking past the edge of the metal wall and triggering a burning arc of jellied gasoline towards the airships.

As both of the Mastersons were speaking, I withheld comment. Reaching over my shoulder, I grabbed a plastic tube with no fluted ends and gave them a LAW. Streaking in between a Corsair and the Harrier, a Curtis Helldiver was hit and went to its namesake. Damn, I had been aiming for the Harrier. And advancing from behind the burning wreck of the old Grumman antique was a state-of-the-art Grumman Tomcat, currently the finest fighting plane in existence. That thing used a Harrier for target practice! What the bloody freaking hell was a line-ship like the Tomcat doing in a goddamn navy museum? An exhibition?

"Trouble with a capital *T*," said George as a .50 round banged off his helmet, knocking him askew. The muzzle of his weapon went wild for a second, the armor-piercing shells chewing paths of destruction in decks and bulkheads.

"Got a clever plan, Mr. Renault?" asked Ken, calmly triggering controlled bursts of caseless HE.

I did. "Don't die, and win!"

"Good plan."

"Thanks. I got it off a gum wrapper."

Our weapons kept a constant barrage going, and it was not a problem hitting the planes. This was easy as shooting ducks in a barrel. Only these ducks shot back, more, and better.

Holding on to a stanchion with both hands, Tina exclaimed something in Russian and mage.

"Will that work?" asked Jessica, our universal translator.

Feet braced against a hatchway, Raul strained to hold on. "How do I know? Nobody was ever dumb enough to try before!"

"Do it!" cried Blanco.

Stretching from their precarious positions, the two mages managed to grab hands as racing lines of ethereal power poured straight through them. In unison, they began to chant, and the majority of streamers now arced around the pair. The few glowing ribbons that went in didn't come out the other side.

Firing off another 40mm shell of thermite, I nearly did a dance. Holy mother of pearl, the two were retaining snatches of the limitless energy flowing past them. Recharging themselves to who knew what level of magic. And the closer we got to the nexus, the more ethereal power would pour into them. It wouldn't work against LaRue, he'd only absorb the energy. But it might save our butts in this particular instance.

"Kill those planes!" shouted Blanco, internally glowing from the endless power passing through her trembling form.

George and Sanders gave a start, then boldly charged towards the amassed fighter/interceptors.

Bullets bounced off their adamantine bodies, missiles impacted and only crumpled their warheads—no explosion. Repaired and backed by the quintessential, concentrated river of magic, the two indestructible soldiers waded forward, their Masterson assault cannons firing nonstop. Over four thousand rounds a minute of armor-piercing, high-explosive, caseless ammunition spewing from the pitted maws of the deadly weapons.

The oncoming missiles were shredded, the explosion and shrapnel forced back towards the warplanes. The jets cut loose with everything they had: missiles, rockets, 40mm shells, .50 rounds, .75 depleted uranium slugs, blinding magnesium flares. The determined planes even dropped their payloads of bombs onto the deck beneath them, the tons of high-explosive thermite and napalm blockbusters only adding to the general destruction.

Boldly marching, the two soldiers took it all and gave it back, compounded with interest, their bulky coffers of ammunition refilled the microsecond the packs were exhausted.

Indomitable, the pair advanced upon the clustered million-dollar jet fighters. And as each machine was drained of ammo, it was destroyed. The Saber was torn to bits under the horizontal rain of 20mm rounds, its fuselage split apart and the fuel tanks exploded into a strident fireball. The Hellcat and the Corsair were slammed against the bulkheads and burst into kindling. Ripping free from their mountings, the great motors bounded along the corridor as insane things, the spinning propellers smacking into the deck and bulkheads, throwing the roaring engines hither and yon, with no rhythm or reason.

Nimbly, Ken ducked under a ton of spinning metal, and George tracked the other engine's wild flight, peppering the motor with caseless HE rounds until it jammed and burst. The Delta Dagger died next, then the Corsair and the Harrier. A chunk of canopy went skidding by and I saluted the tiny American flag painted on the Armorlite windshield as it passed. So I'm a patriot. Sue me.

Incredibly, the Tomcat turned tail, shoved its wings into a pair of opposite hatchways and throttled up both engines.

"Oh shit!" cried George.

"What?" I shouted, banging away with my .357 Magnum.

"Know the difference between a flamethrower and a jet engine?"

"*Nyet!*"

"A flamethrower doesn't have as much hard thrust!"

Uh-oh. Time to fry.

And the twin turbo engines seemed to disintegrate into a boiling wave of reddish flame that completely filled the corridor, as the Tomcat blew hundreds of gallons of half-burned fuel out its turbines in a last great effort to toast us alive.

The very force of the flames served to deflect the 20mm rounds from the Mastersons. So Raul and Tina upped their chanting, and George and Ken dug their heels into the metal deck. Step by step, meter by meter, they charged straight into those yawning pits of hell, and shoved the stuttering muzzles of their dire weapons straight into the thundering engines!

There immediately followed a quite spectacular explosion.

When I could see and hear again, only a steaming hole in the twisted metal deck remained of the rogue defenders. The Tomcat was totally destroyed, plane and simple.

Ugh! sent Jessica.

Sorry, it had to be said.

No, it didn't.

Gathering ourselves together, we grabbed ahold of the mages, and the team levitated over the jagged gap to land on the smooth undamaged deck beyond. Ahead of us was a set of double doors large enough to comfortably pass a cargo plane. And on the wall a neatly stenciled sign told why.

"Vehicle Storage?" cried Mindy.

Exasperated, Donaher rolled his Irish-green eyes. "Saints preserve us! This is where they park the squadrons of extra planes. Hundreds of them!"

Panting from the constant exertion of keeping the two mages in tow, I thumbed my last 40mm round into the breech of the grenade launcher. It was a special shell that I had been reserving for Mr. LaRue, a low-yield explosive canister of an outstandingly virulent military nerve gas outlawed by the U.N. Security Council as inhumanly painful and deadly. If this didn't kill Wild Willy, then he deserved to rule the earth. Or, at least six feet of it, positioned directly over his head.

"Screw the planes!" I snarled, clicking the breech shut. "Let's take the bastard!"

The doors were thick, veined steel, but two satchel charges and a LAW did the trick, and we stormed into the acrid smoke just as the ethereal winds died.

Utilizing fully half of the carrier's middle deck, the vast place was mostly empty, with only a poor navy jeep sporting a mounted .50 machine gun waiting for us. That trifle hardly even slowed us.

Standing there in a sketchy pentagram was Wilson LaRue, three times human size and glowing as if he were fluorescent, torrents of scintillating mystical energy pouring into him from every direction. And sprawled about him were the guards.

Or, rather, what remained of them.

Lying on the deck, the humans were physically linked to form a pentagram about the mad alchemist, their hands fused together into an unbroken circle of flesh. And bits of the guards were missing, eyes from one, hair from another, the chest of a third. Lacking critical ingredients from his laboratory, LaRue must have made do with live human beings for his hellish diagram.

But not everyone was dead. Scattered about in the five-pointed star, a few still moaned or screamed in their torment. Living links in the corpse chain.

His hated visage filled my sight and even as I raised my gun, God help me, I paused for a moment, desperately fighting the swirling emotions within. LaRue had to die, would die, but it meant killing more civilians. I could have gunned down my beloved Jessica without a qualm if it got Wilson also. That was our job. But we were sworn to die if it meant saving a single innocent life. And it took me, all of us, a full solid second to overcome that oath of allegiance.

Which was what LaRue had probably been hoping for.

Even as we fired, a last wisp of visible magic snaked across the hangar to enter his body. Suddenly, Raul and Tina slumped to the deck unconscious, my sunglasses went dark, Mindy's sword ceased its rainbow display, my body armor became fantastically heavy and a copper bracelet fell off George's wrist.

"Success," said LaRue, watching the lightning play between his fingers with mad eyes. "Success! *Success!*"

It was over. The spell was done. And Wilson LaRue possessed every last drop of magic on Earth.

We had lost . . .

17

. . . the battle, not the war. Ruthlessly, I pumped the nerve-gas grenade at LaRue. Not even looking in my direction, he caught the projectile and tossed it into his mouth, munching on the 40mm shell as if it were a gumdrop. Wisps of vapor spurted from round his lips. Then I smacked myself in the head. Chemical weapons against an alchemist? Alvarez, you putz!

Aiming so as not to kill, Father Donaher hosed the legs of the mage with flame, and both Mastersons cut loose, a fusillade of explosions peppering the kimono-wearing space suit. Not much damage was done to either.

"Routine four!" I shouted, dropping the spent M-203 and unlimbering my heavy HAFLA four-shot.

The team separated and attacked from different directions.

Callously, LaRue threw a lightning bolt, and it missed Jessica by a yard. He seemed as surprised as she. Stupid librarian didn't yet realize it took practice, and lots of it, to control the higher magiks. LaRue may have the power of a god, but not the skill. Like a baby with a bazooka, he was more dangerous to himself than to us. So we still had a fighting chance. But it decreased with every passing moment.

A HAFLA rocket impacted on the ceiling above LaRue, raining napalm down upon him. His clothes and hair caught fire.

Ken sprinted off into the distance. Trying to get behind our foe, I thought, but then he circled completely about and rejoined us. That was when I noticed his spray gun was pointed at the ceiling. I glanced up and saw a sizzling ring in the steel deck above LaRue. Obviously, we had had similar ideas.

With a loud metallic crack, twenty tons of metallic plating plummeted onto the nasty nitwit, crushing him flatter than a bug under your shoe heel.

We shouted in victory.

Then the steel disk levitated into the air and the ceiling coalesced into a homogeneous whole. Smiling in a cocky manner,

LaRue stood as before, quite undamaged. His kimono and battlesuit weren't even rumpled. Hoo boy.

On command, my team threw the satchel charges, and as they hurtled towards the mage, the canvas packs became smaller and smaller until button size, and the bags landed at his black boots and went snap-snap-snap.

I let fly the three remaining HAFLA rockets, tossed the launcher and cut loose with the .44 AutoMag, spent shells the size of cigar butts jerking from the injector port.

During this, Jessica had been steadily firing her Uzi at the madman, the 9mm Parabellums flattening against his body and staying there like little lead buttons.

Holstering the empty .44, I shrugged and started triggering my twin Magnums at the walls, angling for a ricochet. Maybe his shield, or whatever, only operated in the front. But the heavy-duty combat slugs merely hit his back as roses, the harmless bouquet falling limply to the deck as if some pagan offering.

In a tumbling roll, Mindy sliced the man in half along the waist with her sword, and then rolled away again. Blood spurted for only a moment. Mages were always quick healers. As the only mage alive, I guess his repair factor was magnified geometrically. What we needed was a full body death blow.

Or a Brain Blast. Yeah.

Turning, he gestured and twin saber-toothed tigers leapt from his palms. Suddenly, Mindy was embroiled in her own private war.

Now in his right hand there appeared a crystal staff. No, a diamond staff, with a crystal ball atop, the illuminated globe pulsating with shimmering radiance. Eek!

"Jessica to me!" I cried, and she came arunning, firing every step of the way.

Hydrofluoric acid tanks empty, Ken slapped the chest release button and threw the entire assembly at LaRue. Leveling his wand, the tanks, hose and spray gun stopped in flight and streaked backwards at Sanders. He ducked, and they lowered in trajectory. Kneeling motionless, at the very last second he jumped straight up, and the equipment impacted into the deck, indenting the thick metal floor in a meteoric strike.

Shotgun and pistols maintained a steady discharge. In the background, the tiger growls were down to meows, and in bloody sword slashes they soon ceased. LaRue cast a Flame Lance, an Ice Storm, Flesh-to-Stone and a couple of modified Death spells.

Only hitting the bulkheads, the lethal conjures dispersed in the standard gay pyrotechnics of a failed spell. But the armored walls were discolored from the raw brute force of the magic.

"Mine is the only voice you can hear," I said softly, pulling my small wife close. "Mine the only voice which commands." Jessica's face softened as she entered the primary stage of the trance.

Grenades raining around him, LaRue erected a prismatic dome. Mike rolled a bottle of holy oil under the bottom lip of the dome, LaRue stomped on it and slipped, nearly falling. With his bare fists, Sanders pummeled the dome with trip-hammer blows, making the magic green barrier ring. A transdimensional portal appeared in the air and out charged a huge roaring hydra, standing bigger than LaRue. The legendary dragon's seven heads writhed and hissed, as some drooled acid or poison, others breathed frost or belched flame, one screamed with sonic fury, another stared at us hypnotically and the biggest launched a salvo of spines from its brow. Crouching low, Jennings stabbed Wilson in the boot with a poisoned dagger. With a yelp, the portal winked out and the horrid beast faded away. Whew. Thankfully, this was a private party. Attendance by invitation only.

Donaher slid his wristwatch to Mindy, who stuffed it and hers under the dome. Ken added his, bodily grabbed the prismatic shield and slammed it flat against the deck. There was a loud whump, the dome bulged and jumped.

Then the curved shield vanished and an angry smoking LaRue let off a Body Boom. With only tatters of cloth clinging to their combat armor, my friends went flying. In a wild frenzy, LaRue fired an uncoordinated barrage of red laser beams and golden disrupter rays. The lasers slagged holes in deck and walls everywhere. The touch of the disrupters made the ship metal implode with violent fury. The alchemist didn't hit anybody, but my .44 AutoMag and holster were disintegrated, and my helmet was blown off my head with stunning force. As recommended by Renault, I had left the chin strap dangling, just for this type of situation. Too many soldiers in the past had lost their heads in battle trying to look prim and proper, instead of being comfortable and functional.

"The command phrase is 'Armageddon,'" I spoke fast and low, using my aching jaw as little as possible. "The activation word is 'Apocalypse.'"

Sitting upright, Tina fired her Bureau special derringer into

LaRue's stomach. The composite mage staggered, and then Raul stood. Swinging his drained staff in the manner of a baseball bat, he bent the steel shaft over the alchemist's head. Wilson fell trembling to his knees, and a thorny thicket sprang into existence around Horta. Instantly, I heard Raul trying to start a motorized hedge trimmer. A garish light encased Blanco, and she slumped to the deck.

This was going to be close.

"Jessica, the go code is—"

. . . and searing agony hit me in hands and feet. Dimly through the red fog of pain, I could tell I was now stark naked and against the cold metal wall of the hangar, steel spikes driven through my wrists and ankles. More were positioned under my armpits, groin and knees. There was no way I was going to fall free. And the rest of my team was pinned spread-eagled along the wall, hanging helpless as animal skins on display.

"Surprise," wheezed LaRue, a trickle of blood oozing down his cheek. "I win."

Panting for breath, his staff pulsing, Wilson stood whole and healed. His battlesuit spotless, the kimono pressed and crisp.

"And none will be allowed to die!" he screamed, spittle spraying from his mouth. "Ever! Ever, ever, ever!" Deep breaths. "Until I know more, all, about this Aztec book and the Bureau 13 which once captured it."

Struggling against the racking throbs in my limbs, I tried to tell him to stick it where the sun don't shine, but fainted instead.

Ice-cold water splashed onto me, and I came awake shivering, trembling and nailed to the wall. No, it had not been a terrible nightmare. Argh.

Human size once more, LaRue eyed us dispassionately.

"You have given me a great deal of trouble," he said with deceptive calm. "But a god has no need for revenge. Tell me what I want to know about this possible danger, and I will kill you painlessly. This, I solemnly promise. Where is the Bureau located? Who is in charge? What resources do they possess?"

Somehow, this time I did manage to give him the proper directions for insertion, and George added a fillip about his mother and a diseased camel.

Amused, Wilson only laughed. "Ah, I see the loss of blood has made you irritable. Well, let's cauterize those nasty wounds."

And the spikes glowed white hot. I writhed from the unbearable agony, then choked and vomited from the stink of my own roasting flesh. Somewhere in the distance, I heard other members of my team screaming and crying. But I was lost in my private world of pain and could think of nothing else.

A million years later, the spikes cooled and I weakly returned to panting, sweaty consciousness. LaRue had us trapped and was trying to wring out information we wouldn't give him even if we had known it. Our Bureau-implanted mind blocks prevented him from reading our thoughts. Not even the dread Mind Rape could get the data he wanted. He could only kill us. Eventually.

"Perhaps you do not fully realize the situation," LaRue stated dramatically. "With but a gesture, I have countered every bit of the damage done in our little altercation and repaired my loyal fleet of warplanes. They are now also armed with forceshields and lasers, an oversight I will not repeat. Any rescue attempt will be met with massive resistance. And if necessary, I will take part. I learn from my mistakes."

Talkative bastard. But then, amateurs always were.

Summoning her resolve, Tina spit at LaRue, and Donaher hit him with one of those damn-your-soul-to-perdition curses that only a fighting-mad Catholic Irish priest ever seems to be able to do correctly. And this one was a doozy. It could have boiled water at twenty paces.

Frowning in annoyance, Wilson glared, and the priest became bumpy from head to toes. Then the freckled skin burst as thousands of barbed quills slowly grew out of his skin. The priest screamed for an eternity. Then LaRue blinked and Donaher was as before. Only much paler.

"I was hoping you would become my first priest convert. Perhaps even my pope!" offered the sly mage. "Your false lord will not save you. Worship me, and you may have Ireland for your very own! Mayhap England as well! I am generous to those who are loyal."

Father Donaher got so furious, he couldn't speak for a moment, so Mindy pinch-hit for her friend and rattled off a long phrase in Japanese. Whatever she said, it must have been good, 'cause LaRue gasped and bathed her naked form with a flickering cone of purple light from his staff. In silent torment, Jennings began to split apart like rotten fruit.

Shutting my ears to the noise, I turned my head to avoid watching. The finest fighting team the Bureau had, and we were only toys for him to play with. There was no rescue coming, no hope of escape. And death would not be quick, no matter what he said. We had failed. Totally. Utterly.

I had done it before jokingly, but now I silently offered my soul to anybody, anybody at all—good, evil, or indifferent—if they would only give us one last fighting chance. As always, silence was the only response.

The howls stopped, and Mindy hung limp from her spikes, great open festering wounds lining her body.

"Answer me!" yelled LaRue in childish impatience. "Haven't you had enough? You have no more magic! You are only normal humans now!" His brows furrowed. "Or are you?"

Gliding closer, his wand played a spectrum of lights over our tortured forms. "Ah, this man is a human, but his wife is a telepath! The muscular bitch with the big mouth is a martial artist of some kind. Fatso is a professional soldier, and of course the big redhead is a cleric!"

LaRue placed a hand akimbo. "What a strange band you are! This man is a royal prince of the blood and a medium-level wizard. The actress is a beginner mage, previously with the power of three full wizards! Yet the giant . . ." His voice trailed away. "What are you doing with these people?" For some reason the mage stressed the last word.

In raw terror, Ken's face went dead white, and he trembled, but not from the pain of the spikes.

Wilson leered in delight. "So . . ." he hissed. "They don't know, do they? How amusing! How pitiful."

Lowering his head as if in battle, Ken growled a response too soft for me to hear.

"So you say," acknowledged LaRue. "But that does not make it true. Tell me what I want to know and I shall continue the process! You shall be a demigod!" An evil smirk. "Or perhaps I should reverse the process, and let them see you as—"

In a hideous ripping noise Sanders tore free from the spikes and dropped to the deck, gushing blood. Even Wilson was caught totally by surprise. Screaming that jungle roar of his, Ken bared his teeth and sprang for the alchemist's throat.

And the student agent almost succeeded. But just in time, LaRue recovered and frantically gestured. A lightning bolt, laser beam, disrupter ray, Death spell, Flesh-to-Stone crackled from his gloved fingertips and blasted Sanders into a charred husk while still in midflight.

But the remaining two hundred pounds of dead cooked flesh

continued on by sheer inertia and slammed into Wilson's chest. Off balance, the bastard mage stumbled backwards and tripped over one of the dead guards in the pentagram. Falling, the would-be world conqueror dropped to the deck and smacked his head on the metal with a resounding *crack*!

For a moment, we could only stare. Then, hesitantly, LaRue drew a ragged breath. Hell's bells. Not dead. Only stunned.

"Jessica," I croaked from parched throat. "Mine is the only voice you can hear. Mine the only will to obey."

In a trance, she dumbly nodded assent.

"The activation code is 'Apocalypse.' The command phrase is 'Armageddon.' The go word is 'Ragnarok.' "

Jessica gritted her teeth, there was a cracking noise and she swallowed. Her whole body became flushed, and she started gulping air.

"What?" demanded Mindy, tears of pain running down her cheeks. "What are you doing?"

"Hollow tooth filled with a massive overdose of MCD, the brain-booster drug," I rasped. "Jess blocked its existence from her own mind. Only I can make her remember."

My wife was hyperventilating, her eyes rolling into her head until only solid white showed. Her nude body spasmed, jerking and twisting against the wall, almost succeeding in tearing herself free. Anew, the blood gushed from her wrists and ankles.

"It'll kill her!" denounced George. "Or worse!"

Not for at least . . . five minutes, sent Jessica. *No more . . . pain . . . my friends.*

And the searing agony in my hands and feet was gone. I wanted to thank her, but there was no time to waste on niceties.

"Brain Blast him!" I ordered.

Can't . . . too weak . . . he might survive.

"Link us together," suggested Tina. "Many minds better than one."

. . . still dangerous . . . maybe a Death Dream . . .

"Do it!" I commanded furiously.

In a swirl of thoughts, our conscious minds joined, and as a fighting unit Team Tunafish began to mesh with the living, insane mind of the multiple personalities of the fledgling god.

Kill or be killed, we were going in.

18

The "I" of me became a "we" as the team gestalted into a single identity and, guided by the adroit control of the "Jessica" part, smoothly, tracelessly, meshed with the dreaming brain of our woozy enemy. We had only seconds in which to act. A Death Dream, eh? Okay. Let's make it a doozy.

In his disoriented thoughts, LaRue was reliving the events which had just happened a moment ago. As Sanders leapt, he stepped aside. No. As Sanders leapt, he hit the man with a Disintegration spell. No. As Sanders leapt, LaRue used a Death spell and—

We took over his subconscious.

—the two of them crashed through the paper hull of the aircraft carrier and tumbled into the dirty water of the Hudson River.

Floundering and splashing, the surprised LaRue turned Ken into lead, and the big man sank into the murky depths. Wilson started for shore via a dog paddle when a violent tug on his leg jerked him down. In the jumbled blurred view of underwater, smoky tendrils of blood muddied the river, and the horrified alchemist saw a blue-gray shark swimming off with his leg. LaRue screamed and polluted water filled his lungs. Gagging, the new wizard formed a platform beneath himself, and more sharks shot out of the stygian river depths. The ultra-mage tried to cast spells, but his arms moved with nightmarish slowness through the water.

At this point, he almost understood that was only an illusion in his mind, so "we" had more sharks attack. Jerk, and another leg was gone. An arm went, taking the diamond staff along. Then his head! The sharp teeth—

No!

Alive and whole, a dripping-wet LaRue was standing on the pier trembling from exertion when a car horn blared. He turned and a taxi rammed into him. His body wrapped around the hood, bones crunching audibly. With a squeal of brakes, the car stopped and LaRue was airborne, tumbling head over heels. Brutally, he crashed through a window, the glass shards slicing him to ribbons. He landed on an electrical outlet with a thump and hard current zapped into him. Rolling away, the alchemist pulled himself together when a piercing whine rapidly built to a deafening volume, and suddenly a jumbo jet smashed into the office building!

Subtlety, I love it.

In an explosion of pain, the navy librarian was crushed and violently slammed-slammed-slammed through numerous walls to reach the outside. Pulped to jelly, he fell to the street, stopping himself an inch above the sidewalk. From the core of his being, LaRue extended a Heal spell, and twisting about, landed on shaky feet.

Damnation, this guy was hard to kill.

Just then the city disappeared in a blinding atomic flash. Horribly burned by the thermal wave, his charred remains were blown into the sky as a second nuclear bomb detonated. In a desperate time jump, LaRue moved backwards to avoid the bomb blasts.

Okay, no more Mr. Nice Guys. Time for the nightmare from hell.

. . . and a hundred thousand thermonuclear detonations dotted the entire North American continent only seconds before the moon crashed into the Earth. Whole oceans left their beds from the meteoric impact, continents split, mountains erupted, gouts of primordial magma vomited into space and the planet cracked in half. A heartbeat later, the cleaved world closed its two halves like snapping jaws to crush the rogue moon with a vengeful force.

Spinning out of orbit, Earth plunged into the sun, tongues of nuclear flame annihilating chunks of the world until only molten residue remained. Caught in the hellish crushing gravitational field of the staggering astronomical body, the boiling elements splashed into an atomic sea to be further rendered into random nuclei. Then the violated solar orb went nova—a blinding cosmic fire storm whose starkly incalculable fury extended to fill the planetary system, and went beyond, expanding to reach another star. All stars! In a wild chain reaction, the whole galaxy flared into a supernova of raw cosmic energy whose unbridled chaos threatened to destroy the very fabric of the time space continuum!

Then the Creator of the Universe closed a mighty hand about the tiny flame. And making a fist, squeezed with prodigious strength until even the immortal souls of the trillions dead screamed in limitless anguish and died, winking out of existence.

Nothingness.

Absolute and infinite.

Mentally, "we" heard a pitiful wimpering cry, then sensed Wilson LaRue, and all of his multiple personas, die-die-die.

19

In echoing silence, the "we" separated, and I became myself once more. Utterly fatigued, I felt no physical pain, only a type of soulful weariness, a mental exhaustion I had not experienced since my infamous date with those Swedish triplets during college finals. Ah, youth. Wish I had some left.

Still attached to the wall, I forced apart my gummy eyelids, but could see only a blurry whiteness. Then I realized that it was the colorless smear which was pressing on me. A gentle warm pressure, but one which held me motionless in its encompassing grip.

It was the magic! With LaRue dead the magic was returning to the world! Caught here at the epicenter, the reverse vortex was a tangible force to even nonmagical beings.

At least, that's what I sincerely hoped was happening.

In gradual stages, the velveteen hurricane diminished in magnitude, until I was allowed to slide down the wall and slump onto the cold metal deck. Hey, I was free!

Glancing about, I found the rest of my team and some handsome stranger sitting on the metal floor. I felt odd, but there was no pain, and I was wearing clothes. Only the bare essentials, but at least I wasn't naked. Tina and Raul must have recharged from the outpouring and done a few quick conjures. Mages. Ain't they wonderful? I hoped they both increased a level or two from the experience.

The overturned jeep wreck was whole and undamaged once more, and beyond the bloody pentagram of guards was Wilson LaRue in street clothes, Rashamor Hoto in his kimono and the TNR battlesuit. All individuals again and each looking very deceased.

There was no sign of the Aztec book.

Scrambling closer, I found Tanner limp and heavy. I yanked out his powerpack just to be safe. Hoto proved to be a desiccated corpse weighing about as much as a dry leaf. He crumbled to the touch. So I touched him. A lot. Wilson LaRue had his ugly head split asunder. Inside the cranial cavity was only a gnarled lump of flesh, vaguely the size and shape of a fried raisin.

Deciding that a dose of lead poisoning couldn't hurt, I reached for my Magnums. Or rather, I thought of reaching for my weapons, but my hand went over my shoulder and produced a sword whose razor-edged length shimmered with rainbows. Eh?

That was when I noticed my hands were slim, muscular, covered with tiny scars and a dark rich brown. Glancing down, I was in the loose black cloth of a ninja, combat sneakers, and had small pert breasts . . . *Jumping Jesus, I was Mindy!*

No, I was in Mindy's body.

Hey, Jennings! You in here also?

Silence.

Now I understood why I was so clumsy. My mind was giving directions to muscles which responded differently from my own. Geez, it was a wonder that I could even walk upright!

Moving carefully, I diced and sliced the alchemist into convenient chunks and then kicked the pieces away from each other. I was far from finished with him, but this would do for starters.

In a half glide/half lurch, I shambled back to my team. Had to find out who was who and how long this bizarre phenomenon was going to last. Hell! This could get embarrassing!

George, Donaher, Tina and Raul were moving and attempting to stand. The handsome stranger I noticed earlier was, of course, me. I started to ask whoever was in me to turn about so I could get to see the back of my head when I noticed Jessica lying deathly still on the cold deck.

Clumsily, I threw myself to her side, only Mindy's instinctive reactions kept me from falling flat. Quickly, I checked my wife's pulse and respiration. Neither was detectable. Wasting no time, I tilted her head, straightened the tongue and started giving her mouth-to-mouth resuscitation.

Soon Donaher was next to me, his big hands pressing down on her chest with a pause, release, pause, press.

"Mike?" I asked between breaths.

"I'm George," replied the big priest. "Ed?"

Exhale. "How'd you know?"

"Kind of obvious," he said, looking at the still telepath.

Yeah, I guess it was.

"Hey!" hissed George's body from the double doors of the hangar deck. "The police are here!" The plump soldier was standing in an odd position, a fist held at his waist, the other hand slightly extended as if to offer a friendly shake. The cat stance, I believe it was called. Renault must be Mindy. This was getting confusing.

Using his precious staff to depress a button on the small control panel, Raul had an ear to the wall-mounted intercom. "And saints preserve us, it sounds as if that pimple Jules Englehart with his bedamned camera crew is with them!"

Donaher, without a doubt.

"Forget 'em!" I squeaked. "Jess is dying!"

Awkwardly, Christina shoved her way close. "Let me," snapped the redhead.

"Who?" I demanded.

"Raul," she growled, waving her wooden staff. Twinkling fairy lights sprinkled over my wife.

"Well?" demanded George-in-Donaher.

"I can save her life," replied the mage. "But that's all I promise."

Good enough. I nodded. "Go."

Weaving golden trails in the air, the buxom woman consulted her pocketbooks of spells and started to chant in a language not English or Russian. Someday, I would discover what the private language of magic was, and why nobody but a wizard could even pronounce the words.

With a shuddering gasp, Jessica began to breathe again. In seconds, color returned to her cheeks and she softly called my name. Lowering my voice as much as possible, I said her name and gave her hand a squeeze. Alive. She was alive. But at what cost? Only time would tell.

There came sounds from the other side of the hangar doors.

"Who?" I asked in sign language.

"Jewels," came the reply. Mindy had never been a good speller. And Renault had never been very adept at sign language.

"Tina," I asked of Edwardo. "Seal the hangar doors with a Lock spell!"

My head was shaken. "*Nyet*. You have no magic for me to use."

Hell and damnation. "Raul?"

He shook her head, auburn locks swishing. "No can do, chief. I'm drained after fixing Jess."

"Drained! From one Heal? How bad was she?"

He/she paused. "Let's just say she knows the Grim Reaper by sight, and leave it at that."

In angry thought, I closed a hand into a fist, the knuckles cracking and popping. Okay, nothing else to do. Fingering the words for routine one, the team shifted to both sides of the doors and waited for the rush. There was no means of escape, or place to hide. We couldn't use magic, or shoot them, or knock 'em out with sleep gas. That left only one option. The oldest ploy in military history.

Slowly, the double doors parted and as the gang of reporters boldly entered, my team laid into them with fists, feet, teeth and staffs. Professional spectators, the reporters had no ability for bare-knuckle brawling—such as it was—so we were gentle and limited their destruction to a few black eyes, a couple of lumps and a broken nose or two. But down they went, and for the count.

Dusting our wrong hands off afterwards, we tromped on the video camera, smashed the tape recorder, then stole Englehart's pants, took several tasteless pictures with 35mm at F100 at medium focus suitable for eight-by-ten color glossies and pocketed the film. These could come in useful at some future date. And there was always the possibility of a bulk mailing.

"Faith, it's the police!" cried Donaher-in-Raul as the hangar doors cycled shut with a hollow boom. "Lots of them! They must have heard the slaughter."

"Street cops or SWAT?" asked Mindy-in-George, twisting her hands on a sword pommel not there.

"SWAT, with navy SEALS, I think."

Gulp. Then we were dead meat. This ploy wouldn't work twice. Especially on SWAT and SEALS. Even in our prime, these guys could give us a run for the money.

"Can we disguise ourselves as the reporters?" asked George-in-Donaher. "Steal their clothes?"

"None of them are women!" I snapped. "Maybe Mindy could pass, but not Jess, and how are we going to hide those?" I pointed at Raul/Tina's ample chest. He/she blushed.

"Smash the keypad lock," said Mindy-in-George. "That should slow 'em down, at least."

It was done.

"Who's got a watch?" demanded Donaher-in-Raul. But nobody had. Every one had been used in battle.

Limping to the pentagram, Donaher-in-Raul took a hand radio

from the belt holster of an unconscious guard and dialed to the proper CB channel which the Bureau secretly monitored for emergency broadcasts from agents. He pressed the transmit switch. "Alert! Alert! Tunafish on toast! Need immediate evac! Coordinates on request! Respond!"

Static.

"Goddamn thing is broken!" snarled Donaher-in-Raul.

"*Nyet!* Give to me!" ordered Ed Alvarez.

"Faith, you can't use it," said Raul aghast. "No mage can!"

"I am not mage!" snapped the handsome fellow. "I am mage in a human. You are human in a mage!"

Confusing but accurate. I could see that soon name tags would be necessary. Oh Lord, this was weird. And dangerous. One agent had the power, but another had the knowledge to use it. Thus, our own training was working against us. And on the way were squads of grim cavalry who would probably think we were the bad guys.

You ever just have one of those days?

"Bureau, respond!" cried Tina-in-Ed, into another radio. Static. Tossing the communicator aside, she/me grabbed another. "Hello, Bureau!" Another. "Bureau, respond!" Static.

"Use code!" I snapped at myself. "No open transmissions on a public airwave!"

"No matter," Ed sighed. "Most of devices are broken."

"Maybe they're not free from their pocket dimension yet," suggested Mindy-in-George, scratching at a place most women normally did not.

I smacked fist into palm. If only we had some BZ gas. The harmless military hallucinogenic would befuddle the troops long enough for us to escape. No, that was wrong. We had no masks. And they most definitely did.

A pounding sounded on the doors. Then sparks crackled on the dangling wires of the broken keypad. They were trying for a bypass.

"Hey, breaker breaker one-three, there good buddy," drawled a radio on the deck. "This is Dragon Master looking for a ten-thirteen on I-80 west. Kicker back."

Tina/Ed stared at the CB as if it were speaking Martian.

Was it the Bureau, or just some truck driver actually asking for road information? We had to chance it. I snatched the radio from my hands. "Ten-two, Dragon Master. Negatory on the thirteen, friend. This is the Suicide Jockey and we're in ten-one-hundred up to our necks. Got the hammer down with a party of thirty cold friends and the smokies are aknocking on our door. They'll be hanging paper on us till doomsday unless we find a rocking chair to slide into fast! Can you help? Come on.''

''Well, ten-four, good buddy. I ain't Uncle Charlie, but I'm a cousin of his, and always happy to oblige. I got your ten-twenty on the flip-flop. But your voice sure sounds funny for the Suicide Jockey. Is this the Mad Mexican from the Windy City?''

Oh shit, I was Mindy!

''That's part of the problem, Dragon Master. We have switched vehicles. The Suicide Jockey is in the chassis of the Tiger Lady.''

''Say what? Come again?'' Confusion filled his voice.

The warning lights set above the doors began to flash.

''We'll explain later, Dragon Master. This is zero hour. Move it or lose it.''

· ''Well, then.'' A pause. ''I'd surely appreciate knowing what is your favorite type of sandwich.''

''Tunafish!'' we cried in loose unison.

Instantly, an amber oval formed in the air and flexing lines of force spun outward to pass over the moaning reporters and ensnare everybody else: us, the guards, LaRue, Hoto, Tanner, the charred remains of Sanders and even the jeep. We levitated into the magic portal just as the double doors to the hangar slammed open and a single flashbulb went off from a tiny pocket camera held by a rumpled man on the deck.

But all Jules Englehart got was the fuzzy picture of a transparent ghost giving him the finger as it faded away.

Ha! Print that, ya bozo.

Epilogue

As the portal closed, the strands released us gently on a cushioned mat inside a huge pentagram, ringed by armed guards, most of whom I knew. A squad of medics pushed their way through and swarmed over us, hauling Jessica away on a hospital gurney. After a moment, I recognized where we were. The observation tower on the eighty-sixth floor of the Empire State Building. Geez, we hadn't used this place in sixty years!

Jessica spent a week in an iron lung at Bellevue Hospital, but was then moved to the Rehabilitation Ward of the Mayo Clinic. She would live, and there would be no physical damage.

As Wilson LaRue had so kindly repaired the damage caused by our fight with his battle machines, the entire U.S.S. *Intrepid* incident was discounted as mass hysteria augmented by swamp gas. Our favorite cover story. The few civilians killed on the streets were merely considered the normal casualties of New York City. Sad but true.

The files of the missing thirty guards were hastily changed to show that they had been transferred to another post the day before and the *Intrepid* had been totally deserted that night. The attack on Englehart and his crew was attributed to a foiled mugging attempt.

The pictures came out wonderful.

In short order, the Holding Facility was shifted to the far side of the moon, the connecting doorway located two hundred miles into the desert of New Mexico, smack in the middle of the White Sands nuclear testing range. In case of another mass escape, there will be a small, unscheduled H-bomb test.

So there.

As soon as possible, my team led a foray into an alternate universe where we traded junk scrap iron for twelve more tokamac fusion reactors from the peaceful machine culture of Click. Nice folks, but as oil was against a tenant of the local religion, they squeaked something awful. Next trip, I was bring-ing earplugs.

Then Technical Services decompartmentalized the entire Holding Facility with Faraday cages, so this nasty incident could never happen again.

It was discovered that the reason the old car in the hospital parking lot had captured our attention so was that LaRue had coated the vehicle with an alchemical "Steal Me" potion. After we departed, the exploded wreck was stolen a few hours later. Its cross-country odyssey of being swiped from the thieves who snatched it from the crooks who ripped it off from the initial joyriders, was a magnificent exercise in futility. At present, we believe the car to be somewhere in Outer Mongolia.

Jules Englehart got fired from the staff of the *National Gazette* and started immediately his own private newspaper, *The Secret Truths*. Oh well. Win a few, lose a few.

Instituting a massive recruitment drive, we inducted the Ala-bama bus driver, the two Chicago police officers, the kid with the video camera, the tollbooth attendants Lumpy tried to con-sume, the Cincinnati officer who broke into our revelry in LaRue's bookstore, the entire class of Hebrew Union College rabbinical students—now Team Maccabees—and even the traffic cop who gave George a ticket. She did not actually have a su-pernatural experience, Renault couldn't quite drive that fast, but desperately short of personnel, we were willing to bend the rules.

The six navy SP officers who survived LaRue's torture needed microsurgery to separate them from their deceased companions. But afterwards, each was happy to join the Bureau and fight such villains. One man proved to be a latent telepath, and another had become a wizard from the ethereal bombardment she twice received. A bonanza, all round.

Plus, four of the animated jet fighters remained in that aug-mented state, and once free of the master's odious control, the loyal American fighters became machine agents for the existing Bureau techno-warrior division: Cyber-Cops.

LaRue's bookstore was rebuilt into the Ye Olde Magic Shoppe, but this time by a White Witch from Massachusetts, who would keep very careful records of who bought what. She wasn't a Bureau agent, merely an associate who owed us a favor.

During the five minutes that there was no magic in the world, no end of bizarre events occurred. Fairies fell from the sky, Las Vegas casinos started losing money, a dozen werewolves were cured, a hundred crime bosses disappeared and a thousand haunted houses went condo. Republicans became Democrats, Democrats became Liberals, and Liberals got jobs. The aurora borealis winked out, boomerangs stopped returning and countless famous actors aged years instantly.

Then everything precisely reversed as the magic returned.

However, in Manhattan, there momentarily appeared a secret third tower of the World Trade Center: a medieval-style, block stone structure, and placed prominently on top was a giant neon "B 13." It caused quite a stir.

"B^{13} vitamin pills" were released on the health market two weeks later. Yes, of course, the incredibly detailed laser hologram of the building had been only a crazy publicity stunt.

The structure is no longer there. Personally, I now think our headquarters is situated inside the support structure of the Golden Gate Bridge in San Francisco. But it's only a guess.

In the following week, the FBI let leak the information that the young girl in Huntsville was a federal agent on secret assignment to crack a white slavery ring. Her family was astonished by the news that their daughter had died in a shoot-out with international terrorists and had personally saved the life of the President. He actually came and visited them for an hour and gave them a Presidential Medal of Valor, the highest award a civilian can achieve in peacetime. The politician was glad to do it. Plus, the parents were consoled a bit by the million dollars they received as their agent daughter's backlog of danger pay. Her name was Veronica Harmond.

Jess and I plan to call our first girl child that.

It isn't much, but it helps me sleep at night.

Eventually, we returned to our original bodies. But not quite soon enough, and I now have new respect for ladies who quietly suffer through that time of the month. Me, I'd rather get hit in the head with a baseball bat every twenty-eight days. Ugh.

Christina Blanco graduated and was permanently assigned to our group. Mr. Renault and the Russian beauty took residence with each other. Oddly, according to the security monitors in the apartment, something invisible from Raul's room went to visit Mindy in her room every single night, and twice on Sundays.

Gosh, whatever could that be?

And, in an unprecedented move, Horace Gordon himself told

Father Donaher that his next sabbatical had better be to Hell-
sinki, Finland, but leave the original alone. I wonder why?

Pizza-Pizza in Chicago canceled our account and will no longer deliver to our pet pirate. Serves him right for undertipping.
Justice will always triumph.

And I received a letter in the post, no return address, no
canceled stamp. Inside was a plain piece of paper which simply
told me to stop offering my soul for assistance. Or else. Then it
crumbled into dust and was blown away by an unseen wind.

A crank letter obviously. On the other hand, it was a stupid
habit of mine, so what the hey.

Unfortunately, as the weeks passed it became apparent that
Jessica had been rendered psionically dead from the overload of
MCD. Her mental powers would never return. My wife would
remain a Bureau agent, but her personnel records have been
shifted from "Unique" to "Normal: Previously Unique."

From the bombardment of raw magic that had coursed through
our mages, Horta's staff went to silver topped with gold, and
Blanco was elevated to a stainless-steel mage.

Contrarily, the remote-control photocopier machine Raul had
used to duplicate the Aztec manual was hauled away by the
garbagemen in many small broken pieces. And the book Blanco
had saved from the fire at LaRue's store proved to be a first
edition of *The Kitchen Magician: Basic Alchemy in the Home
for Fun and Profit*. Surely, the volume that had started LaRue
on his journey to hell. However, chained to the andirons in our
fireplace, the animated book made a small but pleasant blaze.

I can only tolerate so much nonsense from a wizard.

Upon returning to our Chicago apartment, at dinner on our
first free evening, we held our ritual toast welcoming Christina
Blanco into our ranks. Then, from another more special cup,
we bid farewell to Kensington Sanders, the student who died
giving humanity its fighting chance against a mad god.

The name of Field Agent Ken Sanders was placed on the Bureau 13 Roll of Honor, we hung his picture in our trophy room,
and a dignified monument to the brave soul was erected in his
ancestral hometown of Lokitaung, Kenya. Funny, he hadn't
looked African.

We never did discover his terrible secret, and perhaps it was
for the best. But Ken was a good man, a top-notch agent and a
damn fine friend.

Personally, I was going to miss the big gorilla.